Mysterious House *on* CANNON HILL

DIANE WILLIAMS GORDON

Black Rose Writing | Texas

ISBN: 978-1-68433-775-0
PUBLISHED BY BLACK ROSE WRITING
www.blackrosewriting.com

Printed in the United States of America
Suggested Retail Price (SRP) $18.95

Mysterious House on Cannon Hill is printed in Chaparral Pro

*As a planet-friendly publisher, Black Rose Writing does its best to eliminate unnecessary waste to reduce paper usage and energy costs, while never compromising the reading experience. As a result, the final word count vs. page count may not meet common expectations

Mysterious House on
CANNON HILL

CHAPTER ONE

Just after 2 am on a Friday morning, Lena drove down Diversey Avenue. The streets were empty, but she noticed a homeless man huddled in a corner of the entrance to an old grocery store. From where she was, it looked like he was only wearing a light jacket. The poor guy didn't even have on shoes. Lena thought to herself, "I'm really cold inside this car. I **know** that poor man must be freezing. It's only 38 degrees out there." She started thinking about her own situation and wishing there was something she could do for the man. Lena had just stolen $100,000 from the company she worked for. "I need to get out of this town as soon as possible," she thought, "Come morning Mr. Wilson will realize the money is gone and call the police. When I don't show up for work, he's going **.....** **to** come up with...me."

Lena's conscious began to worry her. She hadn't seen many homeless people before. She couldn't stop thinking about that poor unfortunate man. As she continued her get away drive, she noticed a Walmart just a couple of lights down. It was only 2:30 in the morning, so nobody would know about the money yet. "I think I'll run into Walmart and buy that poor man a blanket and maybe something for him to eat." Her thoughts kept on racing as she headed to her new destination. "I wish I knew what size shoes he wears. Oh well, I can just get him some socks. At least they'll keep his feet a little warmer." Lena turned into the Walmart parking lot. She got out of her car and hurried into the warm store.

First, she found a nice heavy blanket. Back in the men's department, Lena found some crew socks. She made her way to the front of the store. Located right behind the checkout lanes was one of the food warmers. There was the perfect solution for a cold night's meal. A warm baked chicken would feed that poor man huddling in the cold and darkness. She thought, "I wish

I could do more, but I just don't have the time. As it is, I'll have to back track just to give these things to him." After paying for all the goods, she got in her car and headed back down Diversey Avenue toward town. As she approached the area, she spotted a big streetlight right in front of the old grocery store. "At least I'll be able to see what I'm doing." She pulled up right in front of the grocery store.

The old man was still huddled in the corner next to the door. Lena got the packages out of the back seat of the car and walked to where the man lay shivering. She laid the packages down beside him and without looking back, hurried to her car. She turned the car around in the middle of the road and headed out of town. She was back on her planned route. She had finally made it to the highway going north. She planned this route before she ever stole the money. She would continue going north until she reached the Canadian border. Lena was beginning to get tired, but she knew she couldn't stop to rest. "No, I'll keep going until I reach the border. Then I'll find a place to sleep for a few hours. I want to find someplace I can stay and not be noticed."

Several hours passed as she drove as fast as was legal. She could barely hold her eyes open. She had fifty more miles to get to the border when she noticed a roadside café. It had a big sign across the top of the building that read "Open." She decided to stop there since she needed coffee to stay awake. She pulled up in front of the café and got out of her car. She noticed two police cars sitting side by side in the parking lot. Lena decided they probably didn't know anything about the robbery. After all, Mr. Wilson wouldn't even be at work yet. She opened the door and went inside for her hot cup of coffee. There were just two women behind the counter. No one else was inside the café. She took off her coat and sat down in one of the booths. One of the waitresses came over and asked her what she could get for her. Lena said, "I think I'll just have a cup of coffee please."

The woman first looked to be about 60 years old. She was most likely in her 40's. She had teeth that were stained yellow and horrible breath. It was all Lena could do to keep from putting her hands over her nose. She remembered what her mother use to tell her. "Lena; it will soon pass." The badge on her shirt said her name was Brenda. She asked Lena if she would like to try some of their famous lemon pie. Lena just wanted her to go away, so, she said yes, she would try a piece. As she sat waiting for her coffee and pie, she looked out of the café window and noticed the two police cars had left the parking lot. A wave of relief came over her.

Brenda finally brought her coffee and pie. Lena said thank you to her and picked up the sugar container. She poured two tablespoons of sugar in her coffee and a couple of drops of cream. The coffee tasted good and seemed to revive her a little. She ate the pie and was surprised at how delicious it was. She leaned back in the seat and tried to relax a little. She noticed her hands were shaking so much that she could hardly pick up the cup. After sitting quietly for thirty minutes she decided she'd better get back on the road. It was almost daylight and she had intended to be a lot farther away from Chicago than she was. According to her calculations she had only gone about 175 miles.

Her body ached as she got up from the booth. She walked over to the counter where the cash register was and laid a twenty-dollar bill down with her ticket. She told Brenda how much she enjoyed the pie. Lena asked her if she had baked it. Brenda said she did. Lena said, "Well it was delicious. You are a fine cook." Brenda's face began to get red even though she apparently was pleased with the compliment. Her red face and yellow teeth for some reason made Lena want to laugh. She got her change and made a much-needed trip to the restroom. When Lena got back into her car, she got the map out of the glove compartment. She studied it a few minutes. There was a small town in northern Michigan called Escanaba. She had heard it was a nice quiet little town and not far from the Canadian border.

CHAPTER TWO

Lena decided she could drive there before morning. If she felt safe there, she would be looking for some place to stay for a short rest. "I don't think anybody would think of looking for me in Escanaba. All the same, I am glad I changed my name and got all new identification papers. I just have to get used to being Jessica Harris." She hoped no one would be looking for someone with such a nice simple name. "Lena Montgomery is no more." Before long she realized she had gone nearly 300 miles. She quickly estimated she was probably only about 30 miles from Escanaba. "Well, I guess I had better get going. In less than an hour I can be in a safe place and get some rest."

Lena glanced at the package laying on the passenger seat of the car. She continued thinking about her future. "I'm going to have to be very careful how I spend the money. One hundred thousand dollars plus what I saved over the past year won't last forever. Eventually I know I'll have to find a job, if only a part-time job. More importantly, something very inconspicuous." As she continued her drive, she started thinking about what she had done. "I never wanted to hurt anyone by taking that money, especially Joyce, but I really needed it. I just needed to get away from all the anxiety and confusion in my life. It was the same old thing every day: the job, the people I had to deal with at the finance company and worst of all Mr. Wilson always bothering me. I just got tired of it. I had to do something about it."

A year before, she had started saving her money. She didn't buy anything unless she just had to have it. Though she loved the little coffee shop near work, she saved that coffee money and put it towards her nest egg. The only way out for her was to leave and get as far away as she could. To do that she had to have more money. So, she took the money from work. She began to think about it all. "Well, now I'm a free woman. Oh, I know in time the police may catch up with me, but I'm free for now and I'm so much happier. I'm out here driving in this beautiful country and I have no one mistreating me. Mr. Wilson was always after me in the office. He just wouldn't leave me alone. I just had to do something." Her life had become a complete disaster.

Meanwhile back in Chicago, Mr. Wilson was just getting into his office. He wondered where Lena was as she was always in the office before him. He brushed it off and proceeded to open the safe as he did every workday. Trying to account for everything, he suddenly realized some of the money was missing. It was exactly 100,000 dollars. His first thought was he had miscounted the money. He carefully counted everything again. After the second counting, he knew for sure the money was missing. "Where is Lena, why is she late this morning?" He went to his office and picked up the phone and called her residence. A voice came on the line that said the number had been disconnected. "That's funny," he thought "why would her phone be disconnected?"

He called her sister Joyce and asked if she had heard from Lena that morning. Joyce replied, "No I haven't Mr. Wilson. I haven't heard from Lena since yesterday. She seemed to be okay, then."

"Well, she hasn't come in this morning and I just found out we have 100,000 dollars missing from the safe."

"Oh no, Mr. Wilson, I'm sure Lena wouldn't have taken the money. She isn't that kind of a person. Surely you don't believe she took it, do you?"

Mr. Wilson answered with "Joyce, all I know right now is I have 100,000 dollars missing and an employee who has not shown up for work. I'm going to need to report this to the police. If you hear from Lena, have her call me immediately. If she doesn't, the police are going to be looking at her as my number one suspect."

As Joyce began to put down the phone, she started to tremble. She just couldn't believe her sister would ever steal money. She wondered where Lena could be right now. Mr. Wilson had said her cell phone was disconnected. This can't be true; she wouldn't do something like this. But it was true. Lena was long gone and never would answer her cell phone. She was a missing person and wanted to stay that way. Mr. Wilson decided to inform the police of the theft. When they arrived, he told the detective his secretary, Lena Montgomery was the only person he could think of that would take the money. "And even more reason to suspect her is that Lena hasn't shown up for work today." The detective noticed the door to the company had not been broken into; it had to be an inside job.

The detective asked Mr. Wilson to sit down and see if he could describe Miss Montgomery to him. The first thing out of his mouth was, "Oh, she is a very sexy woman."

"What color was her hair and eyes Mr. Wilson; did you ever notice that?"

"Well of course I did detective, what kind of man do you take me for, anyway? She had long dark brown hair and brown eyes. Very pretty sexy eyes."

"Okay, I think that will do for now. If you think of anything else that would help us find her, please give me a call." The detective handed Mr. Wilson his business card. As the two detectives walked outside, they discussed Mr. Wilson.

The first one said, "That man is creepy. I don't much blame Miss Montgomery for not wanting to be around him. I don't know if she took the money or not, but she was wise to get away from him."

"Carl, you are so right, that guy even creeped me out." After they returned to their car, Carl picked up his microphone and reported Lena as being a missing person of interest. He turned to the other detective and said, "David, I say let's go talk to the sister, Joyce. I want to see if she knows anything about Lena."

CHAPTER THREE

The two detectives arrived at Joyce's house a little pass five o'clock in the afternoon. Joyce had just gotten home from a doctor's appointment. One of the detectives knocked on the door. Joyce was hesitant at first, but she thought it may be someone with good news about Lena. She opened the door to see the two men standing there. The two detectives showed Joyce their badges and asked if they could come in for a moment and speak with her. "Yes, of course, come in and have a seat. How may I help you, gentlemen?"

"Joyce, may I call you by your first name?"

"Yes, that's fine."

"We are here to ask you some questions about your sister Lena. Have you heard anything from her recently?"

"No, I have not. I have been worried sick about her. I just can't believe what she is being accused of."

"Well, she hasn't been accused of anything yet. She is just a person of interest."

The detective spoke up and advised her to give them a call if she should hear from her sister. "Mr. Wilson is the one accusing Lena of taking the money, that's why we wanted to speak to you. Maybe she did and maybe she didn't. We must investigate these accusations brought against her."

"Joyce said, "I understand fully, sir. I will also tell you that Mr. Wilson is a scum bag. He was always touching Lena and wouldn't leave her alone. She hated the man. He also held back her vacation pay this year and last year just because he didn't want her taking off work. So, if my sister did take some money, it was to get away from that jerk and because he owed it to her."

Joyce sat quietly on the sofa as tears ran down her face. One of the detectives patted her on her shoulder and handed her his card. "Thank you,

Joyce for speaking to us. Please let us know if you should hear from Lena. We'll go now and leave you alone." They opened the front door and stepped out into the sunshine. As they were walking to their car, Carl spoke up and said, "I don't believe Joyce knows where Lena is. Lena may use one of those throw away phones to stay in touch with her and we don't have any way of tracking them." David shook his head and mumbled under his breath.

Escanaba, MI was a quaint little town with lots of tall trees and pretty homes. She kept driving until she came into the busier part of town. It was there she started looking for rooms to rent or a hotel she could stay in for a few days. Her thoughts were still on her safety. "For all I know, there may be an all-points bulletin out for me including my picture. I wouldn't put anything past Mr. Wilson. He is a conniving old man." She spotted a pretty white hotel called the Magnuson Grand Pioneer Inn. There was a sign out front that read, "Rooms for Rent". "Oh wow, such a beautiful place. I think I'll go check about a room."

Lena noticed the parking lot was around the back of the house. She drove her car around to the back making her feel less conspicuous. She walked back around to the front door and knocked. A short plump lady answered the door. She had a red face and a sweet smile. She said, "Hello Love, what can I do for you today?" Lena gave a big smile back to the woman and asked about renting a room for a couple of nights. "Of course, come on in and lay your things down on the side table. I'm Mrs. Galloway. Just follow me into the living room where we can get comfortable."

Lena followed the pleasant woman into the living room. The room was very old fashioned. The furniture was brown, gold and red. It was old fashioned but beautiful. It reminded her of her own home growing up. She remembered that her Mother was always cleaning and redecorating the house. It didn't have fancy furniture in it, but everything was in place and clean. It was so homey and comfortable. This place was the same way. She loved it and the aroma from the kitchen smelled heavenly. "Mrs. Galloway must be making pumpkin pies or something else with that wonderful spicy aroma."

In the living room, Mrs. Galloway asked her to sit down and make herself comfortable. She asked her if she would like to have a cup of tea and a piece of pumpkin pie. Lena told her she thought that was what she smelled coming from the kitchen. "It smells so good; I believe I'll have a piece, if it isn't too much trouble."

"Oh no, Dear, no trouble at all. I'll be right back." While she sat waiting for Mrs. Galloway, she could hear the birds outside the window chirping away. The window was open and there was a beautiful bird feeder that looked like a gazebo hanging right outside the window. The lace curtains fluttered in the light breeze.

As she watched the birds come and go, she noticed a lot of red birds on the feeder. She thought maybe there must be a family of them close by. Mrs. Galloway came into the room carrying a large tray. Lena jumped up and tried to help her. Mrs. Galloway said, "It's okay, Dear, I'm used to carrying these big trays." She sat it down on a corner table. She handed Lena a cup and a small plate with a piece of hot pumpkin pie on it. She then poured her a cup of tea. "Do you use sugar in your tea?"

"Yes, one teaspoon would be nice." The woman handed her the sugar bowl and then poured herself a cup of tea.

As they sat in this beautiful room enjoying their tea, Mrs. Galloway spoke up.

"So dear, would you like to rent one of my rooms for a few days?"

"Yes, I would. I'm not sure for how long, but probably a couple of days."

"Well that will be fine and if you should decide to stay longer, that will be fine too. Now, I serve breakfast at 8 am every morning and dinner is at 8 pm every night."

"That sounds wonderful, Mrs. Galloway. I want to go ahead and pay you now for two nights. If I should decide to stay longer, I'll pay you then. Is that okay with you?"

"Yes, dear, that will be just fine. Now when we finish our tea, I'll show you my rooms.

I have one that's overlooking the street or there is one in the back of the house.

It's your choice." Lena decided she would rather be in the front of the house. That way she would be able to watch for the police or anything unusual. "I prefer the front room, Mrs.

Galloway. I like people watching."

"I understand, dear. The front room it is then."

CHAPTER FOUR

After Mrs. Galloway left the room, Lena went down to the parking area and got her small bag out of the car. She went back up to her room and took a shower. She felt dirty from driving so long. She got her map out of her bag and sat down in front of the window.

She planned out the route she would take when she left this place. It was a nice little town, but it just wasn't far enough away from Chicago. She started planning the next stage of her escape. "Tomorrow I'm going to go buy one of those disposable cell phones so I can call Joyce. I know she must be worried to death about me." She rested, while waiting for dinner time. "I sure hope Mrs. Galloway has something good for dinner; I'm starving."

As she sat down to dinner, there were two men and one other lady at the table. Mrs. Galloway introduced her to everyone there. "Ladies and gentlemen, this is Jessie Harris. She is staying with us for a couple of nights." Before she had eaten the first bite of food, one of the gentlemen spoke up and asked, "Where are you heading, Miss?" Lena was stunned at his question and didn't immediately answer him. For one thing she didn't know how to answer the question. She didn't know herself where she was headed. The gentleman asked her again, "Where are you heading, Miss Jessie?" She looked down at her plate and finally spoke in a low voice. "I'm going to visit a friend north of here."

"Well, I hope you have a safe trip."

"Thank you."

Mrs. Galloway came into the dining room with a tray of fresh baked cookies for dessert. The crowd at the table started to clap and raised their voices to praise her. She smiled and nodded her head to everyone. After dinner, everyone went into the living room to watch television. Mrs.

Galloway asked Lena if she would like to join them. "There is a game show we all love to watch. You are welcome to join us, Dear." Lena said she was tired and excused herself. She went up to her room and changed into her pajamas. She sat on the side of the bed and looked at the map again. "Tomorrow I'll go buy one of those disposable cell phones and call my sister. Then they can't trace my calls. I'm so glad I bought my tickets ahead of time. I'll take the bus to the border and then switch to the Amtrak train which will take me into Sault Ste. Marie. I can hardly wait to get there."

Lena pulled back the covers on the bed and crawled under them. She was so tired she fell asleep right away. She woke up around 6 am and couldn't go back to sleep. She just laid in bed for almost another hour before getting up. She planned to get dressed, have breakfast and then go buy one of those phones. "I think I will leave here tomorrow morning. I'll tell Mrs. Galloway today that I'll be leaving." She looked in the mirror and saw dark circles beginning to form under her blue eyes. "Oh my gosh, just look at that face. It's all sunken in and so pale." She put lotion on her face and smoothed it out gently. Then she put on powder, liner, mascara and a small amount of rouge. She took one last glance in the mirror and decided she looked okay.

She went down to the dining room and sat down for breakfast. The guests seemed joyful and talkative this morning. Lena just said good morning to everyone and ate a small amount of eggs and potatoes. She excused herself and left the room. One of the gentlemen, Mr. Atkins spoke up and said, "Well, she sure was quiet again this morning." Lena saw Mrs. Galloway in the hall as she started up the staircase to her room. She called out to her to wait. "Yes, Dear, how may I help you?"

"I just wanted to let you know that I have decided to leave tomorrow morning. I wanted to thank you for such a lovely room and the nice time I have had here with you. You have been most hospitable."

"Well thank you, Dear, but I am sorry to see you leave. I have enjoyed you being here. I want to wish you best wishes on your trip. May you find what you're looking for."

She reached over and gave Lena a hug. Lena thanked her again and turned and went up the staircase to her room. Lena grabbed her purse and started back down the steps. She wanted to purchase the cell phone before it got too late. She knew her sister, Joyce would be worried to death about her. Joyce was expecting her second child in a few months and Lena felt badly about not being there for her. As she approached her car, a tear began to roll down her cheek. Suddenly it hit her what she had done. She thought to herself, "Joyce is the only living relative I have left in this world and now I might have ruined everything. I am a selfish woman. But I can't turn back now. It's too late for that."

As she drove down the street, she saw a merchandise store. She parked the car and went inside. She found the untraceable phones on a shelf near the checkout area. She decided to buy three of them, so she could stay in touch with Joyce. That evening when she went down to dinner she decided since this was her last night there, she would join the other guest in their conversations. Mr. Adkins was surprised and delighted to hear Jessie join in. She told them she would be leaving first thing in the morning. When dinner was over, she said her goodbyes and went up to her room. She decided to look at the map one more time. She wanted to make sure everything was correct in her mind before she left in the morning. She set the clock because she wanted to leave at first light.

Lena had decided she would call Joyce after she took her shower and got into her pajamas. She sat down on the side of the bed and dialed her sister's number. "Hello, Joyce, its Lena."

"Lena, where are you, what have you done? I have been worried sick about you. Are you okay?"

"Yes, Joyce, I'm fine. I can't tell you where I am; I just wanted you to know I love you and I'll call you again soon. I must go now. Take care of yourself, and little Jessie."

"Lena wait, please wait; Lena don't hang up." The phone went silent. Joyce was so relieved to hear from her sister. But even if she had to lie, she knew she couldn't tell anyone about the call.

CHAPTER FIVE

The following morning, Lena wanted to get up early. The alarm clock by her bedside rang out at 5 am. After dressing she packed everything she brought in and then crept down the steps. She didn't want to wake anyone up at this early hour. She took her bag to the car and then went back up to her room. She looked all around to make sure she hadn't left anything. Even the cell phone she used to call Joyce the night before was in her carrying case. She had decided to throw that phone away after she was well into Canada. She didn't want to leave any evidence that she was ever there. Lena had signed the registry as Jessie Harris. She was so glad she had gotten that new identification.

As she started out the bedroom door, she stopped and looked back one last time. Lena again crept down the steps as not to wake anyone. When she finally got into her car, she took a deep breath. What a relief to be leaving the United States. She was about to enter a whole new country where she hoped Mr. Wilson would never find her. She lowered her head and said a silent prayer. "Lord, I know I have done wrong and embarrassed my family and friends. Please forgive me and guide me to safety. I pray that Mr. Wilson will pay for what he did to me. Please Lord, let me live in peace and do what's right from now on."

After leaving the bed and breakfast, Lena drove over to the rental car company. She returned the car she had rented and called a taxi to take her to the nearest bus depot. There she boarded a tourist bus to the Canadian border. When crossing the United States Canadian Border Lena would have to have certain information, including her date of birth, gender, and country of citizenship. She had to memorize all the information on her new identification papers. She wanted all traces of her old self left behind. She was glad she had already bought her ticket to take Amtrak into Sault Saint Marie. Lena couldn't wait to be in Ontario, Canada and a long way from Chicago. The thought made her smile for the first time in quite a while.

Lena thought the city of Sault St. Marie was beautiful with its many sandstone buildings. She decided she would walk around the city and look at all those fine-looking old buildings. She had also looked forward to having lunch in one of the many cafes that lined the streets. She sat down at one of the tables outside one of the street cafés and waited for someone to take her order. In just a little while a quite handsome young man approached her with a menu. He asked if she was ready to order. She asked him for one of the veggie burgers and a cup of coffee. The weather was a little cool but pleasant. She felt so relieved just being this far.

After she had eaten her lunch, she decided to look at the map again. She thought to herself. "I think I better find out how to get to Prince Edward Island. I will go talk to someone at a travel agency first. Yes, that's what I'll do. I'm sure they can steer me in the right direction." She decided to ask the waiter if he could tell her how to get to the nearest travel agency. The young man gave her directions and said she could walk there. Turned out there was an office just around the corner from the café. She paid her tab and walked around the corner to the tourist agency. The lady behind the desk greeted her with a big smile. "Hi, I was wondering if you could advise me how to get over to Prince Edward Island?"

The woman was delighted to help Lena. She looked on her computer and then gave Lena a map of the island. "I guess you know that it's a long way from Sault St. Marie. Your best bet is to take a flight to Charlottetown from here. It's nearly a five-hour flight. You could drive it or take the Amtrak. Either of those ways, it's going to be a very long trip. Lena wasn't really concerned about the distance she had to go. She just wished she was already there. "Okay, I think I will fly to Charlottetown."

"That is a good decision, Miss Harris. Your flight is not until seven o'clock this evening. It's just three now so you might want to go kill a little time shopping."

"Yes, I think I will do that." She paid for her ticket and thanked the woman for her assistance.

She enjoyed walking around the town while she waited. She loved the old buildings and the atmosphere she felt around her. Lena decided to have dinner at one of the local restaurants. It was nearly six o'clock by the time she finished eating. She realized she didn't have much time and called for a taxi to take her to the airport. Once settled in on the plane, her thoughts looked ahead. "I can hardly wait to get to the island. I can't believe how free and happy I feel already. I guess the first thing to do when I land will be to rent a car. Maybe I can find a bed and breakfast I can stay in for a few days. Just think, a few hours from now and I will finally be on Prince Edward Island." When she landed in Charlottetown, she checked with the airline people to see where to rent a car.

Charlottetown is the capital of Prince Edward Island and a lot busier than she had imagined. She followed instructions to get to the car rental area and rented herself a nice-looking SUV. She knew the first thing she had to do was to find a place to stay for the night. As she drove around the Island, she stopped at a red light and took a big deep breath. She started thinking, "The traffic here is so different from Chicago. Let's hope nothing but good can happen in a place like this. I know I am going to love living here, at least for a while." Just on the outskirts of town she saw a white two-story house with a porch that wrapped all the way around the house. It had white Wicker rocking chairs across the front porch and beautiful potted plants lined the steps leading up to the porch.

CHAPTER SIX

The shutters on the house were a pale blue and were perfect with the rest of the house. Lena thought the place was one of the most beautiful homes she had ever seen. She pulled in the little parking lot out front of the house and got out. There was a sign in front of the house that read, Prince Edward Island Bed and Breakfast. Under that it read, "Vacancy." She walked up the steps and tapped on the front door. A young boy answered the door. Lena said, "Hi there, I'm inquiring about a room." The boy looked at Lena and then asked her to come in the house. He said, "My name is Jackie. My grandma runs this place. Come sit down and I'll go get her." She could hear Jackie telling his grandma they had a visitor. The grandma told Jackie to go outside and play and she would take care of their visitor.

Jackie's grandma finally came into the parlor and introduced herself as Maggie. "Hi there, Miss, how can I help you?" Lena told Maggie her name was Jessie Harris, and she was interested in a room for a few days. "I am delighted to meet you, Jessie. We do have a vacancy right now. Follow me into the lobby and we'll fix you right up."

"Thank you, Maggie, that would be wonderful." Maggie pulled the notebook out from under the counter and laid it on top of it. "Miss Jessie, I am going to give you one of my favorite rooms. It's very lovely and feminine and I know you are going to love it."

"Oh, I'm sure I will, Maggie."

"I serve breakfast at 8:30 every morning and dinner at 7:00 in the evening. Both are included with the room. There will be fresh towels outside your door every morning. If there is anything else you need, just let me know."

The following day, Lena decided to drive out in the country and do a little site seeing. She had taken a turn on a whim and ended up on Cannon Hill Road. She wasn't sure where she was. Cannon Hill began to get more and more secluded as she drove along slowly. She had come to a T in the road and wasn't sure which way she should turn. As she sat at the stop sign, she began to look around. "What in the world is that over there? It looks like an old mansion. That's odd, seeing a place like that way out here. I think I'll go have a peek." She backed the SUV up and turned into the driveway of the old abandoned house. She just sat in the car looking at it. She first thought it was big and spooky looking.

Then she became intrigued by what was behind the overgrown yard. "I'll bet no one has lived here for a really long time, and that's why it looks so bad. Just look at all those vines growing all around the old place. I sure would love to see the inside of it." She got out of her SUV and started walking around the old house. Suddenly she saw an old, faded sign laying in the grass. It was battered and worn, and you could barely make out the phone number. She dialed the number and waited to see if anyone would answer. A lady's voice answered the phone. Lena casually said, "Hi, I found this number on an old faded for sale sign."

The voice on the other end of the phone asked her where she found the sign? "I'm way out in the country. I suddenly came upon this old, abandoned house on Cannon Hill Road."

"Oh well, that makes sense. I'm Delores, the realtor who has been trying to sell that old place for a very long time."

"Really? I would love to see inside the house. Do you have time to show it to me, Delores?"

"Sure, why not. I could meet you there in about an hour."

"Okay, I'll wait for you." Just before she hung up Delores asked, "By the way, could you please tell me who I am meeting at the Cannon house?"

"I'm Jessie Harris. I'm new to the area."

"Okay, Miss Harris, I'll see you in about an hour."

"Thank you, Delores, I appreciate getting to see the inside this quickly."

"No problem, I'm just happy someone is interested in the old place."

Lena stood in front of the old house just looking it over. It was a Victorian style home, mostly brick. She walked all around the outside of the house and noticed it had a fenced in backyard. "Wow look at that. I could get a dog for protection. I don't think anyone would look for me here; it's such a secluded place. Listen to me, talking myself into a comfortable life." The real estate lady didn't show up until an hour and a half later. Lena just sat on the front porch to wait. She had her arms draped around her knees. She closed her eyes and drifted off to sleep. She was so tired from her journey and felt comfortable being on this beautiful island. She dreamed about Mrs. Galloway. Over and over in her dream, Mrs. Galloway kept saying "Are you okay, love, are you okay, love?"

CHAPTER SEVEN

Suddenly she was awakened by a noise. Lena looked up to see a car coming in the driveway. It was Delores, the real estate lady. "Finally," she said whispering under her breath. The two women approached each other with their hands out. They shook hands and walked over to the front porch of the house. Delores turned to Jessie and said, "Now don't be too surprised when you see the inside. Remember no one has lived here for an awfully long time. Probably about seven years." Jessie said, "Oh, really, that has been a long time."

"What in the world would a young woman like you want to be way out here by yourself, anyway?"

"I'm a writer and I need someplace that is quiet and peaceful. It's hard to think and write when there's so much going on around you." Delores replied, "I certainly understand. It just seems like such a lonely place away from the city."

As they walked from room to room, Lena knew in her heart she wanted this house. "I love this house, Delores. What are you asking for it?" Delores looked at Jessie like she thought she was crazy or something. "Well, I have been wanting to get rid of this place for a long time. Let me go home tonight and go back through my paperwork and give you a call tomorrow." Jessie immediately said, "No, let me call you." Delores said, "What would be a good time?" Jessie told her she would call around eleven o'clock in the morning. "Any questions before you go?" asked Delores. Jessie said, "Does the furniture stay with the house?"

"Yes, everything stays," replied Delores.

As Delores was walking away, she mumbled under her breath, "It's beyond me why anybody would want to live way out here, especially by themselves." She shook her head in amazement and got in her car. Jessie waved goodbye and said she would call her tomorrow. Jessie took one last look at the old place and decided she would go back to the bed and breakfast and get some rest. She was still tired from her flight. Prince Edward Island was just as beautiful as she had imagined. The people were friendly and nice and treated her like one of their own. She thought to herself, "This is the kind of place I could live in forever. I've been missing for four weeks and I bet Mr. Wilson hasn't given up yet. He's always out for revenge. I wish I had never taken that job, but I was desperate at the time and needed the work. Now I am a fugitive from justice because of him."

The police in Chicago had come to a dead end. They sent two officers to speak with Mr. Wilson. One of the police officers, Greg Parrish, began to tell Mr. Wilson their results on the investigation of Lena Montgomery. "She gave up her apartment with no forwarding address. Discontinued her cell phone service. She closed all her bank accounts and closed her accounts with her pharmacy. There just isn't any trace of her. Her sister seems to be telling the truth about not hearing from her. So, sir, we have reached a dead end. Oh, and she has no other family either."

Mr. Wilson was surprised and shocked when he heard they had nothing to go on. He couldn't believe Lena had been planning her escape while working in his office. "Okay gentlemen, I guess I'll have to hire a private investigator since you guys can't seem to find her." Officer Parrish spoke up and said, "Sorry Mr. Wilson, but there are no other leads. If you come up with something, don't hesitate to call me. Here's my card." The two officers left the office as Mr. Wilson just stood there shaking his head. He said out loud. "Lena, you are a smart woman. A lot smarter than I gave you credit for."

The following day, Wilson got on the computer and started looking for a private investigator. He was determined to find Lena and get back his money. The investigator he picked was a guy named Jim Brown. Mr. Brown checked into all the information already gotten by the police. Finally, he had to tell Wilson that the police were right; there were no more leads. Maybe the woman had gone out of the country. Mr. Wilson didn't like what Jim Brown had to say. He was getting irritated with everyone telling him there were no more leads. "I don't care if you think there are no more leads, do your job and find something. You'll get paid well." Brown had nothing else to go on and suggested to Mr. Wilson it was possible she had gone to Canada.

They had no jurisdiction in Canada: so, Jim Brown decided he would get a map of Canada, close his eyes, and point to a spot on the map. It was as good a way as any to find a starting point. Lena was in luck. He headed to Halifax to have a look around. Brown had been there a few times, so he felt comfortable. "This city is a lot bigger than I remembered." He started thinking to himself as he drove down the middle of town. "I would think she would want to stay in a big city like this. With all these people here, she could probably hide out and never be found. I'll show her photo to some hotels and Bed and Breakfasts in town." But no one had seen a woman who fit her description or matched the photo. After three days of searching, he decided to go back to Chicago. Prince Edward Island never even entered his mind.

The following morning Jessie couldn't wait to talk to Delores about the Cannon Hill house. By then, Delores had decided to let the old place go. She was tired of fooling with it. "Jessie, I've been trying to sell that old house for the past seven years. Everyone says it's haunted and too far out of town. So, I'm going to do both of us a favor and let the place go pretty cheap."

"I want a place away from town and I'm not afraid of ghosts. I don't believe in them anyway."

"Well, why don't I meet you out there around 2 this afternoon? Then we can talk it over."

"Okay, Delores, I'll see you at 2." It was just after eleven when Jessie hung up. She decided to ride into town and pick up a few things she needed.

CHAPTER EIGHT

The people of Prince Edward Island were very friendly. As she walked up and down the aisles of the store, everyone she passed said hello to her. Some even asked how her day was going. She didn't plan to get too close to anyone for fear of being discovered, but it was nice to be around such pleasant people. Even so, she knew it was best to keep a low profile. After she finished her shopping, she decided to ride around the area. She wanted to find the house that was in the series Anne of Green Gables and the Lake of Shining Waters. She started talking to herself, "When I was a little girl and didn't feel well, my mother would put Anne of Green Gables on the television for me to watch. It always perked me up and made me feel better. I have always wanted to come to this place. Not as a fugitive though."

As she drove through the streets of Prince Edward Island, she thought about how beautiful the area was. "I hope I never have to leave the island. It's so peaceful and quiet, and the people are just so friendly. My heart wants to stay here forever." Jessie thought about Jackie and how he was getting attached to her. "I think I should probably leave the bed and breakfast as soon as I can. I don't want to get close to anyone. And Jackie is getting way too close to me." It was 12 o'clock and Jessie was getting hungry. She decided to grab a sandwich at the local cafe. She pulled up in front of the store and just sat there for a moment. She could see through the window that there was one policeman sitting at the counter. She certainly didn't want to go in while he was there. She waited patiently for him to leave.

After fifteen minutes the officer got up from his stool and left the cafe. Jessie got out of her car and went inside. She ordered a chicken salad sandwich on rye with curly fries and got it to go. She paid the cashier and left the cafe. She decided to ride out to the house on Cannon Hill Road and wait for Delores. She would eat her sandwich while she waited. She pulled up into the driveway of the old house and parked the car. She ate her lunch and then began to get sleepy. She laid her head back against the headrest of her car and dozed off. Again, she began to dream. She seemed to always dream about her escape from Mr. Wilson. She kept having the same dream over and over. She dreamed he was chasing her around the office and threatening to kill her if she told anyone about it. In her dream she was screaming and crying and trying to get away from him. He was always grabbing her and saying terrible things. A car pulled in the driveway as she is waking back up. It was Delores.

Jessie had tears in her eyes when she woke up. She wiped her face with a tissue before getting out of the car. She didn't want Delores to notice she had been crying. "Hi Delores, how are you?"

"Hello, Jessie, isn't it a beautiful day?"

"Yes it is," she replied."

"Well, let's go inside and sit down so we can discuss business." Delores unlocked the front door, and the two women went inside. They took off the sheets covering the sofa and sat down. Jessie noticed the furniture was old but didn't look too bad at all. She was both surprised and delighted. Delores pulled out the paperwork from its folder and sat it on the sofa between them. "You know this old place has been sitting empty for several years. It's been a struggle trying to find a buyer.

After almost three years of trying to sell it, I just gave up. I haven't been out here in four or five years until you called. I just want to make sure you know what you're getting into before we continue with this." Jessie assured her that the house was perfect for her needs.

"It's far enough away from town and has the privacy I want." Delores heard all she needed to hear. "Okay, then let's get on with it. Go ahead and look over the rest of the house before you make your final decision." At the end of the speedy walk through, Dolores was ready to get the place sold! "I have drawn up all the necessary paperwork for you to sign if you decide to take it. You said you wanted it as is, so we don't need an appraisal on it."

Jessie was getting anxious and just wanted to hear what the final price would be. "Can we discuss the price. I need to get all of this settled as soon as possible. I have work to do." Delores looked at Jessie and remarked at how impatient she was. "I am impatient and anxious and just want to get settled. I have books to write and I need a place like this to get started."

"Okay, then what do you think you can afford to pay for this place? I am going to leave it up to you." Delores kept fishing for the best price Jessie was willing to pay. "I have no idea what a fair price for a home would be this size on the island." She still didn't want to show her hand, hoping that Delores would name her best price.

"Well, since it's been sitting here for all these years, and because it needs a lot of work, I think maybe somewhere around seventy-five thousand dollars would be a fair price. You won't get a better deal on this island." Delores thought to herself, "I was hoping for more money for the old place, but I need to go ahead and get rid of this eye sore." She spoke up and said, "Okay, let's just make the deal. You can have this old place for seventy-five thousand."

Jessie was so excited she reached over and gave Delores a hug. "Thank you, thank you. I'll be paying cash for the house. Are there any fees or anything else I need to pay?"

"Well, there are taxes and insurance you'll need to prepay. So, the final cash you'll need will be seventy-eight thousand. Does that sound good to you?" Jessie was trying to look calm, while her heart raced with excitement. "Yes, that's just fine. Let me go and get the money." Delores told her she'd go ahead and get all the paperwork ready for Jessie to sign. "You can move in here right away. Sound good?"

CHAPTER NINE

Jessie was on her way to the car and didn't say anything after she heard the "you can move in here right away!" She was so happy to have this place. She tried to reassure herself, "I really think I'll be safe here and hopefully no one will find me. Delores is the only person who knows where I am, and she only knows me as Jessie Harris from California." Again, she was glad for the new identification. She thought to herself, "Hm, I wonder if I should explain why I'm carrying around that much cash."

Jessie went back in and started to explain. "Delores, the reason I have so much money in cash is…"

"Stop right there, Jessie, there is no need to explain anything to me. I know you are new here. I would think you probably closed your account in California before you left and haven't had time to open a bank account here"

"Yes, that is exactly right," Jessie was happy with Delores' explanation. "I just haven't had time to establish myself here yet. Thank you, Delores for all your help. I can't wait to move in here and get started on my book. I have so many ideas floating around in my head right now. I've just got to get them down on paper." Delores finished the conversation, "I do understand writers. I have a good friend who writes, and he also lives out in the country."

After all the papers had been signed and Jessie paid Delores for the house, she took a deep sigh of relief. The two women said their goodbyes as Delores walked to her car. In a flash she was out of the driveway and gone. Jessie was left standing in front of the big mysterious house. "Well, here we are alone at last. It's just you and me, mysterious house. And you know what? I am going to write a book. It's going to tell my whole story and why I did what I did. I want to expose that awful Mr. Wilson for what he is. Everyone thinks I'm the villain of this story but I'm going to prove them wrong. Mr. Wilson will be the real scoundrel when the truth comes out. Yes ma'am, I'm going to become an author of a bestselling book."

Jessie stood just looking up at the house with the keys in her hands. She walked up to the front door and put the key in the lock. She entered the house with caution as if not to wake someone up. "What in the world am I doing. There's no one here but me. I think I'll go into town tomorrow and pick up some paint and cleaning supplies. This place needs a good scrubbing. I think I might even go to the local shelter and find me a puppy...one that will get big and be protective of me. Yep, that's what I'm going to do tomorrow."

After she looked the house over and decided what she needed to get at the store, she drove back to the bed and breakfast. She would spend the night there and check out the next morning. As Jessie was entering the front door of the hotel, she ran into Maggie and Jackie. "Hello there, how are you today?"

"Oh, we are fine as rain, Miss Jessie. Jackie and I are heading to the store. Would you like to come with us?"

"Thank you for asking Maggie, but I think I'll go upstairs and lie down for a while. I wanted to let you know that I'll be checking out in the morning. It's time for me to move on."

"Oh, I'm so disappointed, Jessie. I was hoping you would stay longer."

"I want to thank you for everything, and I know I am going to miss you and Jackie." Jessie knelt and hugged Jackie. "I'll miss you Jackie and I promise I'll come by to see you every now and then. Please be a good boy and mind your grandma." Jackie returned the hug and asked, "You promise you'll come see us, Miss Jessie?"

"Yes, I will Jackie, I promise." Jessie went up to her room to lie down. She was feeling a little anxious about the house. Her stomach was in knots. Maybe it was because she had never owned her own home. On top of that, it was under strange circumstances. She was hoping that after a short rest she might feel differently.

As soon as she fell asleep, she began to dream. It was something that seemed to happen every time she closed her eyes. The dreams would not stop. In this dream she was running to get away. Suddenly she found herself in the woods, running full speed as if someone was chasing her.

CHAPTER TEN

It was almost dinner time when Jessie woke up from her nap. She was very restless and anxious when she got up. She decided to take a shower and put on some fresh clothes. Then she would go down for dinner. She walked into the dining room with a smile on her face. She thought it was better to smile than to always look like she had been crying... The other guests were friendly and polite to her. Mrs. Johnson said, "Jessie, you should try some of that trout Maggie fried for us. It is delicious."

"It certainly looks good; I believe I will try it." At the end of the meal, it seemed like everyone started talking at once. One lady talked about her daughter, while another one talked about her deceased husband. Some of the others talked about the weather. It got so loud at the table that Jessie began to get a headache.

She stood up and excused herself. "I've enjoyed meeting all of you and I want to wish all of you well. I am leaving tomorrow and won't be back." Everyone at the table was stunned to hear of Jessie's leaving. Mrs. Johnson said she wished Jessie good luck. They all said their goodbyes as Jessie finally left the dining room. As she went upstairs to her room, she realized how tired she was. "I don't know what is wrong with me. I feel so restless tonight. I'm scared to death of moving into that house by myself. I know what I'll do. Tomorrow I'll go to the shelter and find me a nice little dog. I need one that will grow up and be good company and my protection."

Early the next morning, Jessie woke up and glanced at the clock on the bedside table. It was 6 am already and she decided to get up and start the day. She needed to make a list of things she needed at the store. She couldn't wait to go over to the shelter and look for a puppy. She was anxious to hurry through her shopping. She decided to ask Maggie where the animal shelter was located. She took one last glance around the room just to make sure she hadn't forgotten anything. She opened the door and went down the stairway to see Maggie. "Okay Miss Jessie, are you sure you didn't leave anything behind?"

"Yes, Ma'am, I made sure to look around several times."

"Okay then, all you need to do is sign out on the top sheet."

Maggie wished Jessie good luck and said she hoped she would see her again one day. "Thank you for a lovely room and very nice stay. Please tell Jackie goodbye for me." Jessie reached over and gave Maggie a hug. "Oh, could you direct me to the animal shelter on the island?" Maggie gave her directions and wished her good luck with whatever new animal she decided to get. Jessie said goodbye to her and left the bed and breakfast. She got into her car and sat there for a moment just thinking about the past three months.

"I've met so many nice people along the way. I wish I could stay in touch with them. I think I will miss Maggie and little Jackie the most. So much has happened since I left Chicago. It's a place in time that I just as soon forget. I miss Joyce and little Jessie and wish I could see them, but other than those two, I never want to look back. This is my home now and I'm Jessie Harris, Lena is no more." Jessie gave herself a pep talk. "You've got to stop thinking about things you can't change. Every time you fall asleep you start dreaming about that awful old Mr. Wilson." She said a silent prayer that no one else would ever endure what she had experienced over the past few years. She pulled out of the parking area and headed south down Mulberry street.

The private detective Mr. Wilson had hired sat in a chair in front of Wilson's desk. Mr. Wilson asked, "So Brown, did you check the airlines or travel agencies here in town to see if a woman of her description bought a ticket. I know she could have gone most anywhere. You've got to check every angle. You said you went to Canada and found nothing to lead you to her. So, man, are you just going to give up?" The detective got up from his chair to leave. He turned to Mr. Wilson and said, "Look, I have checked every angle I can think of, but I'll keep on checking because you're paying me, AND I know you are the kind of man that will never give up."

"No, I won't give up until I have my money back, and I see that woman severely punished."

Brown left and went back to his own office. He sat down in his chair, propped his feet up on his desk and crossed his arms. "That Wilson is really peculiar. In a way I don't blame that woman for disappearing. I bet he drove her crazy every day. Well, I don't know what else to do. She sure has covered her tracks. I'm just going to sleep on this mystery." The following day, Jim Brown decided he would check the mortuaries around town. "She could have died, and even her sister doesn't know. Maybe she changed her name and who could ever be able to figure that one out. I need the money, but I sure don't like that old guy Wilson. Who knows, he could have killed her and then stole the money himself. I just wish he would give up and leave me alone."

But Wilson was not going away. He was determined to find Lena and get his money back. Wilson didn't care what it took or how long either. Mr. Wilson needed help in the office, so he decided to hire another woman. This time he hired an older lady who was a Christian and had several grandchildren. He reasoned to himself, "I think I can trust this lady. I figure she won't run off with my money because she has children and grandchildren. Lena was all alone with no children or a husband. She was always telling me she needed a raise. Why should I give her a raise? She wouldn't do anything for me. I suppose she thinks she deserved that money. Well, I've got news for her. She's not going to get away with this, I'll see to that."

Wilson knew that the odds of finding Lena or his money were getting slimmer with each passing day. Still, he kept the anger in the front of his mind and tried to think of any other possible ways he might use to find them both.

CHAPTER ELEVEN

She saw a sign that read Animal Shelter one mile. She decided to stop at that little store she saw on the corner just before she reached the shelter. She could pick up puppy food and the few other supplies for the house. She pulled over and parked in front of the grocery store. She reached into her purse and pulled out a list she had made earlier of the things she needed. Jessie went in and easily found all the items she needed. She wasn't sure what kind of puppy food she should get and decided on the Purina puppy food. She hoped the puppy wouldn't be too picky about his food.

When she finished her shopping, she headed to the shelter. Jessie was so excited! It was time to pick out a puppy and head back toward the country. Every time she thought about the house, she got a lump in her throat. "I wonder why I feel so nervous about the house. It's going to be a challenge for me, but in time it will be home." She walked into the animal shelter and started looking around at all the puppies. She came across a cage that had a German shepherd mother dog and three puppies. "Oh, what a beautiful dog and she has such cute puppies."

She went out into the lobby and asked the lady behind the counter if the German shepherd puppies were adoptable. "Well, as a matter of fact, they just became adoptable. They are six weeks old and ready for a new home."

"I would love to have one of the male puppies, if possible." The lady behind the desk called for one of the attendants to bring one of the male puppies out into the gated area. "You can wait here, and someone will bring the puppy to you." It wasn't long before the attendant brought the cutest little fat puppy out to her. She knelt and picked him up. He licked her face and wagged his tail. "You are adorable, little guy. I think you'll do just fine."

She thanked the attendant and told him she would take the puppy. After filling out the adoption papers, she led the puppy on a leash to her car. "Your name is Rusti, and you better be a good boy in this car." She put Rusti in the very back of the SUV and told him to stay there." Rusti laid down and never made a sound. Jessie was relieved because she wasn't sure what she would do if the dog started to act up while she was driving. After arriving back home, she led Rusti to the backyard.

"Now I know the grass needs cutting but this is your yard now, Rusti. So, you be a good doggie while I take things inside the house. Rusti, you are going to be a good protector for me, I just know it." Jessie had not had the electricity turned on yet, so she decided she would just use candles for a while. She would put one in every room of the house. She got all the packages she could carry and took them into the house.

Rusti as a puppy.

She was glad it was only late afternoon and there was still a lot of daylight left. After setting all the packages on the kitchen counter, she went into the living room and started taking the old sheets off the furniture. The room was large and airy. The furniture wasn't new, but it would do. The curtains on the windows were filthy but they too would do for the moment. As she walked from room to room, she noticed the floors and doors creaked. As she went up the staircase, the steps also creaked. "Oh, my goodness, the whole house creeks. Makes me feel a little creepy. I think I'll go let Rusti come in the house. At least now I won't be alone in the place. Maybe after I get things put in place, it will not be so scary."

Jessie went to the back door and called Rusti to come in the house. He wagged his tail and was very happy to get back in. "Now don't you go pee on the floor, boy. I have enough to do without having to clean up your mishaps." Jessie had bought a dog bed and three rubber toys for the dog when she went to the store. She put them down on the kitchen floor and told Rusti to go get his toys. The dog ran over and started playing. It was as if he had always been there.

She worked all afternoon cleaning the kitchen. She scrubbed the stove, the old refrigerator, the cabinets and the floors. She then went upstairs and cleaned the first bathroom which led into the master bedroom. "This looks like a nice room. I think Rusti and I'll take this room." Rusti had started following her all over the house. At one point he growled at the wall and made Jessie a little uneasy. "What is it, Rusti? Do you hear something? You know this house has been empty for a long time." She reached down and patted him on his head. "It's okay, boy, we won't let anything bother us way out here."

The master bedroom was a very airy room with four windows overlooking the front lawn. She sat a candle on the side table and lit it. It gave out enough light to change the bed linen. The bed had been covered up with a big white sheet. She pulled it off the bed and dust filled the room. Jessie began to cough and ran over and opened the windows. "The fresh air will help this place. I think I'll open a few more windows before it gets dark. Rusti, tomorrow I'm going to call the local electric company and have the lights turned on. We'll just have to use the candles tonight."

CHAPTER TWELVE

Summer was coming to an end and the nights were beginning to get cooler. There was a big fireplace in the living room, so she decided to gather some firewood. "I sure hope this fireplace works. Come on, Rusti, let's go out back and see if we can find some wood." Jessie put her boots and heavy coat on. She and Rusti walked out behind the house. She began gathering the wood, she found lying around on the ground. Rusti sat by the fence watching her. As she was coming back toward the house, she thought she saw someone in the upstairs window. "That's odd. Well, it must have been my imagination. They say old houses like this one are haunted. It's probably that old Mr. Wilson come to haunt me. Come on, Rusti, let's go in the house and try to get a fire going."

Jessie put the wood in the fireplace and lit it with a match. The wood began to slowly catch fire. "I sure hope the chimney isn't stopped up." Before she finished getting the words out of her mouth, smoke began to fill the room. The fire got bigger. "Oh no, it's been so long since it was used, it might be stopped up." She jumped up and opened the windows in the room. She began to fan the smoke. After ten minutes the smoke had disappeared from the room. The fire in the fireplace was burning as it should be. Jessie thought leaves were apparently blocking the smoke. She was thankful it wasn't a big blockage. Now that she knew it was okay to use, she could gather more wood and use it at night when it got colder.

Jessie loved the house and worked hard to make it livable. She scrubbed windows, washed curtains, mopped floors and waxed all the furniture. She transformed the Cannon Hill house into a beautiful warm and cozy home. As she sat in the living room one winter evening, she began to think about her journey. "It's hard for me to believe, but I've been gone from Chicago for almost a year now. I wonder if Mr. Wilson has ever given up looking for me. Knowing him, I doubt it."

Jessie began to think about her sister. "I need to call Joyce and check on her and Jessie. I think I'll go to town tomorrow and pick up some supplies and a couple of burner phones too." Rusti was laying in front of the fireplace when his ears went up as if he heard something. He jumped up and started barking. "What's wrong, Rusti, did you hear a noise?" Jessie had chills go up her spine. She was frightened by his barking. "I always thought I was so brave, but I'm finding out I'm not." Rusti finally calmed down and laid back down on the floor. "It was probably the wind blowing a limb against the house. Rusti, you're a good watch dog."

The following day, Jessie got up early and as she stood in front of the mirror, she could see more stress lines on her face. "Give me another year or two and I'll look twice my age. Oh well, there's not much I can do about it." She put on a pair of blue jeans, a purple sweater, and tennis shoes. She then pulled her hair back with a scarf. She was ready to drive to the store. "You ready to go, Rusti?" The dog started wagging his tail and turning around in circles. "Okay, let's go." She was rarely seen without the dog.

Whenever Jessie went out in public, she wore her hair pulled back. She would wear thick rimmed glasses and no makeup. "Who would ever recognize me like this? I look completely different from the way I use too." She reached over and patted Rusti on his head as she drove towards town. Jessie had made an agreement with the store manager to bring Rusti with her each time she came into the store. She claimed to have problems with her eyesight, and she needed the dog to help her.

She finished shopping for supplies for the house and bought a thick tablet. She wanted to start writing about everything that had happened over the past year. She figured between her story and the info about previous owners, it would make a great novel. That would be an interesting story to read. Before heading home, she decided to buy a paper. She wanted to catch up on news from the US. It took her an hour and a half to drive to the Cannon Hill house from town. She really didn't mind the drive; it was worth the long drive if it kept her safe.

She pulled into the driveway and just sat there for a moment. She got out of the car and walked up to the front door. She noticed the door was ajar. "Rusti, I know I locked this door before we left. You go in and check the house." Rusti went inside the house and ran from room to room. Then he returned to Jessie wagging his tail. "Well buddy, I guess that tail wagging means it's okay to go in. That really is strange though. I just know I locked this door." As she walked in with her eyes looking everywhere, she continued talking to Rusti. "There have been things happening that I do not understand. Maybe this house is haunted after all. What do you think, boy?"

After she carried all the new supplies into the house, she decided to turn all the lights on. She felt something in the air that just didn't feel right. It felt like a curtain hanging over her. It was heavy and depressing. "What in the world could be causing this feeling? I don't like it, whatever it is." She started a fire in the fireplace and sat down in her favorite chair. She unfolded the newspaper and started reading the headlines. She began to scroll through the inside of the paper until she came to the news section about the United States. Way down at the bottom of the paper was a small news article about a prominent business owner in downtown Chicago. It said he died Friday evening from a head injury, after an unknown assailant had attacked him.

CHAPTER THIRTEEN

She continued to read the article when suddenly she said out loud. "Oh my God, it was Mr. Wilson. Oh, it can't be! But there's his name: Robert J Wilson, owner of Liberty Finance Company in Chicago. I just can't believe Wilson is dead. He was so terribly mean. I wonder if his attacker knew him. Could this mean I am finally free of him?" She wasn't sure if the police would stop looking for her. Until she knew for sure, she felt the need to stay put and be careful. She folded her hands to pray and said, "Thank you God for taking this evil man out of my life. He made my life miserable and caused me so much pain. God, forgive me but I am so glad he is gone from this earth. Amen."

Jessie felt so relieved by the unexpected news. She just sat in the chair by the fire until she fell asleep. When she woke up, she noticed Rusti was gone. She called to him several times before she heard him bark. He had gone upstairs and was sitting in front of one of the back bedrooms. "What's wrong, Rusti? Did you hear something again?" She slowly opened the door to the bedroom and went inside. "There's nothing in here, Rusti, but phew, do you smell that musty odor? It's horrible." She quickly ran to the bathroom and picked up a can of deodorizer. She sprayed the room thoroughly and opened the windows. "Come on, Rusti, let's go." She shut the bedroom door and went downstairs. Rusti followed close behind.

"Where is that paperwork Delores left for me to read. There's a folder in there that lists all the people who have lived here. I better read it because someone may have died here. Who knows, maybe this place is haunted. I'm beginning to think it is. Let's go make some lunch an then I'll go back up and check on that room. I want to make sure the smell has gone away." Jessie made a sandwich for herself and put some dog food in a bowl for Rusti.

"There you go, boy. You are such a good dog. You are always alerting me to things. I'm so happy I chose you at the animal shelter." She patted Rusti on his head and told him she loved him.

It was late afternoon when Jessie decided she would go upstairs and check on the bedroom. She opened the door and walked into the room. The horrible odor had disappeared, and a flowering smell filled the air. "What's going on in here? First there was that terrible odor and now the flowers. I like the flower smell but even it's strong. I think I'll just leave the window open a little longer and keep the door shut. There's something fishy going on around here and I sure would like know what it is."

After lunch she went into the living room and sat down in the chair near the fireplace. She had been out back cutting wood which made her body ache. "I guess the last residents left that shack of wood piled up." She decided she needed to buy a wheelbarrow so she could haul the wood up to the house. As she stood up, she rubbed her back. It was aching so badly she could hardly walk. Carrying all that wood yesterday had made her sore. She ached from her head to her toes whenever she moved around. "Next time I go into town, I'm going to buy a reasonable wheelbarrow to haul wood and save my back!"

She sat down in her favorite spot and picked up the folder Delores had given her. It had been sitting on the table beside her chair. She had wanted to read it ever since she moved in. Jessie opened the folder and started reading about the first family that lived in the Cannon Hill house. As she read, she kept hearing noises from upstairs. Rusti started barking and ran up the staircase. She was a little uneasy at first, but decided she was going up there and find out what was going on. She spoke to Rusti as she headed up the steps, "I am sick and tired of all these noises and crazy things happening around here."

As she climbed, she shouted out to whoever and whatever was up there. "Whoever you are, you'd better go before I call the police. I'm sick and tired of you ghosts disturbing me all the time. I can't get a minute's peace in this house." Rusti was still barking and standing outside the bedroom door that had smelled so badly and then changed to the smell of flowers. "What is it, Rusti? Let's just go in there and see what's going on. These ghosts have got to go."

She opened the door, and the horrible smell was back. "Good grief, what a terrible smell. Okay you guys, get out of my house. I'm tired of this. Get out, now." She kept shouting "Get out, Get out." Suddenly the smell disappeared. "Well now, what about that, Rusti. The smell is gone. Well, it may not be gone for good but for now it's gone. You ghosts had better leave this place now. I'm not afraid of you. I just want you gone."

Jessie remembered her Aunt Louise having a conversation with her about ghosts. She told Jessie if she was suspicious her home was haunted, she needed a plan. "Go to the center of the house or wherever the ghosts were seen the most and ask them to leave. Sometimes ghosts haven't passed over to the other side, so they linger in familiar places. Aunt Louise might be right about that." Jessie had thoughts of her own in this house. "Of course, I guess they sometimes come back. That's okay, because I'm ready for them. I just wonder which family it is."

CHAPTER FOURTEEN

Jessie and Rusti went back downstairs. She picked up the folder again and sat down to read it. She started reading about the very first family who lived there. There was a husband, wife and little boy about five years old. They were from Nevada. She was a dealer at one of the casino's and he owned a pub of some kind. During their stay at the house on Cannon Hill, the husband was very rarely seen. He went out at night supposedly to work and came home very early in the morning. One day they just up and moved.

She continued reading about the next family who also seemed peculiar. "There were four of them, a mother, a father, a teenage daughter, and a son about eleven years old. The father traveled and was rarely seen. He was lazy and even had his own son cut the grass while he watched. The mother worked part-time and was unfriendly to everyone. When she went to town; she wouldn't speak to anyone. They left the house in shambles when they moved out. Hmm, this family doesn't sound very good either. Well, Rusti, are you ready for some more of this story. Somebody had to have died along the way. I wonder who it was?"

"Here we go, Rusti. The third family was even stranger. A man and woman lived in this house for ten years. They both drank and partied a lot. The wife had numerous affairs and the husband knew all about it. They argued a lot about her affairs. The wife would just ignore the husband and continued her wild lifestyle. In 1986 the couple had a big Christmas party. They invited several prominent people to the party, including, now listen to this, Rusti, Mrs.

Carmichael's two lovers."

Jessie continued reading to her dog, "One of them was a famous businessman from Nova Scotia. The other one owned a hardware store in

Charlottetown. With all the music and laughter going on, no one heard the shot that killed Mrs. Carmichael. Some say she had unfinished business and has never left the premises. Rusti, that's it. That woman was killed here. I bet she thinks her husband's the one who killed her. It says here that the husband was never convicted of the crime. Several people saw him at the party and gave him an alibi for the time of the murder. Hey, wait Rusti, there's more to the story."

The dog laid his head on the edge of Jessie's chair cushion as if he was listening and understood everything she said. "It says here their names were Robert and Naomi Carmichael. The husband continued to live in this house after his wife's death. He lived here for five years until he died of a heart attack." She looked at Rusti and said, "You know what that means? His ghost could be here too. No wonder Delores didn't tell me about all this before I signed the papers. I guess she didn't because she was afraid I wouldn't take the house. If I have you here with me, I'm not afraid, Rusti. I'm still glad I took this house. I really don't know who the ghost is. For all I know, it might be old Mr. Wilson's ghost. He may have found me and has come here to get me."

Jessie decided she would go and make some hot tea to drink before she read any more stories. She got up from her chair and went into the kitchen. Rusti followed closely behind. She filled the kettle up with water and placed it on the stove. After her tea was ready, she went into the living room and sat back down in her chair. Rusti laid his head against her leg. "Let's see now, I wonder if the following story is also going to be disturbing," she said as she yawned. Evidently the house had a long history of crazy residents. She sipped on her tea as she spoke to Rusti. "I don't know if I can finish these stories tonight. I'm awfully sleepy. Why don't we go up to bed?"

She got up from her chair and put the fire out in the fireplace. She left the light on in the living room and walked up the staircase to her bedroom. "Come on, Rusti, get in your bed."

Jessie was not afraid if Rusti was beside her. She changed into her pajamas and crawled into her bed. She laid there thinking about all these people she had read about. "I wonder how many more crazy people lived here?" After a while, she finally fell asleep.

The same old dream came to her as if a cloud of doom had fallen all over her. Mr. Wilson was chasing her around the office. She tried getting her work done, but he wouldn't leave her alone. Then she saw the police coming towards her. They had their guns out and were pointing them right at her. Her sister Joyce was calling to her to give herself up. Then suddenly she woke up, as always, with tears in her eyes. "Surely the police wouldn't be looking for me after all this time. Now that Mr. Wilson is dead, I would think the case has been closed. I'll make a call to Joyce tomorrow. Maybe she can find out for me."

CHAPTER FIFTEEN

Jessie woke up early the next morning. She sat up on the side of the bed, stretched and yawned. "Come on, Rusti, let's go take you outside." Rusti wagged his tail and ran down the staircase. Jessie followed behind him with one arm in her bathrobe and the other one hanging behind her. She didn't realize it had snowed while she slept. "oh look, Rusti, it snowed last night. Isn't it beautiful outside, boy? Go on out in the yard while I put on the coffee." Rusti hesitated for a moment then ran and hiked his leg. He immediately wanted to come back in the house. "Too cold outside for you isn't it, boy? Come on, let's go build a fire in the fireplace."

She added firewood to the fire as the flames rose higher and higher. It felt so good. She decided to read some more of the folder while she drank her coffee. She sat down in her chair, picked up the folder and started reading aloud to Rusti. "I couldn't stop thinking about all these people last night. I dreamed about them all night. But my dreams always turn to Wilson. I seem to dream the same old dreams. I wish I could forget about him and everything that happened back then. Look, Rusti, there's more about the Carmichaels. The last thing I read last night was the husband lived here for five years after his wife died."

Rusti laid by her side as if listening to her as she continued to read from the folder. "It says the ghost of Mrs. Carmichael tormented him until his heart gave out. The man must have been guilty of something. That's probably why his soul isn't at rest. Good grief, Rusti, we are living in a house of horrors. I'm going to have to figure out how to get rid of all these ghosts." She sat back in her chair and drank her coffee. She couldn't stop thinking about all the people who had lived in her house. She decided to drive into town and go to the local library. She thought she might find some more information on the Carmichael family.

Jessie went upstairs and opened the back-bedroom door. That horrible smell had disappeared at last. She went to the hall closet and got a big candle out and took it into the bedroom. She sat it on the dresser and lit it. "This will make this room feel and smell so much better." She left the door open so she wouldn't forget to blow the candle out before she left the house. She wanted to go into town early and get home before dark. She decided to stop by the hardware store and pick up some flood lights. It was dark outside with only a porch light on.

Jessie drove the long drive into Charlottetown. She stopped at the gas station to fill up the car. While there, she decided to ask the attendant where the local library was located. "I believe it's near City Hall, Miss. I haven't been there in several years."

"Thank you, I'll check it out." She knew how to get to City Hall. She parked her car, and from there she saw the library just across the street. She put Rusti's leash on and then got her glasses out of the glove compartment. She hated disguising herself every time she went to town, but she didn't want to take chances.

She went into the library and asked the lady behind the counter if she could direct her to old newspaper articles. "What years are you looking for? I can help you find them."

"Well, I think it would be in the 1980's. Somewhere around 1986."

"I believe I know just where they are. Yes, here they are, Miss. My name is Ruth if you need anything else. I'll be glad to help you."

"Thank you, Ruth, I appreciate that." Jessie sat down at the table and started scrolling through the newspapers. Finally, she found an issue that talked about the Carmichael's. On page 43 she got to learn more about the house on Cannon Hill.

Jessie read the article over and over. It spoke of all the distinguished people from the island that came to their parties. It told how the couple drank all the time and then got in fights with each other. She murmured softly, "It says here they had a son. His name was John, and he was sent to school in Halifax. I wonder if he is still alive? I need to talk to him, if I can find him." She continued to read the article. She read about all the parties they had. "No wonder they sent their only son away to school. Rusti, we have a mystery on our hands, and I mean to get to the bottom of all this. This is our house now and I won't put up with the past ruining it for us."

Jessie began to gather all the information she could about the house, especially about the Carmichaels. After leaving the library she sat in her car and picked up the throw away phone. "This would be a good time to call Joyce." She dialed her number and waited to hear her voice on the other end. Joyce answered the phone. "Hello."

"Joyce, it's Lena."

"Lena, how are you? We haven't heard from you in such a long time. Are you alright?"

"Yes, I'm fine. How are you and the kids?"

"We're all okay."

Now she got down to the main reason for the call. "Joyce, I was wondering if you know if the police are still looking for me."

"As far as I know, Lena, they have closed the case. Wilson has been dead a while, so they stopped pursuing it two or three months ago. Are you coming home?"

"No Joyce, I'm happy where I am, and I plan on staying here. I love you and the kids. Please give them a hug for me. Got to go now, goodbye." Lena hung the phone up, as she sat there with tears running down her face. She missed Joyce so much, but she did not want to go back. She loved it on the island and wanted it to be her permanent home.

She laid her head back against the seat and closed her eyes. She was thinking about when she and her sister were little girls. They would chase each other and play hide and seek. Joyce always found her, no matter where she hid. She was her protector and confidant. Now she was all alone except for her sweet Rusti. She reached over and gave the dog a hug. Jessie backed out of the parking lot and drove down the street to Freeman's hardware store. She went inside and bought two flood lights. Before she left, she decided to ask the cashier if she knew of anyone that would be willing to put those lights up for her.

CHAPTER SIXTEEN

The woman behind the counter told her she had a teenage son who might be willing to hang them for her. "I would be willing to pay him of course. The problem is, I live way out in the country. I could come to town and pick him up."

"Well, let me check with him when he gets home from school today. He's a good boy and I know he will be willing to help you out."

"That's wonderful. My name is Jessie Harris, by the way. I'll come by tomorrow and check with you, if that's okay?"

"Yes, of course"

"Thanks for your help. I forgot to ask your name."

"Lorraine Jenkins and my son's name is Scott."

"Thank you, Lorraine, I'll see you tomorrow."

Jessie and Rusti left the hardware store and walked down to the local café. She went inside and ordered a chicken salad sandwich on rye and curly fries to go. The waitress behind the counter had gotten to know Jessie and knew what she would order before she came in the door. "Hi Janice, I guess you know what I'm going to order."

"You bet I do. You always order the same thing." Jessie laughed as she paid for her food a short while later. "See you in a couple of days." She picked up her lunch and walked over to the little grocery store on the corner. She picked up a few things she needed, then she headed home. She was amazed at how friendly everyone in town was. Stranger or no stranger, the people of Prince Edward Island were the same to everyone they met.

Jessie loved living here and was beginning to know a few people that had lived here their whole lives. As she drove home she began to think about the Carmichael's. "Rusti, I have got to solve the mystery of the Carmichael family. I need to find out if their son is still living or not and where I can find him." Rusti sat in the seat beside Jessie and lifted his head each time she said something. It was as if he understood every word. As they pulled in the driveway, Jessie noticed the front door was open. "This is the second time that door has been opened when I got back home. Rusti, go in the house, boy, and check it out for me." He jumped out of the car and ran inside the house.

Rusti stood at the bottom of the steps barking. Jessie went inside the house and looked up the staircase. "Rusti, go get'em." The dog ran up the staircase barking as he ran. Jessie went into the kitchen and got a butcher knife out of the drawer. She ran back into the hall to see what was going on. Rusti roamed from room to room. He went into the bathrooms and all the bedrooms. Finally, Jessie decided to go upstairs herself. "Well, Rusti, it looks like the ghosts have been naughty again." Jessie yelled out as loud as she could, "If you think you are going to scare me out of this house, you have another thought coming. This is my home now and I am not going anywhere. Come on, Rusti, let's go eat our lunch."

She filled Rusti's bowl up with his favorite dog food then filled the kettle with water and sat it on the stove to heat. She poured herself a cup of tea and ate her sandwich and curly fries. "I've got to do something about the ghosts in this house. They think they are scaring me, but they aren't. Well, I must admit maybe they are scaring me a little. It's just so creepy knowing they are here. There must be a way of getting rid of them. Maybe if I could solve the mystery of Mrs. Carmichael's death, they would go away."

After dinner that evening, Jessie and Rusti went into the living room and sat down by the fireplace. The weatherman on the radio said it was 28 degrees. "I believe it, Rusti, because it is freezing in here." When she blew her breath out into the air, it almost froze. "It can't be that cold in here. The fireplace has always warmed up this room. I think I know what's going on. Mrs. Carmichael is paying us a visit. Okay, Mrs. Carmichael, I know you are here. I don't care what you do, I'm not going to leave this house. Go away, you are going to freeze us to death." In a short while the frosty cold disappeared from the room.

"Now that's better. Come sit by my side and I'll read some more stories from this folder." Rusti understood and leisurely walked over to sit down by Jessie's chair. "Well, let's see who lived here after the Carmichael's. It says here a family from Iowa moved in here in 1997. The family consisted of mother, father, teenage son and grandfather. They had an online flower business and at one point dug up the whole backyard. They tried to get plants to grow out there but with no luck. The grandfather got sick and died in the upstairs bedroom. Oh no, Rusti, there may be another ghost in that room. Who knows, his spirit might still be here too."

Jessie continued to read from the folder. "After the grandfather died, the family moved out of the house. So, there's really nothing significant about these people other than the grandfather passing away. Now I know why my backyard is so bumpy. They only lived here a year, so I'm not sure they left any bad vibes behind. I think I'm going to concentrate on the

Carmichael family. Rusti, we need to find the son, John Carmichael. I think he may have the answer to a lot of this. If we can find him, we may have some clue about who the killer was."

CHAPTER SEVENTEEN

The cold was relentless during the month of November. The snow and ice on the ground made it difficult to get around outside. The weather made Jessie decide to put up a Christmas tree. "You know, Rusti, I think a Christmas tree would look beautiful in the living room. I haven't had a tree in twenty years. I remember Joyce and I always had a tree at Christmas. When I became an adult and left home, I never had one again. Ghosts or no ghosts in this house, we are going to celebrate the holiday season. It will help to brighten this old house up a bit. What do you think, Rusti?" The dog wagged his tail and gave out a bark as if to say he was excited too.

"Rusti, as soon as the weather lets up a little, we are going into town and get all the decorations and a Christmas tree. In the meantime, I am going to read some more of this folder and see if I can figure out some things. There have been so many people living here in the past, there's no wonder the house was in bad shape. I'm going to write down the important facts about the Carmichael family. And each time I discover something new, I'll write it down. Let's see now, first there is the wife.......Naomi Carmichael – Killed by gunshot on Christmas Eve 1986. Robert Carmichael died in this house five years after his wife's death.

A son called John –

Murder unsolved?

Restless ghost – could be Mrs. Carmichael?

Where is John, the son?

"Looks like my list is getting longer and longer. I can't think of anything else right now, why don't we turn in. I'm really tired and cold." Jessie checked all the doors to make sure they were locked and put the fire out in the fireplace. "Come on, Rusti, let's go upstairs and get ready for bed. Rusti went over and got in his bed. He turned and turned until he was comfortable. Jessie put on her pajamas and crawled into her bed. She sat up in bed for a while writing her story. "If anything, ever happens to me, at least people will know the truth about why I did what I did." She wrote for over an hour. Her eyes were getting so tired she could barely hold them open. She decided that she should write a little each night, but for right now, she was going to sleep.

The following morning Jessie got up early. After she showered and dressed, she motioned for Rusti to go downstairs with her. She let him outside for a few minutes while she put the kettle on for hot tea. Rusti was anxious to get back in the house. "I know why you want to come back in so fast, Rusti. It's freezing outside. Cold as it is, I really need to drive into the heart of Prince Edward Island today. I want to buy a Christmas tree and decorations. I'm also supposed to stop by Freemans's hardware to find out about that boy. I really need those flood lights. That porch light just isn't enough." After she had a bowl of cereal and cup of tea, she was ready to head to town.

She arrived in town just in time to see a Christmas parade. "Look Rusti, a Christmas parade. I did not know they were having one today. Why don't we park and watch for a little while?" The parade brought back many memories of her and Joyce when they were little girls. She started thinking about her younger days. As usual, she spoke to Rusti. "Mama and daddy would always take us girls to the Christmas parade in downtown Chicago. They would buy us cotton candy and a little bottle of Coke. I'll never forget those wonderful days of our youth. Oh, how I miss Joyce. I wish there was some way I could bring her and the kids here to live with me. Wishful thinking, I guess."

Jessie and Rusti walked through the crowd until they reached the hardware store. All the stores in town were decorated for Christmas. She walked into the store and the lady behind the counter said hello, how are you today? "I'm just fine, Lorraine, thank you. I didn't know the town was having a Christmas parade today. Everyone seems to be having a really good time."

"Yes, Ma'am, the island has one every year, and they really put on a nice one. I came into town today to pick up some Christmas ornaments for my tree. While I was here, I wanted to stop in and see what your son's answer was."

"Oh, he said he would be happy to come out to the house on Saturday and put the flood lights up. He has a car and seems to know where the Cannon Hill house is located."

"That's wonderful. I'll be more than happy to give him some gas money because it really is a long way out there."

Jessie and Rusti left the hardware store and went into one of the merchandise stores. She picked out three packs of Christmas lights and a beautiful star ornament for the top of the tree. "I want to buy a nice tree skirt too, Rusti. Look at these beautiful ornaments. I think I'll buy two boxes of these." After she finished shopping she went to her car and loaded all the packages. She stood by her car and watched the rest of the parade. There was a Santa Claus with his little helpers throwing candy out to all the little kids. A school band dressed in red Christmas outfits playing traditional Christmas songs.

"White Christmas sure seems to be appropriate with all this snowy weather we're having. Rusti, when we get home I'm going to find Christmas music on the radio, make some hot chocolate and decorate the tree. Maybe that will drive the ghosts crazy, and they will leave us alone for a while. Wouldn't that be something? Okay, boy, get in the car and let's go home."

CHAPTER EIGHTEEN

After arriving home, Jessie unloaded the car. She went back out to the car and dragged the Christmas tree up to the porch. She picked it up as best she could and brought it into the living room. After several tries, she finally got it in the stand straight. It stood there in the corner of the room just waiting to be decorated. "I don't think this old house has had a Christmas tree for a long time, Rusti. I can't wait to get it decorated. It's going to be beautiful. Let's turn the radio on and listen to Christmas music." She went into the kitchen and put the kettle on the stove to heat. "Hot chocolate is just the thing I need right now. It's so cold in here. I better put some wood in the fireplace and warm the house up. Mrs. Carmichael may be visiting us and causing it to be cold. She may be offended by the Christmas tree since she was killed on Christmas Eve. Oh well, she will just have to get over it."

Jingle Bells was playing as she hung the lights on the tree. She went around and around with them until she had all three strung like she wanted them. "That looks nice, Rusti, now let's put these pretty ornaments on the tree." She continued hanging the shiny ornaments and stood back to admire her work. "Well, Rusti, I'll get a chair from the kitchen so I can reach the top." She climbed onto the chair and placed the star on top of the Christmas tree. She climbed down and stood back away from the tree to look at it. "Rusti, what do you think. Isn't it pretty?" Rusti let out a bark as if to say it looked nice. Jessie patted him on the head and told him he was a good boy.

"The Carmichael's fought a lot in this house. It appeared Naomi had several boyfriends she was associated with and Mr. Carmichael found out about it. But there was one guy she was in love with. She went behind Mr. Carmichael's back and saw this guy a lot more than the others. I wouldn't doubt one bit if Mr. Carmichael didn't hire someone to kill her. The whole thing is weird to me and I just know her husband had something to do with her death. I wish I knew who the guy was she was in love with. I've just got to figure this out."

The clock on the mantel struck eleven. Jessie was tired and decided to take all the empty boxes upstairs to the hall closet.

She put the fire out, turned off the radio and unplugged the tree. Then she checked all the doors to make sure they were locked. "Come on, Rusti, let's go up to bed. It's late and I'm very tired." Rusti followed behind her as she went upstairs. Jessie opened the hall closet and started to stack all the boxes behind the clothes when she noticed a line in the back wall. "Well, Rusti, I never noticed that line in the wall before." She knelt and ran her fingers down the line. Suddenly the wall moved backward as if to open. It was a little door that opened into a secret compartment in the closet. "Oh my gosh, I think I've found a trinket box. I know I shouldn't be snooping into someone's personal things, but I believe this belonged to Mrs. Carmichael."

She picked up the trinket box carefully. She carried it to her bedroom and laid it on the bed. "Okay Rusti, it's time to open it and see what's in here. Maybe it will have a clue to her death." Jessie opened the trinket box and saw several letters tied together with a piece of string. She picked up a picture of a woman and a man hugging each other. She turned it over in hopes it had names on the back. Sure enough, it read Naomi and Richard, Spring of 1985. "Naomi Carmichael, wow, she was a beautiful woman. Blond curly hair, blue eyes and a very slender figure. This Richard was nice looking too, but I'd like to know what Mr. Carmichael looked like. I may have to go back to the library one day and look through some more newspapers."

As Jessie fumbled through the trinket box, she found a lovely diamond watch. It had an engraving under the band. She picked it up and held it under the lamp so she could read the writing. "It says, 'To Naomi with all my love, Richard'. Rusti, the plot thickens. This Richard must have really loved Mrs. Carmichael to give her something like this. You can tell the watch is very expensive. I know I shouldn't, but I have got to read some of these letters. They may have a clue we need to solve this case." She got undressed and put on her pajamas. She then crawled into her bed, propped her pillows up, and sat back so she could read.

She opened the first letter which was dated July 10, 1984.

Dear Naomi,

I miss you so much my heart aches. I'll be back in town in three days, and I pray I can see you. Does your husband suspect anything? I love you so much, I don't even care anymore. I'll call you when I get in and maybe we can meet someplace.

Farewell my love, Richard.

Jessie just sat there in her bed feeling kind of sad. She wanted to read the rest of these letters, but she was too sleepy then. She put them back into the box and decided she would read them tomorrow. She reached over and turned the light out and fell quickly asleep. She dreamed about the box and the letters all through the night. In her dream, Mr. Wilson would always appear, and she would be running to get away. When she woke up the following morning, she felt like she had been up all night. "I don't know why I am so tired this morning. I slept all night, but I had terrible dreams. I guess that's why I feel so tired today."

CHAPTER NINETEEN

Jessie just laid in bed for a while thinking about the box. "Mrs. Carmichael must have hidden the box so her husband couldn't find it. What a shame someone killed her. She must have been a lovely lady for Richard to love her so much. I don't think Richard killed her." The following day was Saturday and Lorraine's son Scott was coming out to put her flood lights up. She hurried and got her shower and dressed. "Come on, Rusti, let's go outside and potty." As Jessie and Rusti started downstairs, she noticed a picture laying on the steps. She reached down and picked it up. It was a picture of a man standing on the front porch of this house. She turned the picture over to see if there was a name on it.

Robert Carmichael was written on the back of the picture. "Look, Rusti, our ghost gave us a picture of her husband. Now we know what he looked like. Looks to me like she is trying to help us solve this mystery." Jessie looked around her and said, "Thank you, Mrs. Carmichael." Jessie was curious to know who the other men were that Mrs. Carmichael was seeing. "I don't want to go to the police and ask questions. There could be a warrant out for me. Even here in Canada, I'm not completely safe. How long has it been now, Rusti? It's almost two years since I came to Prince Edward Island. I don't think I'll ever feel safe again."

It was ten O'clock in the morning when Jessie heard a car pull into the driveway. She instantly ran up to the upstairs landing to look out. It was a blue pickup truck. Two young boys got out of the truck and walked up to the front door. "That has got to be Scott. Who else could it be?" As he rang the doorbell Jessie stood on the other side of the door. She quietly asked, "Who is it?"

"It's Scott, Mrs. Harris. I'm here with my friend Frank to put up your flood lights." Jessie opened the door and told them to wait a moment. "You know you can never be sure of anyone. I try to be very careful who I open my door too."

"I don't blame you, Mrs. Harris."

"You boys go ahead and get the ladder out of your truck." Scott climbed up the ladder and put the flood light in the socket. "You're lucky the light equipment has already been installed. All we had to do is replace the bulbs."

"I am so grateful to you both for doing this for me. There is no way I could have climbed up a ladder that tall. I want you both to have a ten-dollar bill for coming way out here to help me out."

"Thank you, Mrs. Harris. Can I ask you a question about this place?"

"Of course, Scott, what do you want to know?"

"Well, we have always heard this house was haunted. Is that true?"

"Well sometimes Rusti hears things, but I have never seen or heard anything. I heard that rumor before I bought this old place and was hesitant at first. Tell me everything you have heard about this house if you don't mind. I'm curious now."

"Well, not much except."

"Except what Scott? Frank, Scott, what did you hear about this place. Please tell me." Frank spoke up and said, "I heard about a lady that was killed here and her ghost roamed the halls at night longing for her lover."

"Did the police ever find out who killed her?"

"They accused her lover, Richard, but it was never proven."

"Do you know if he is still alive or living here on the island?"

"Yes, he lives over on Murray Street, I believe."

As they headed back to the truck, she waved and said, "Thank you boys again for your help and the information about this old place. The stories have been very interesting."

Jessie didn't want the boys to know the truth about this house. She was afraid they would go tell other friends of theirs. "The next thing you know curious people would converge on my place." She was so glad to get the new lights up and hoped it would discourage uninvited people. After Jessie finished feeding Rusti, she got a cup of hot tea and decided she would read the other letters she found in the trinket box.

She plugged the Christmas tree lights up and started a nice fire in the fireplace. She sat down in her chair and opened the next letter. As she read the letter she felt a slight cold come over her. "Rusti, I think we have company this morning. Mrs. Carmichael is here with us. I guess she wants me to read the letters." Jessie started reading the next letter.

Dear my darling Naomi, September 14, 1989

I have returned from my trip and want to see you. I have missed you so much. Please meet me at our regular place tonight at 9 pm. If you have a problem getting away, I'll understand. But please try to come. I need you my darling.

Love Richard

"Wow, Rusti, this guy was really in love with Mrs. Carmichael. These letters are heartbreaking to me." Suddenly a cold frost descended upon the room. "I'm freezing. I'm going to get a blanket for both of us, Rusti. I know you must be cold too." Just as she got up to go get the blankets, the frost disappeared from the room. "The room is warming up again. She must have left the room, Rusti. I wish she would let us know who shot her. I wonder if she could leave us a message somehow. Come on, Rusti, let's go to town and look up this Richard. I want to ask him some questions, Maybe I better try to call him first and make an appointment to see him."

CHAPTER TWENTY

As Jessie and Rusti were driving into Charlottetown, a car passed them that looked like a detective car. "I have seen so many detective stories I can spot one of their cars. It was solid black with dark tinted windows. I wonder if they were going to our house. Maybe I better head back that way and see where they went." She turned the SUV around and headed back to Cannon Hill road. She pulled off the road just before her house. "Look, Rusti, that black car went right passed our house. Let's just wait a little bit and make sure they don't come back here." Jessie waited for almost an hour before she decided the car wasn't coming back. "I wonder where they were going, Rusti. That highway just circles around the island and goes back into the middle of Prince Edward Island. But it's the long way around. It takes about two hours to get back to town that way."

Jessie was a nervous wreck by the time she drove into town. She stopped at the café to pick up a sandwich when she overheard the waitress talking to the mailman. "I heard a government official was visiting our island today. They are looking for land to develop."

"I heard they were going to look out in the countryside to see if it would be worth building a new subdivision."

"Well, I'll be, can you believe that." Jessie was relieved to hear this. She just knew it was detectives coming after her. She ordered her sandwich and curly fries.

When the waitress brought her food, she casually asked her about the conversation she just overheard. "I don't mean to be nosy, but I couldn't help overhearing your conversation with the mailman. Is it true about the government officials being on the Island today?"

"Yes, they are here but they never do anything around here. They just come and look around and then we don't see them again for another year." Jessie bowed her head and said, "Thank you, God." She was relieved because they were not looking for her. She had already looked up Richard's home address and spoke to him on the phone. He told her she could come by today any time after 2 pm. It was 1:00 so she had time to eat her sandwich and curly fries.

There was a nice little park located close to the town square. She pulled into a parking space and decided she would eat her lunch and then go see Richard. "Rusti, I hope I can eat this sandwich, my stomach is in knots right now. I guess I got so nervous over that black car, it made me sick." After she ate, she began to feel better. "I think I'll go over what I intend to ask Richard about Mrs. Carmichael." She thought about all the things she wanted to know. "Okay, Rusti, I think I am ready to go meet this Richard and find out a few things about our ghost."

Jessie pulled up in front of Richard's house. "He must be in his sixties now but surely he remembers his love affair with Naomi Carmichael. Well, come on Rusti, let's go meet this man that was suspected of shooting her." Jessie knocked on the front door. A handsome man with gray hair and a gray beard opened the door. "Mrs. Harris, I presume. Come in and have a seat."

"Thank you, Mr. Mitchell."

"May I ask you what info you need, Mrs. Harris. My affair with Naomi was a long time ago and I was acquitted of all charges."

"I know that, Mr. Mitchell. You see I live in the house on Cannon Hill."

"Oh, I see, well what does that have to do with me?"

"I know this is going to sound crazy, but I have a ghost living there that I believe is Mrs. Carmichael."

"Good lord, woman, are you serious?"

"Yes, I am, and she needs to go, but I believe she wants me to solve her murder before she will leave the house." Richard Mitchell was hesitating before answering. "Well, I have heard rumors the old house was haunted, but I just thought it was something some kids made up. Tell me some more about this ghost of yours, Mrs. Harris."

"No one knows what I have endured since I bought that house. She has left me things, you know clues. She left a picture of her husband lying on the upstairs steps. She also led me to a secret compartment in the back of my hall closet."

"Really, what was in there?"

"That's what I wanted to talk to you about. It was like finding a Pandora's box. There were pictures of you and Mrs. Carmichael. Also, I found several letters from you."

"Oh my gosh, those were personal love letters to Naomi many years ago. I would like to have those back, Mrs. Harris. If you are wondering if it was me that shot her, you're wrong. In my opinion, I always suspected her husband, Robert."

"I'm not here to accuse you of anything, Mr. Mitchell. I'm here to see if there was anybody else that may have wanted to kill her, besides her husband, of course. I have got to solve this murder for her or she will never leave my home. I think her husband's ghost is there too. I really believe I have two ghosts living in that house." Richard was very interested in helping Jessie. "I just don't know what to tell you. There were other men who went out with

Naomi. Oh, I knew she was seeing other guys while I was out of town. But I loved her, and I thought she loved me. That's why I overlooked it as much as I could."

"Do you remember any of their names?"

Richard paused to think about the past. "Let me think about all this and give you a call in a day or two. I'll see if I can remember the men's names. I believe it was only two other men she was seeing." Jessie didn't want to give out her number. "Let me give you a call in a day or two, Mr. Mitchell. My phone is giving me problems right now." Jessie knew she needed to keep this information private. "Mr. Mitchell, can we keep this information to ourselves. I really don't want any of this to get out."

"Of course, Mrs. Harris, I would never discuss any of our conversation with anyone. I've already been accused once, and that was enough. But I can assure you, it wasn't me that shot Naomi. I loved her and still do. I never married because of how much I loved that woman. Please keep me informed of any information you may stumble across. And Mrs. Harris, if you need me to come to Cannon Hill house let me know. I may be able to communicate with her in some way."

CHAPTER TWENTY-ONE

As Jessie and Rusti drove back to Cannon Hill house, she wondered if she should let

Mr. Mitchell come to her home. "I'm a fugitive, so I need to be careful who comes to my home. Even though It's been two years, I still need to be extremely cautious. Yet, it is possible he could help me find out who the killer was." When she arrived home, the house seemed still and quiet. Snow was still coming down but seemed to have slowed down some. As she entered the house the bitter cold hit her in the face. "Oh no, Mrs. Carmichael has been at it again, Rusti. She must know I am doing my best to solve this mystery. Why won't she leave us alone? Guess I better put some more wood on the fireplace and try to warm the house up."

As she went out on the back porch to gather some wood, the back door slammed shut behind her. She tried to open the door, but it was locked. She could hear Rusti barking and running around inside the house. "Oh, good grief that ghost has got to go. Lucky for me and

Rusti, I still have my keys in my coat pocket. If it isn't Mrs. Carmichael, it's her husband doing these tricks." She unlocked the back door and went inside the kitchen. Jessie yelled out, "That's not funny, Mr. or Mrs. Carmichael. What if I didn't have my keys? What did you want to do, freeze me to death?"

As she walked through the house the cold disappeared. She put the wood in the fireplace and lit it. She hugged Rusti and said, "I'm so sorry these ghosts are tormenting you, Rusti. I'm doing the best I can to find out who shot Mrs. Carmichael. I need to read a few letters to see if Richard mentions anyone else. If I could just get the names of the other two men she was seeing. Maybe he will remember who they were. I'll give him a couple of days to remember and then I'll call him."

After dinner that evening, Jessie and Rusti went into the living room. She turned on the

Christmas tree and stoked the fire. "Okay, Rusti, it's time to read some more letters. You know, Richard asks me for these letters, but I'm not going to give them to him. This trinket box is going to stay hidden where no one can find them." She pulled out the third letter and proceeded to read it out loud. Rusti laid at her feet with his head resting on his paws. The room was warm and cozy now, and the lights from the Christmas tree gave it a festive atmosphere. Jessie read the letter out loud to Rusti.

Dear My Darling, Naomi,November 12, 1989

I miss you so much. I know it's hard for you to get away, but I need to see you, my darling. Try to meet me tomorrow night at the Roadside Inn out on highway 154, at 8 pm. I'll be waiting for you in our regular room.

Love forever, Richard.

"Wow, these letters are getting more and more personal. I feel strange reading them. I feel like I'm invading someone's privacy. In a way I am, but I need to solve this mystery for

Naomi. I just feel obligated to do that. I need to give this house peace again. Right, Rusti, we need peace in our home too." Rusti raised his head and let out a low bark as if to say he agreed. Jessie patted the dog's head as she pulled out another letter. "I'm going to read one more tonight and then we're going to bed." She opened the letter and began to read.

My Darling Naomi, February 10, 1990

I saw you last night with that James Walton. You both looked like you were having a good time at that Restaurant. I wanted to come in and yank you out of there, but I knew better than to do that. I must see you soon. I love you Naomi and I thought you loved me. Please meet me tomorrow night at our usual place. I'll wait for you until 9 pm. If you don't show, I'll know it was because you couldn't get away. Until tomorrow, my darling Naomi.

Love forever, Richard.

"This was a long letter to Naomi, and he mentioned a name. This will help me a lot now that I have another name. I just need that third person she was seeing. I want to keep reading,

Rusti, but I am so tired. I can barely hold my eyes open. I guess we better go up to bed, it's eleven O'clock." Jessie put the fire out in the fireplace and turned off the Christmas tree lights. She always left a light on in the kitchen and living room. It had become a habit for her. She then turned on the front porch light and the flood lights. "Come on Rusti, we are finally ready to go up to bed."

She had accidentally left the trinket box on the table next to her chair. Usually, she took it up to her room and set on the table next to her bed. While she slept, the ghost of Mrs. Carmichael crept into the living room and took the letters from the box. Jessie woke up around 7:30 the next morning. "Come on, Rusti, let's go take you outside." Rusti was so comfortable in his warm bed, he just laid there. "I know it's cold, boy, but you need to go outside and do your business. Come on, boy, get up." Rusti finally got up from his dog bed and followed Jessie downstairs. "I think I better make a fire in the fireplace this morning. It's freezing in here." As she walked into the living room, she found all the letters scattered around on the floor.

Jessie picked the letters up off the floor and placed them in the box. "I guess I forgot to take them upstairs with me. Mrs. Carmichael must have thrown them on the floor. That woman never ceases to amaze me. Look, Rusti, there's one letter lying way over by the Christmas tree. It is a good thing I found it. I wonder if she is trying to tell me something. Let's go take you outside and then we'll read this letter and see if it gives us a clue. Come on, boy, let's go."

CHAPTER TWENTY-TWO

Snow was falling outside and the weatherman on the radio said it was only thirty degrees. "Rusti, I think this would be a good day to stay in. It's way too cold to be outside. We can finish reading these letters. Maybe there's a clue in them somewhere." Rusti went over and laid down in his bed. "I don't blame you, boy; it's still freezing in here. I'll put some wood on the fire and stoke it a little. It's good thing I bought you that big warm bed to keep in here. Now you have one upstairs and this one down here." Rusti wagged his tail and let out a bark as if to say he was thankful too. "I don't know what I would do without you here with me, Rusti. I would be so lonesome and probably very scared."

Jessie went into the kitchen and put the coffee pot on the stove. She filled Rusti's bowl with dry dog food. The dog was so warm and comfortable he didn't want to eat. He just laid in his bed all curled up. Jessie scrambled two eggs and made a piece of toast for herself. After everything was cooked, she took her coffee and eggs into the living room and sat them on the side table next to her chair. "Okay, Rusti, are you ready to hear the rest of the letters?" Rusti wagged his tail and let out his usual bark. Jessie curled up in her chair and proceeded to open the letter she found by the Christmas tree.

As she sat there opening the letter, a slight breeze surrounded her. Jessie knew Mrs.

Carmichael was present in the room. She continued to open the letter and read it out loud to Rusti.

My dearest Naomi, June 1990
I just returned from Italy and want to see you as soon as possible. I heard you were seen around the island with Jeff Parks. I am disappointed in you and wonder

how you can say you love me yet go out with the likes of that man. Naomi, Jeff Parks has a horrible reputation and I fear for your life. He is an alcoholic and a thief. I need to talk to you in person. Can you get away tonight and meet me at our usual place. I'll wait for you until 9 pm. If you can't make it, I'll try to understand. I love you my darling and miss you very much.

Richard

Jessie understood why Mrs. Carmichael wanted her to read this letter first. "I wonder if this Jeff guy could be the one that shot her. I need to check up on this man. I guess we'll have to wait until the weather clears up, Rusti. Besides, it's only four days until Christmas. I wouldn't want to disturb anyone during the holidays." She sat there and wondered about the letter. She forgot about her breakfast, and now it was cold. "This letter is an eye opener for sure. I hope Richard remembers something about this Jeff. We'll solve this mystery one way or another, Rusti. I may go ahead and call Richard because it's been three days since I was at his home. Hopefully he remembers something by now. Rusti, we didn't eat our breakfast. Guess I'll go warm up my coffee. Come on, Rusti, you need to eat too."

The dog climbed out of his doggie bed and reluctantly followed Jessie into the kitchen. The house was still a little cold and the bad weather outside looked like it was here for the long run. After Jessie and Rusti finished their breakfast, they went back into the living room. The warmth from the fireplace felt good as Rusti settled back into his doggie bed. Jessie picked up her throw away phone and dialed Richard's phone number. A lady's voice answered the phone. "Hi, my name is Jessie Harris, may I speak to Richard Mitchell?"

"I'm sorry, Mrs. Harris, but Richard suffered a heart attack yesterday morning. He died in the ambulance on the way to the hospital. I am his sister Grace."

"Oh no, I am so sorry to hear this. I just met him three days ago. I was supposed to call him today about a situation we were working on. Can you give me his funeral information?"

Grace hesitated but finally told her all the information was in the Prince Edward Island local newspaper. Jessie thanked her and hung up. Jessie stood there with the phone in her hand. She was filled with disbelief and despair. "I can't believe this. I just spoke with him three days ago. I hope it wasn't the news about Naomi that caused him distress. I may have been the very one that caused his heart attack. I told him about finding the letters and Naomi's ghost living here in my house. I feel so horrible about all this. I didn't mean to cause anyone any harm. The man was only about sixty-five years old. I didn't know he had heart problems." Tears started to fall down her face as she sat down in her chair. "Oh, God, I am so sorry about Richard Mitchell. I pray I didn't cause his death."

CHAPTER TWENTY-THREE

The anxiety Jessie felt about the situation with Mrs. Carmichael was unbearable. She rubbed her neck and wrung her hands. "I let my guard down one time and went to talk to Richard Mitchell about this dead woman, and now he's dead. I just don't know what to do. This house will never be at peace until these ghosts are gone. If I start talking to other people about all this, they will be suspicious of me. Tonight, I'm going to finish reading all the letters. Maybe there is another clue in there someplace. Come on, Rusti, let's get finished with dinner so we can read the letters. There must be a way I can solve Naomi's murder."

Jessie continued to think out loud, "I love this house and feel so safe here on the island and I don't want to have to give it up. If I have you, Rusti, I know I'm safe and unafraid here. Whatever happens, I'll lie and do whatever it takes to keep my shameful secret. If the police hear about me meddling in their investigation, they will want to talk to me. I sure don't want that to happen. They may find out who I really am. Oh, Rusti boy, this whole situation has got me so unsettled. I have got to find out who killed Naomi, or her ghost will haunt me forever."

Jessie felt so anxious and mentally stressed. She didn't have any appetite for dinner but managed to feed Rusti. "I'm determined to read the rest of those letters tonight. But I feel confused and I just can't understand how all this happened. I'm worried about what will happen to us." She went into the living room and sat down in her chair. She forgot to stoke the fire and turn the Christmas tree lights on. She sat there feeling powerless and numb. Rusti licked her on the leg and whimpered as if he was sad for her. "Rusti, I'm sorry for being this way tonight, boy, but everything that has happened with this ghost and Richard Mitchell has got me feeling so hopeless and helpless."

She managed to pull herself up from the chair and walked over and plugged the lights in on the tree. "Are you trying to tell me you're cold, boy? I guess I'd better put some more wood on the fire." She walked around in circles as if she was trying to figure out what she was doing. She stopped in the middle of the room and just stood there. Suddenly she burst out crying. She cried so hard, she began to shake and had to sit down. All the guilt and shame she had bottled up inside of her began to boil over. It was Christmas and this incident with Richard Mitchell tore at her heart. The situation with Mrs. Carmichael's murder all came tumbling down on her. She sat there in her chair until she fell asleep. She dreamed about Mr. Wilson chasing her and the trinket box she'd found. She dreamed about the love letters and Naomi's murder.

She woke up unexpectedly and found she was in the chair freezing. "Oh my gosh, Rusti, how long have I slept here. It's so cold in here. I'm so sorry, Rusti, I forgot to put wood on the fire. What time is it anyway?" She got up from her chair and went over to the mantel to look at the clock. It was four O'clock in the morning. "Come on, Rusti, let's go upstairs and get in our beds. It is too cold down here." As she laid in bed, she began to think to herself, "These dreams have got to stop. They leave me so drained and depressed. I've been carrying around the guilt and shame of my crime for all these years. Add trying to solve a murder of a ghost that lives in my house, and now the guilt of Richard Mitchell's death. I am so depressed and exhausted. I just want to flee or hide. She finally fell back to asleep.

The following morning, Jessie woke up around nine o'clock. She sat up on the side of the bed and stretched. "I feel like a big weight has been lifted off my shoulders this morning.

Everything came down on me last night till I could hardly breath. "Rusti, it is Christmas Eve and I'm going to try and forget all about the past. I'm going to call Joyce in a little while. I can't let the guilt and shame overpower me again. I must be strong for myself and you Rusti, my best friend. Even though it was cold downstairs, you stayed with me. You are such a smart dog and you always seem to know how I feel." She reached over and hugged the dog and said, "Rusti, I don't know what I would do without you. I love you so much and thankful I found you when I did. Come on, boy, let's go put the kettle on. Let's make this a good day. I will go put wood on the fire too. With all that snow outside this house seems even colder than usual." After feeding Rusti, she made herself a cup of tea. She then went into the living room and put wood on the fire. She stoked the fire until it was roaring in the fireplace. It warmed the living room up right away. She then lit the Christmas tree and turned the radio on. Christmas music was playing. "Now, Rusti, what else can I do to make this house more pleasant." Rusti wagged his tail and started to turn in circles in the middle of the room. "You silly dog. Come on now and settle down. We are going to call Joyce and then I'm going to read some more letters. How's that sound boy." Rusti barked a couple of times to show Jessie he was pleased.

She picked up her burner phone and dialed Joyce's phone number. Joyce answered right away. "Merry Christmas, Joyce."

"Merry Christmas to you too, Lena. I'm so glad to hear from you. Are you alright?"

"Yes, Joyce, I'm fine. How are you and the children? Have they seen their Santa Claus gifts yet?"

"Yes, they are playing with their toys. I wish you could see them Lena. They are getting so big now."

"I really have to go, Joyce, I just wanted to wish you and the family a very Merry Christmas and to say I love you and miss you."

"Please don't hang up, Lena. I miss you so much."

"Goodbye, Joyce, I'll call another day." Lena hung the phone up and stared at it as if it was going to melt in her hand.

Every time she called Joyce, she cried as she hung up the phone. It was Christmas day and she was all alone except for her best friend, Rusti. She was determined to make it a nice day despite the weather outside and all the circumstances surrounding Cannon Hill House. "Rusti, Santa brought you a nice big bone." Rusti wagged his tail and barked as Jessie gave him the bone. "Merry Christmas, Rusti: I love you so much." Rusti laid by the fire gnawing on his bone for the rest of the day. "I think I'll work on that book I've been trying to write for the past two years."

CHAPTER TWENTY-FOUR

Back in Chicago, Joyce was disappointed Lena had hung up before she could share her good news. Joyce had wanted to tell Lena that her husband Bill was taking her on a trip to

Prince Edward Island. Ever since they were little girls, they had both wanted to go there.

Lena and Joyce always loved watching the series of Anne of Green Gables. It was their favorite thing to do as sisters. She talked about it with Bill as soon as Lena ended the call. "I wish I had a way of telling Lena about the trip. I don't know when she will call back. Oh, Bill, I wish she was going with us."

Jessie was sad and sorry she had cut her sister so short. "Every time I call Joyce, I feel sad. If only she knew I lived here on this Island, she would be jealous. When we were little girls, we always wanted to come here." Jessie had no way of knowing that Joyce and her husband would be coming to the Island the following spring. Jessie decided to make the rest of the day as pleasant as she could for herself and her dog. "Next week if the weather is better, we'll drive into town and look up this James Walton fellow. I need to ask him a few questions about Naomi." Rusti looked at her with eyes that said he disapproved. "I know, Rusti, but I've got to get to the bottom of this. That ghost upstairs is never going away or leaving us alone, at least until her murder is solved. It makes me depressed and sad but it's something I feel called to do."

In the meantime, Joyce and her husband continued planning a trip to Prince Edward

Island in the spring. "I'm so excited about the trip, Bill, but at the same time I'm sad."

"Why,

Joyce, you should be looking forward to this trip?"

"I am looking forward to the trip I just wish my sister was going with us. I wanted to at least tell her about it. She hung the phone up before I had a chance."

"Well, next time she calls you can tell her. It's only the end of December, Joyce." Jessie decided to drive into town. She had two names to check out now, James Walton and Jeff Parks. First, she wanted to see what she could find out about James Walton.

Jessie went to the local library again to see if she could find out anything about this man. She went through all the newspapers dating back to the night of the Christmas Party. There in black and white were all the names of the people who attended the Carmichael party.

The newspaper article told of all the events surrounding the party. The band they had playing the music, the menu, and the beautiful dresses the women wore. It was exciting for Jessie to read all this. "It's hard to believe all this happened in the Cannon Hill house, in this very house that is now my home."

She scanned down the list and found the name James Walton. The newspaper said he was an executive with the local power company in Nova Scotia. "Looks like he was a very influential person during that time. He must be retired by now. I'm going to have to do some digging to find a phone number and address for this man." She read through more of the newspapers looking for any information she could fine about Mr. Walton. She jotted down a few numbers and decided to leave and go by the local grocery store. As she was walking out of the library, snow started falling. The streets already looked almost impassable. "Oh, no, how are we going to get home, Rusti. The snow is really coming down hard and the streets are already covered with the white fluffy stuff."

She walked slowly to her car and backed carefully out of the parking lot. "Well, so far we are doing okay. I think we better go see Mr. Walton another day. I'll try these phone numbers when we get home and see if I can talk to him. In the meantime, let's see if we can make it to the grocery store." After picking up a few items from the grocery store, she decided to pick up a sandwich and curly fries from her favorite café. Thinking out loud Jessie said, "I don't think I'll mention the letters and the trinket box I found. I'm afraid it would be too much of a shock to Mr. Walton. I just want to ask him a few questions about Naomi and the night she was shot."

Jessie hoped that Walton wouldn't be offended enough to call the police. She certainly didn't need that to happen. If Walton thinks no one knows about his affair with Mrs. Carmichael, he probably felt all that happened that fateful night had been forgotten. He doesn't know Jessie, so he would be cautious about speaking to her about something so personal. "Just look at this beautiful town, Rusti. The white snow and the Christmas lights as the background would make a lovely Christmas card scene. Well, I think we have everything we need, Rusti. Let's head home to Cannon Hill."

CHAPTER TWENTY-FIVE

After arriving home, Jessie and Rusti hurried to get inside the house. The weather had gotten even worse than when they left. The snow had started to fall harder again. Everything in sight was covered in snow. Cannon Hill house looked lonely and depressing to Jessie. "Let's get a fire started in the fireplace and light that tree up. Maybe the house won't seem so depressing." Jessie realized she should wait until after the holidays to get in touch with Mr. Walton. He might not appreciate her calling him during the holidays. Jessie had bought a local newspaper before she left town.

She settled down in her chair and started reading the paper. She turned over to the United States news which was always located in the back of the Island's newspaper. Almost everything she read about was murders, or drug gangs being apprehended. "I am so glad I'm not in Chicago. It was a horrible place to live, Rusti. Why I stayed there, I'll never understand. The only thing worse than living in Chicago was living there and working for a man like Wilson. It was tough finding a good job in that city. Times were bad in those days and I felt I didn't have a choice." Suddenly the room turned cold, and Jessie knew Mrs. Carmichael was there.

Jessie just sat in her chair and didn't move. It was as if she was frozen in time whenever the ghost came into the room. The room was freezing for almost five minutes then it began to warm up again. "I think Naomi wants us to read some more letters, Rusti." Jessie began to look through the trinket box when she noticed a letter laying on the bottom of the box. For some reason she had not seen this one before. It was separate from the other letters. She opened the letter and started to read it.

"To whomever finds this letter, I want you to know why I think I'm about to be killed. I am married to Robert Carmichael and have one son, John. My son is away at the University now. My husband and I have not gotten along for many years. I have been unfaithful to him, but he knows all about it. I love another man, whom I'll not mention. I have also been going out with two other men. One of whom has been very angry with me for not leaving my husband, Robert. He has beaten me and cursed me on several occasions. His name is James Walton. I have tried to stop seeing him, but he follows me everywhere I go. He insists I meet him, and if I don't meet with him, he threatens to kill me.

If I am found dead, James Walton is probably my killer. I have also been seeing Jeff Pike on occasion. He is a good man and has never hurt me. James came to the Christmas party tonight. He got very drunk and started cursing at me in front of our guests. My husband had to have him thrown out of the house. He was very angry and drunk, and I believe he will come back and hurt me. Whoever finds this letter will know the truth if I am found dead."

Naomi Carmichael December 24, 1991

Jessie sat there confused. "Mrs. Carmichael wrote this letter and put it in this box.

She had a feeling James was going to come back and do something to her. He must be the killer. I wonder why the police never accused him of it. This mystery just gets more and more confusing to me." The room got cold again. Jessie knew Naomi's presence was there. She just sat in her chair without moving until the ghost went away. "It seems every time I read one of the letters, Naomi appears to be in the room." Jessie didn't know what to think about the letter. She sat there with it in her hands wondering what she should do.

"I could send it to the police anonymously. They would reopen the case and investigate Mr. Walton. Maybe they would find out who the killer was. If he is the killer and I start asking questions, he may come after me." Rusti looked up at Jessie with sad eyes and let out a bark. It was as if he understood what she said. Jessie began thinking about the letter, "I'll have to wait until the weather gets better to take it to the post office. I also want to make a copy of the letter to keep for myself. In no way, do I want the police coming here asking questions. If they reopen the case, they may want to come out here and look around. I hope they won't do that."

CHAPTER TWENTY-SIX

Darkness came early to the Island. Jessie and Rusti turned the outside lights on and looked out the door. The snow was so white and bright it lit up the yard. "Rusti, if this snow continues, we won't be able to get out of the house tomorrow. It's a good thing we stopped for groceries today. Come on, boy, let's go read some more letters." Rusti followed her into the living room and crawled into his bed. "The fire sure does feel good tonight." She sat there wondering what she should do about that letter from Naomi. "I wish I could talk to Joyce about this situation. She would know what I should do. I know I should turn this over to the police, but I'm afraid they will start asking questions and find out who I am. Even if I send it to them anonymously, they will want to come out here to Cannon Hill house and speak to the owner."

That night as Jessie slept, it was as if Mrs. Carmichael was showing her what happened in a dream. Jessie was standing outside the house looking in through the window. The women had on beautiful long flowing dresses. The couples danced a waltz across her living room floor as she watched. There was nothing in the room except a piano and few small round tables off to the side of the room. There was a table set up on one side of the room with all kinds of liquor displayed on it. The living room seemed very large in the dream. A big Christmas tree sat in the corner of the room. It had beautiful lights and decoration on it. A tall slender man was talking very loudly and getting extremely unpleasant. Mr. Carmichael walked over to the man and asked him to leave. It was obvious, the man was drunk. The two men started to argue and get violent with each other.

Suddenly two other men went over to the tall slender man and took him by his arms and escorted him to the front door. As he started to fight, they pushed him out into the front yard. Jessie heard someone walking on leaves and making a succession of short, rapid sounds in the bushes. She couldn't see who it was, but she knew someone was near her. A gun shot went off and everyone in the house started to scream and run toward the door. It was so dark outside she never got a glimpse of the person who shot the gun. She didn't realize what had happened until she heard someone say, "Mrs. Carmichael has been shot."

She woke up sweating profusely and frightened. She sat straight up in bed and looked around to see if anyone was there. "What a strange dream. Rusti, are you okay over there in your bed?" She was trembling so bad she couldn't go back to sleep. "If it wasn't James Walton that shot Mrs. Carmichael, then who else could it have been. It had to be Naomi trying to show me who shot her." Jessie pondered the dream for the rest of the night. It played over and over in her mind as she tried to shut her eyes. As soon as daylight appeared she got out of bed. She made coffee and sat by the fire thinking about the horrible dream she had. "I don't think I'll ever get over the feeling that I was left with after that dream.

Since we can't go outside today, I think I'll clean house and try to get my mind off that dream. Maybe tonight I'll be so tired I'll be able to fall asleep." Jessie vacuumed the floors, mopped the kitchen and cleaned all the bathrooms. She started thinking about the trinket box she found in a secret compartment of the hall closet. "I wonder if there are any more secret compartments in this house. I think I'll check all the closets first, go up in the attic and look around in the basement. Who knows, I just might find something related to this mystery. I'm so thankful to have Rusti here with me. I don't think I can go down in that basement alone. It's really creepy down there."

After Jessie finished cleaning the house, she decided to check all the closets in the house. She first went into the back bedroom where she first noticed the terrible smell. She opened the closet and moved everything around so she could check the walls. She didn't find anything unusual, so she proceeded to go to the next bedroom. The third bedroom was empty except for an old dresser. She opened all the drawers and searched each one thoroughly. Behind one of the drawers was a large yellow envelope. She pulled a paper out and opened it. "Look at this, Rusti. Looks interesting, let's see what's in it."

As she opened the envelope a cold wind swept through the room. "I think one of the ghosts doesn't want us to open this envelope." Jessie took the envelope downstairs to the living room. She opened it and pulled out a large picture. "The plot thickens, Rusti. Look at this, it's a picture of several people in a group. One of the men in the picture is circled. I see Naomi, her husband Robert and Richard Mitchell. There are a few other people I don't recognize. I just wonder how close Richard Mitchell really was to this family. It looks like they are on a picnic at a lake."

She sat down in the chair and thought about the picture. "I'm beginning to wonder if

Richard Mitchell was the murderer. He had the motive and he knew Naomi was seeing other men while he was out of town. He must have been a close friend of the family's too. Why else would he be in this picture with them? It's all beginning to come together now. He wasn't in the dream last night, and when I told him I found the letters, he began to shake a little. Next thing I know he has a heart attack. Oh, yeah, Rusti, I think we know who murdered Mrs. Carmichael."

CHAPTER TWENTY-SEVEN

Jessie decided to keep looking around the house for evidence. She checked all the closets in the house, pulled down the attic steps and climbed up into the attic. "Rusti don't leave me now; you stay right there where I can see you. This is spooky, and I'm scared to death right now." The attic was big and spread out over the whole top of the house. It was floored and had several boxes stored in it. Jessie was thankful it had a light. She opened some of the boxes carefully. She was afraid of what she might find in them. She opened one of the boxes to find some old clothes. She closed it back up and opened another box.

In the box was several items which looked interesting. She found old pictures and folders and decided to take this one downstairs. There was one other box stuck over in the corner of the attic. She pulled it over toward the steps and opened it. There were several books in that one. She started to put it back when she noticed a piece of paper sticking out of one of the books. Jessie picked the book up and put it in the box with the photos. She looked around the attic and didn't see anything else of interest. She climbed down the steps slowly so she wouldn't drop the box.

She closed the attic door and went downstairs to the living room. "Come on, Rusti, let's see what clues and information might be in here." She stoked the fire and then sat down. "It really is cold in here. I think we have company, Rusti. I wish these ghosts would go away and leave us alone." Suddenly, the room became warm again. "Well, it looks like they are gone, I'm tired of being so cold all the time. Besides the cold, every time they come around us, it scares me." She stoked the fire and sat down in her chair. Jessie picked up the book and took out the paper.

She began to read it to Rusti. It was a receipt from an abortion clinic in Charlottesville.

Her face turned red, and the feeling of sickness came over her. "I can't believe this. Naomi had an abortion back in 1989. I wonder who the father was. Could it have been Richard, or maybe James Walton?" She had not thought much about Jeff Parks until now. "There are four men involved and one of them was the father of this baby. After the holidays, I'm going to take a trip into Charlottesville and see what I can find out about this. I wonder if this abortion clinic will tell me the blood type of the father. If they won't, we may never know the truth."

Jessie was really confused by this new information. She thought she had the murder figured out but now finding this out has thrown a new light on the situation. "Rusti, let's read some more letters. Who knows, maybe Richard will reveal something else." Jessie pulled another letter out of the trinket box and opened it up. As she began to read the letter, a cold mist again covered the room. "We have company again, Rusti. Who is here? Are you Mr. or Mrs. Carmichael?" She began to tremble and shake as she waited for a sign from the ghost.

Just as quickly as the mist appeared, it disappeared. "It's gone now. It seems every time I start to read one of these letters, one of the ghosts comes into the room. Rusti, it scares me to death, but I have got to get to the bottom of this mystery somehow. The only way is to read these letters. They seem to have important information in them. The truth will reveal itself eventually. There is no doubt about it. We must keep digging for more evidence, who knows how long this is going to take. If only I wasn't a fugitive myself, I could go talk to these people. Richard is dead and he was my main suspect. What's worse, I may have caused his death." She opened the letter she held in her hands and started to read it out loud.

Dear Naomi, September 1991

I miss you so much. I saw you last night at the restaurant where we used to meet. You were there with Jeff Parks. How can you tell me you love me and then turn around and go out with someone else? Please meet me tomorrow night at our usual place and explain to me what is going on in your mind. I can't continue to go on like this. I don't want to live without you,

Naomi darling. You are the love of my life and I need you. Please meet me at 9 pm.

Love Richard

"It looks like Richard Mitchell is getting agitated with Naomi. I still think Richard is the killer, Rusti. But then we have the drunk James Walton and no good Jeff Parks to consider. Oh, and of course, the husband. I believe all the men were jealous of each other. They seemed to know Naomi was going out with the other men. If only I could see the evidence file the police have. If I got caught, what would happen to you? I can't take that chance. I have to figure this out on my own."

CHAPTER TWENTY-EIGHT

Jessie realizes there is only one more letter from Richard for her to read. "I think I'll go ahead and read this last one. I'm feeling a strong presence in this room, Rusti. This letter must be very important." A mixture of cold and mist filled the room again. But this time with the cold came a horrible smell that took Jessie's breath away. "Rusti, come on, let's get out of this room." Rusti followed Jessie into the kitchen where it was warmer and settled down by the stove. Jessie had been cooking earlier and the stove was still warm. She sat down at the kitchen table and started to read the last letter from Richard.

Dear Naomi, March 19, 1992

I dreaded writing this letter because I love you so much, but I need to tell you how I feel. The anxiety and the depression I have been feeling has caused me to rethink our situation. I can't, and I won't continue to see you. You are unfaithful to me and to your husband. You are a cheap woman with no morals or conscience. But I'll always love you, my dear Naomi, no matter what happens.

This is goodbye, Richard.

"Oh my, this is a powerful letter to Naomi. I wonder how she felt when she read this. So, Richard left her. I wonder if he ever came back or saw her again. I wish my dream would have shown me who was hiding in the bushes the night of the murder. Maybe, just maybe I'll have another dream about that night. I need to know which one of these four men shot Naomi. And of course, why they did it. Was it out of jealously, shame or greed? Maybe one of these guys thought they could get some money out of these people and their little scheme didn't work out. Whatever happened, I have got to know and somehow report it anonymously to the police."

It was getting late, so Jessie decided she would go to bed and try to figure this out in the morning. The smell in the living room had disappeared at last, so she followed her nightly routine to put out the fire in the fireplace and turn out the lights. She turned on the outside lights and made sure the doors were locked. "Come on, Rusti, let's go up to bed. I'm tired and I know you are too." As she approached the top of the stairs, she felt a presence behind her. She stopped dead in her tracks and froze. She started to tremble a little as Rusti barked and growled.

Jessie forced herself to continue toward the bedroom. As she went into her bedroom, the presence disappeared. She stood there leaning against the door as if she was going to faint. "Oh my gosh, Rusti, that was the first time one of the ghosts has ever been that close to me. I was scared to death. I'm still trembling, and I feel so cold." Jessie ran and jumped into her bed and pulled the covers up over her head. As she lay there, she just couldn't get warm. Finally, she slipped off to sleep.

As she slept, she began to dream about the ghosts. In her dream, she turned to investigate the eyes of Mrs. Carmichael. The ghost's mouth began to move as if she wanted to say something to her. Jessie said to the ghost, "Why are you haunting me this way. I am trying to solve your murder as fast as I can. Can't you please go away and leave me alone?" In the dream, the ghost had tears flowing down its face. Suddenly Jessie woke up crying. The dream was very disturbing to her as she came out from under the covers.

She glanced over at the clock that sat on the bedside table. It was 3 am and she was wide awake. "I think I'll go down to the kitchen and make me a cup of hot tea. Sometimes that helps me to sleep. Come on, Rusti, let's go downstairs." She was still a little terrified by the thought of that ghost standing behind her. "Rusti, I am so nervous about this house. I don't want to leave here because I love this old house and truthfully, we really don't have any other place to go. I really feel like it was meant for us to live here." Her thoughts about the house were going through her head as she went down to the kitchen for her tea.

In the morning, Jessie sat at the kitchen table with her head in her hands. She just sat there, drinking coffee and thinking about the night before. "Last night was the first time one of these ghosts have ever got that close to me. It was terrifying and I'm still shaking. Rusti, what are we going to do? I'm trying to solve this murder for Mrs. Carmichael, as fast as I can. I can't go to the police without giving myself away. I just don't know what to do." Rusti laid on the floor by Jessie's chair as if he knew what she was saying. He looked up at her with sad eyes and grunted.

She decided to get dressed and drive into town. Jessie wished she had somebody to talk to about all this. She began to review the situation she was in. "I had Richard to talk to about

Mrs. Carmichael, but now he's gone; so, who can I talk to about all this? The ghost or maybe ghosts, are getting anxious and agitated with me. I just don't know what to do at this point." As she drove into town, she felt hopeless and lonely. "If it wasn't for you, Rusti, I would be all alone in this situation. I am so grateful I have you to talk to. You are really the best friend I have ever had."

CHAPTER TWENTY-NINE

Spring had come at last and the Island was ablaze with color. Flowers were popping up out of the ground all over the island. Visitors from other cities had come to visit Prince Edward Island and Jessie worried she might run into someone she knew. "We need to be extremely careful, Rusti. I need to try to look as different as possible." Jessie wore her hair in a ponytail and had on her thick black rimmed sunglasses. She never wore make-up when she went into town. "Surely, no one would recognize me looking like this!" She wore baggy blue jeans with a floppy blue button-down shirt, nothing she would have worn in her old life.

Jessie thought to herself, "Even my sister Joyce wouldn't recognize me dressed like this. I always wore nice clothes and had my hair done every week when I lived in Chicago. You know Rusti, I don't miss that life one bit. I just wish we could live in peace in our own home. Those ghosts are always disturbing us in some way or another. I've got to solve this mystery as soon as I can." She decided to go back to the library and try to find out what she could about these other two men Mrs. Carmichael had been seeing. "They are the only leads I have right now."

• • •

While Jessie was in town, she decided to stop by the café and pick up lunch. The waitress saw Jessie coming and put the order in for her. Janice knew what Jessie wanted the minute she saw her. Jessie started to walk into the café when she saw a man and woman she knew from Chicago. She stopped dead in her tracks and turned away from them. What were the odds? The couple had been regular customers at the finance company where she had worked. Janice could see Jessie through the café window and wondered what was wrong. She came outside and asked Jessie if she was alright? Yes, I'm okay, I just got a little dizzy, but I'm fine now. Thank you for asking."

"Why don't you come inside and sit down for a few minutes?" The couple had gone into the café, so Jessie was reluctant to go in. "I'll be fine now Janice. Would you mind bringing my order out to me?"

"Of course, if that's what you want. Give me a minute and I'll be right back." Jessie and Rusti leaned against the café wall and waited for Janice to bring her lunch out to her. As she waited, she wondered if Janice was suspicious of her in any way. It wasn't long before Janice handed her the lunch. Jessie gave her the money she owned and said, "Thanks for being so thoughtful, Janice. I'm going to head back home, and I'll see you next time I'm in town."

Janice was worried about Jessie, as she watched her from the window inside the café. As Janice walked back to the kitchen, she wondered why Jessie got so dizzy. "Oh well, I just hope it isn't something serious." Jessie pulled up in front of the library. "This time, Rusti, we have got to make sure we get as much information on those other two men as possible." Rusti sat there in the seat beside her as if he knew what she was saying. The library was empty for the most part, so Jessie walked back to where the computers were and sat down. "Now let's see, we'll start by looking up the Walton man first."

As Jessie put her fingers on the keyboard, she noticed her hands were shaking. "I guess
I'm still nervous about last night. That was the creepiest thing that has happened to me since I've been in that house. The ghosts have never come that close to me before." Rusti looked up at her and whimpered. "Poor Rusti, I know you were frightened. We have got to solve this murder for Naomi as soon as we can. I think she's beginning to get a little impatient with me."

Jessie wrote down as much information as she could find regarding Mr. Walton. She noticed the phone number and address for him were the same ones she had taken down before. "I think I have gotten all the information I'm going to get on Mr. Walton, Rusti. Now we just need to find out as much as we can on this Jeff Parks."

She clicked the mouse for the computer and turned the pages until she found some information on Mr. Parks. "Come on, Rusti, let's go home. I'd better stop by the store and pick up a couple more of those burner phones first. I plan to call Mr. Walton tomorrow and make an appointment with him." It was after four o'clock in the afternoon by the time they arrived home. Jessie remarked how cool the afternoons and evenings still were. "It's almost the middle of March and it's still pretty cold." After getting settled for the night, Jessie put some firewood in the fireplace. "I'm so tired tonight, I believe I'll just sit here by the fire and relax. I have a lot of thinking to do."

The following day, Jessie made a call to the phone number she had written down at the library. A lady answered the phone and asked if she could help her. "Yes, my name is Jessie

Harris, may I speak with Mr. Walton?" The lady replied, "Just a moment please." She put Jessie on hold. Then suddenly a man's voice came on the line. "This is Mr. Walton speaking."

"Hi, my name is Jessie Harris, Mr. Walton. I live in the Cannon Hill house. I understand you knew the Carmichaels?"

"Yes, I used to know Naomi and Robert Carmichael, many years ago." Jessie asked if she could make an appointment to see him. "I have a few questions about the Carmichaels and the house."

Mr. Walton wasn't happy about bringing up old wounds. He was curious about this woman on the phone. He wondered what she wanted from him. "Mrs. Harris, I'll transfer you back to my secretary so you can make an appointment."

"Thank you." Jessie made an appointment for the following day at 2:00 pm.

CHAPTER THIRTY

In the morning, after two cups of coffee and a stale Danish, she was ready to leave.

"Rusti, I know you want to go with me today, but I'm going to have to take the bus, and I don't think they will allow pets." She patted him on the head and made sure he had water and food. "Now you watch over the house for me." Rusti laid by the front door while Jessie was gone. He felt so lonely and lost without her. His ears would go up occasionally from some noise within the house. He would lay by the door until his master returned. Jessie was concerned about leaving Rusti at home.

As she backed out of the driveway, she thought again about leaving him. "I wish I could take Rusti with me today, but Halifax is too much of a trip. Besides the bus, I'm sure the office building wouldn't allow dogs. He'll be better off staying at home until I get back"

After the long drive into town, she boarded the bus which would take her to Halifax. "I sure am glad I left early today. I'm going to be late getting home tonight. It will be worth it if I get the right answers out of Mr. Walton." She arrived at the office building just in time for her appointment. It was 2:30 pm by the time she was called to go into Mr. Walton's office.

Walton was hesitant at first to talk to Jessie about Naomi Carmichael. He invited her to sit down and asked what he could do for her. Jessie spoke up and began to tell Walton her story. "I bought the Cannon Hill house about three years ago. I understand you knew the past owners of the house?"

"Yes, I did know them. I had business dealings with Mr. Carmichael for a while. They liked to give parties and I was always invited. The last one I attended was on Christmas eve. The same night Naomi was shot and killed."

"So, you were there when she was shot?"

"Yes, I was there. Where is this leading Miss Harris? Why all these questions about the Carmichaels?"

Jessie wanted to tell Walton about Mrs. Carmichaels ghost and how she was trying to solve the mystery surrounding her murder. She was afraid he might get suspicious of her if she revealed too much. She had to get answers and he was a good source. "Mr. Walton, I need to ask you some questions that might offend you."

"I don't have anything to hide, Miss Harris, but I am wondering why you are here." She decided to jump in with both feet. "The night Mrs. Carmichael was shot, where were you? I'm asking these questions because I have found evidence in the house that you and two other men knew Mrs. Carmichael very well. Very well indeed, Mr. Walton." Walton's face turned a crimson red. Jessie knew in an instant he knew where she was headed with these questions.

"Look Miss Harris, I don't know you and I don't have to answer any more of your questions. I knew the woman and yes, I was close to her, but I didn't shoot her. I know that's what you are getting at. I think our time is up here." Jessie was disappointed, so she got brave.

"Mr. Walton, I really need some questions answered. You see sir, the house is haunted by this woman." She was surprised she blurted it out. "I'm sorry but that just slipped out. I didn't mean to say it, but it is true and somehow I have got to solve this murder for her."

"Good Lord, woman, do you know what you are saying?"

"Yes, I do, and I can prove it, too. How do you think I knew who you were? I know you had an affair with her. These spirits or ghosts that live in the Cannon Hill house have given me a lot of clues. Even with their help, I still have not been able to solve the mystery of her death." In the back of Jessie's mind, she thought if this was the guilty man, he would want to find out just how much she knew. "I'll be going now. If you remember anything from that night, you'll need to come to the house. I don't have a phone number to give you." Walton was still in shock regarding what she said to him about Naomi's ghost. "I would like to talk to you in private at your home sometime."

"Okay, drop by one day and we can discuss your relationship with Naomi."

Jessie left Walton's office with a puzzled mind. She felt certain Walton was the killer. As she walked to the bus depot; she began to think her life might be in danger. She thought to herself, "If he is the killer, then he is going to want to know everything I know about that night. He may even try to kill me. I'm not worried if I have Rusti with me. I bet that dog is anxious to see me. He's probably wondering when I'm coming home." The long journey on the bus was exhausting. By the time the bus reached Prince Edward Island, she was glad to be nearly home. She was so tired, and she dreaded the drive to the Cannon Hill house.

After an hour's drive out to the countryside, she finally arrived home. Rusti was so happy to see Jessie. The dog was so excited he jumped up and down and turned in circles. "Oh, you precious dog. I missed you being with me today. What would I do without you? I just want to put on my pajama's and go straight to bed." As she spoke to the dog, she reached down and hugged him. As Jessie lay in bed that night, she thought about her encounter with Mr. Walton. She wondered if he would come by one day. She was a little nervous about him coming to the house.

"That man had every opportunity to shoot Mrs. Carmichael. He could have slipped out the sliding doors that lead to the patio. No one would have even noticed. Or he could have hid in the bushes outside the front windows. It's so dark out here, he could have shot her and slipped back into the house without anyone noticing." It was after midnight before Jessie fell asleep. She was restless and tossed and turned in the bed. Around four am, she got up and went downstairs to the kitchen. While she was standing in front of the stove making hot chocolate, she heard footsteps. A cold chill went up and down her spine. The footsteps sounded like they were getting closer and closer to the kitchen.

CHAPTER THIRTY-ONE

Jessie was terrified and couldn't move. She couldn't even turn around to see if someone was there. "Where is Rusti, when I need him. Very softly she started calling his name. Suddenly Rusti started barking. He had a very ferocious bark as he stood at the kitchen door.

Jessie wasn't sure if it was a ghost, or someone really was outside the house. "The footsteps could have been caused by someone walking on the leaves. Rusti kept barking and looking up at the back door. "I would let you go out there, boy, but I'm afraid to open the door." She decided she would start a fire in the fireplace. Instead of going back to bed, she would sit in her chair the rest of the night. Rusti stopped barking after a while and went into the living room. He laid down in front of the fireplace and whimpered for a few minutes. With Rusti nearby, Jessie slipped off to sleep.

The following morning, Jessie decided she would walk around outside the house and see if she could find any footprints or any indication someone had been there. She went to take her bath and dressed. "Come on, Rusti, let's go out in the backyard and look around. You need to go outside anyway." Jessie walked all around the house looking down at the ground. Suddenly she stopped in her tracks. She reached down and picked up two cigarette butts laying on the ground. "Well, here's proof someone was out here last night. I can't call the police because it's too far for them to come way out here. And if they would come, they may start asking questions about me."

• • •

Jessie had a crazy idea it was Walton. After all, she had mentioned the ghost had left clues to her death. "I really believe he is the killer and now he wants to kill me. I think he knows I'm suspicious of him. It's a good thing I bought that gun in Chicago and brought it with me. I think I'll get it out and have it handy in case I should need it." She decided to ride into town and pick up supplies for the house. "I need to stock up on groceries and supplies for the house so I can stay home and not worry about going out again any time soon. Mr. Walton just may come to see me, and I want to be ready for him."

She pulled her hair back into a ponytail and put on her black rimmed glasses.

She was quite sure no one would recognize her. It was only March and the weather was still cold. In Canada it stayed cool for a long time in the spring, so Jessie wore blue jeans and a thick sweater, which made her look heavier than she really was. "I don't think my own sister would recognize me now." She had lost several pounds since moving to the island, and the sweater made her look even heavier than she was. She put Rusti's leash on him and said, "You ready to go, Rusti?"

As Jessie drove into town she thought about her meeting with Walton the day before.

She thought he acted so innocent until she mentioned the clues she had found, then his attitude began to change. "Yeah, I'll just bet it was him sneaking around my house in the middle of the night. The only thing is he would have had to travel from Nova Scotia to the island, and that's at least a four-hour trip. Of course, he could have left right after I did. Who could it be if it wasn't him?

•   •   •

After arriving in town, she decided to put Walton out of her mind for a while. "I must concentrate on what I need from the store and take care of all my business today. I'm just so overwhelmed with everything," she said while bringing a shaky hand to her forehead. She pulled up in front of the local grocery store and noticed a lot of people were in the village. It was the beginning of spring back in the states, so a lot of Americans had come to visit the island.

She realized she was still shaken up by the incident that happened the night before. She felt light-headed and was having difficulty breathing. "I can't seem to get my feet to move. I feel so, stressed I just want to scream.

What am I going to do, Rusti? I'm shaking all over and feel like I can't move." She had tears in her eyes as she sat frozen with fear. "Come on now, get a hold of yourself; you are stronger than this. You have faced so much in the past few years, even ghosts. You can't let this get to you. Someone being outside of my house in the middle of the night frightens me." It frightened her even worse than Mrs. Carmichael's ghost.

She opened the door of the car and moved slowly as she got out. "My feet feel so light, as if I'm walking on air. I can't sit here in the car the rest of the day. I need to get this over with so I can get back home before dark." Jessie finally got up the courage to walk into the grocery store. "Come on, Rusti, let's you and I get this over with before I faint. My head is aching, and I feel so weak right now. I need to get back home and lie down for a while." As Jessie and Rusti walked through the store, she saw a woman that t looked like Joyce. "Oh my gosh, Rusti, that looks like my sister. I think my fears are making me see things. Let's finish getting our stuff."

As Jessie was loading her car with the groceries, she noticed Joyce looking out the store window at her. She hurried as fast as she could to get inside the car. She backed out and headed out of town. "Surely Joyce didn't recognize me? How could she? But she is my sister and sisters usually know each other no matter what." As she drove out toward the country she felt as if she wasn't going to make it home. "My head feels like it's going to explode, Rusti. Now with Joyce on the island, things are even more complicated."

CHAPTER THIRTY-TWO

As she drove, she began to reminisce about their childhood. "Joyce and I loved watching 'Anne of Green Gables' when we were little girls. We always said we would come here one day. Well, I'm already here and now Joyce and her husband are here. Oh, how I wish

I could visit with her. I have missed her so much and now she's so close. But she knows what I did, and I can't take the chance." She began sniffing and wiping at her nose as tears rolled down her face. It was 4:00 in the afternoon when Jessie and Rusti finally returned home. The sun was still shining brightly. She hurried and took the groceries into the house. After putting everything away, she decided to take something for her headache. "Rusti, my head is aching, my throat is scratchy, and I have a runny nose. I think I'll go upstairs and lie down for a while."

As she walked through the dining room she heard a squeak from the floor. "What in the world is that?" She bent down and checked the hardwood floor. There was a loose board in the floor. "Another mystery to follow up on, Rusti. It's going to have to wait a while. I must go lie down or I'm going to pass out." Jessie went upstairs to her bedroom with Rusti in tow. She pulled the covers back on the bed and climbed in. She pulled the covers up over her head. Even the daylight coming in through her bedroom window hurt her eyes. She fell asleep and dreamed about Joyce. She slept for almost three hours. By then, the sun was going down, and it was almost dark outside. Her head felt a lot better, so she got up and went downstairs.

• • •

Joyce and Bill were leaving the grocery store when Joyce said, "Bill, you aren't going to believe this, but I am pretty sure I saw Lena today."

"What? You saw Lena, here on Prince Edward Island?"

"Yes, I did, and I think she knew I saw her. She was disguised, but I still recognized her. She had her hair pulled back and wore black rimmed glasses. She has also changed her hair color, but I know it was her. Remember, we're sisters. I would recognize her in any disguise."

"I am amazed that she would be here on the island. How long has it been now, Joyce? Five or six years?" Joyce was just as amazed as Bill was. "I don't know, Bill, but it has been a long time. I haven't heard from her in quite a while either."

"Didn't you tell her I was taking you to Prince Edward Island for our anniversary the last time you spoke with her?"

"I wanted to, but she didn't give me a chance. She hung up before I could tell her."

Jessie went down to the kitchen and filled Rusti's bowl with dog food. "Here you go, boy, eat your dinner while I make myself a cup of tea. I think I'll have a bowl of soup tonight.

I don't feel much like eating. I still have a slight headache." Rusti ate his dog food and then went to the back door "Okay, buddy, you can go outside for a few minutes." She opened the back door and let the dog out. She continued to heat the soup and pour her tea. Suddenly, Rusti started barking and growling. "Looks like whoever was stalking around here last night has come back." She was frightened and didn't know what to do about Rusti. Jessie wanted to call him to come inside but she knew if he stayed outside, the prowler might get scared and go away.

After a while, the dog stopped barking and started scratching on the backdoor. Jessie felt sure, the prowler had gone away. She opened the door and let Rusti come in. "Too bad you can't talk, Rusti. I sure would like to know who keeps prowling around our home." Jessie's head had started hurting again, so she sat down in her favorite chair and drank the tea she had just made. She laid her head back against the chair and shut her eyes. Rusti laid down by the fireplace. They stayed that way until night gave way to daybreak. When Jessie woke up, it was daylight and the fire in the fireplace was almost out. "I can't believe I slept in this chair all night. My head sure feels a lot better now."

She brought some wood in from the back porch and started a new fire in the fireplace. The house warmed up fast as she put the kettle on the stove to heat. She sat down at the kitchen table and drank her morning tea. "I wish I knew who it was that keeps coming around here. I know I should go to the police and tell them, but I just can't risk that. Jessie couldn't believe she saw her sister, Joyce in the village. She decided to call her and see what she has to say. "Maybe she will tell me if she recognized me or not. I miss her so much. I wish I could see her and talk to her in person. I need someone to talk to about my situation and this house. I feel so lonely and depressed. If it wasn't for you Rusti, I don't know what I'd do. But a girl needs someone to talk to that will talk back occasionally."

Jessie picked up one of the burner phones and dialed Joyce's phone number.

Joyce and Bill had gone for breakfast and had decided to tour the island. Joyce didn't answer at first, so Jessie started to hang up. Suddenly, Joyce answered the phone. "Hello."

"Joyce, this is Lena."

"Oh, Lena, I haven't heard from you in such a long time. Are you okay?"

"Yes, I'm fine. How are you and the family?"

"We're fine. You didn't give me a chance to tell you the last time you called that Bill was taking me to Prince Edward Island for our Anniversary."

Jessie was certain her sister was on the Island now. "I'm so happy for you, Joyce. When are you going?"

"We're here now and I thought I saw you yesterday. Please tell me it was you, Lena." Jessie was quiet for a moment. She missed Joyce so much and needed to talk to her. "I can't talk right now, Joyce; I have to go." Joyce was disappointed that Lena hung up and began to cry. After Jessie hung the phone up, she had tears in her eyes, too. "I wish I could speak with Joyce alone. I don't want her husband to know where I am." Jessie decided to stay away from town. "Joyce and Bill will probably be leaving the Island in a couple of days anyway. I need to get ready for tonight in case the prowler comes back. There's something in this house he wants. Something that will give him away as the shooter."

CHAPTER THIRTY-THREE

She had forgotten about the squeaky spot in the dining room floor. She was making lunch, when it dawned on her that she had not yet checked out that squeaky board. She would do that as soon as she finished her lunch. Jessie was feeling a little depressed about her sister, Joyce. She wanted to see her and speak to her. "I just feel so overwhelmed about all this that's happening to me. I came to the Island and chose this house so I could have a private peaceful life. So far all I have found is turmoil and anxiety. If Joyce was alone, maybe it would be different. I don't trust Bill. He might mention me to someone and that would be all it would take for someone to find me. I know in my heart Joyce would keep my secret forever."

Jessie walked into the dining room and knelt on the floor. She pushed at the loose board.

The board was so loose she could get her fingers under it. She pulled the board out of the floor and saw a shoe box inside. "Look, Rusti, another clue." She pulled the shoe box out of the flooring. She opened the box and found a gun inside. "Oh, no, Rusti, look what I found. I bet this is the murder weapon. Now I know what the prowler is after. He buried the weapon here thinking no one would ever find it. I bet it has his fingerprints all over it. Now what? I can't take it to the police." She put the gun back into the shoe box and placed it back into the flooring.

"If only I could talk to someone about this. I wish you could talk to me, Rusti. This whole situation has gotten out of hand, and I don't know what to do at this point. I need to buy a security system. I need something that would alert me when a prowler comes around. I will have to take the chance of not running into Joyce and Bill." She put her disguise on, added a floppy hat and a put a scarf around her neck. As she looked in the mirror, she thought that she would be well disguised.

After arriving in Charlottetown on her beloved Prince Edward Island, she pulled up in front of the hardware store. She put Rusti's leash on him before getting out of the car. She said hello to the woman behind the counter and asked her about home security systems. Sandra came out from behind the counter and led Jessie to the back of the store. "If you look along these shelves you will find just about any kind of security system you need for your house. Is this for inside or outside?"

"Outside."

"Well, there should be something right over here." Thank you, Sandra, I'll look."

"If you need anything else, let me know."

Jessie looked at everything they had on the shelves. "I can't decide Rusti. Here's one that gives a siren sound when someone gets near the front door. I guess I could install them on both doors. And here's one for the inside of the house if someone tries to get in when we're not home. I don't know what to do. I want to buy all three of these, but they are so expensive." She stood there wondering which one she should purchase. "I think I'll try the ones that you install on the doors. If someone tries to get into the house, the siren will go off and it should scare them away."

She was thankful she didn't run into her sister. She started thinking about the situation. "I'm so overwhelmed with all this. I need someone to talk to, but who? If I go to the police, they are sure to ask questions about me. I know Mr. Wilson is dead now and I have been gone almost five years. I just can't take any chances. If only there was a way to talk to Joyce alone. I think I'll call her again and see if there is any way she could get away from Bill long enough to meet with me. I really want to see her and talk to her about my life."

After arriving home, Jessie and Rusti walked in the house with the two alarm systems. "I think I'll go ahead and try to install these alarms myself. If the prowler comes around again, he is in for big surprise. The alarms will go off if he touches the doorknobs and that should scare him away." It took her only two hours to install the alarms on the doors. "There now, I feel so much safer to have these alarms. Between you, Rusti and these alarms, we should be all set. At least we'll have a warning if anyone is nosing around." She sat down by the fireplace and picked up the burner phone she bought while in town.

Jessie dialed Joyce's number and waited for her to answer. "Hello."

"Joyce, it's me again."

"Oh, Lena, I'm so glad you called back."

"Joyce, is Bill there now?"

"He's actually taking a nap at the moment."

"Can he hear you talking?"

"No, I'm outside on the patio."

"Joyce, I want to see you and talk to you while you are here on the island, but I don't want Bill to know anything about it."

"I understand, Lena. You know me, I have never told anyone anything about you. Bill thinks you went someplace to get away from Chicago. He doesn't even know what happened with Mr. Wilson."

Jessie felt relieved to hear her sister say that Bill didn't know anything. "Is there any way you can get away and meet me? Without Bill knowing anything about it?"

"I'll leave him a note that I have gone to the store to pick up some wine."

"Okay that's perfect. There's a parking lot behind the library. Can you meet there in an hour?"

"I'll try, Lena. I just hope he doesn't wake up before I can leave."

"I'll be there in one hour and if you don't show up, I'll know he woke up and you couldn't get away." Jessie picked up her keys and purse and started out the front door. "Come on, Rusti, we're in a hurry."

CHAPTER THIRTY-FOUR

Rusti ran and jumped in the back seat of the car. "We're going to meet my sister, Rusti.

I'm excited about seeing her, but I'm also just a little leery. I feel like I'm giving up my secrecy by letting someone know where I am." She was silent the rest of the way into the village. Rusti sat quietly and looked out the window of the car. After arriving at the village, she drove straight to the library parking lot. As she pulled into the parking lot behind the library, she saw Joyce waiting in a car. Joyce noticed Lena drive up and got out of the car. She ran over and opened the door of Lena's car.

The two women hugged each other for a long time. "Oh Lena, I am so happy to see you. It's been way too long."

"I know, Joyce, but under the circumstances, it couldn't be helped. I'm happy to see you too. How are the children?"

"Jessie is getting big, and Sally is four now. She's a little spitfire."

" Joyce, you must not tell anyone about us meeting. If you do, I will be found and end up in jail."

"Lena, I know this is all confidential."

"You know, Joyce, when we were little girls we made a pack that we would never tell our secrets. I want you to know I have never told anyone anything you ever told me."

"Neither have I, Lena, and I never will."

"Why don't we get in the car. I would feel better sitting in the car than standing out here in the open."

"So, would I, Lena."

"Joyce, you remember how Mr. Wilson treated me all those years? Chasing me around the office. He wouldn't even give me a raise or let me go on vacation. I don't know why I stayed at that place like I did. I must have been a fool."

"No, you just didn't know what to do. You needed the job and jobs are hard to come by in Chicago."

"I suppose so, Joyce. It was a difficult time for me. So, I started saving every penny I could. Sometimes I would even go without lunch or dinner just to save money."

"Lena, I am so sorry. I had no idea you were going without food. Why didn't you tell me. I could have helped you."

"I didn't want anyone to know what I was planning to do. I decided to steal the money from Wilson and get out of the country. He owed it to me, Joyce, and I was determined to take what I deserved. So now I'm a fugitive and on the run."

"Is that why you are here in Canada?"

"Yes, and I have made a life for myself. I have Rusti and a house now. I stay to myself and never make friends. I can't tell you where I live but I'll tell you the house is haunted."

Joyce was in shock and couldn't believe what Lena was telling her. "The house you live in is haunted?"

"Yes, it's a long story. I wish I had time to tell you more, but I know you must get back to the hotel."

"But I want to hear more about this house of yours."

"Joyce, it would take hours to tell you everything that has been going on. You don't have hours right now."

"You're right. I really must get back to the hotel right away. Bill is going to get suspicious of me and start asking questions. Will I see you again before we leave?"

"Probably not, Joyce. I'll call you when Bill is at work and tell you all about it. I love you and miss you so much."

Lena and Joyce hugged goodbye with tears in their eyes. "I love you too, Lena. Please stay in touch with me. I worry about you all the time."

"I will, Joyce. I promise I'll call you soon. Now you need to hurry and get back to the hotel." Joyce got out of the car and left the parking lot. Lena just sat there with tears rolling down her face. She thought, "I thought I was depressed before I saw Joyce. Now I feel even worse." She cranked up the car and headed home.

After Jessie saw her sister Joyce, she began to wonder if she had done the right thing. "I know I can trust Joyce to keep her mouth quiet. I know in my heart, Joyce has always been on my side. We have confided in each other, our inner most secrets, since we were little girls." She tried to put Joyce out of her mind and think about what she should do about the gun she found. "I think I'll take a trip to Charlottesville and leave the gun at the police department. I'll wrap the gun up in brown paper and leave a note with it. That way the police won't know who left it. Maybe they will run the prints on it and finally know who the killer was."

Jessie hesitated about the whole thing. "If I do that, the police will reopen the case and the next thing you know, they will come here. No, that isn't such a good idea either." She didn't know what to do. It was getting late, and the sun was starting to go down. Jessie dreaded the nights because she knew someone was trying to get in her house. "Well, Rusti, we have the security systems up and the outside lights are on. I have my gun ready, so let's see what happens tonight." Jessie had brought a big load of wood in before it got dark. She started a big fire in the fireplace. Rusti stretched out in front of the fire ready to go to sleep. "I think I'll prepare dinner and try not to think about our prowler. Maybe he won't show up tonight, Rusti. If he does, he's going to get a big surprise."

As she stood in front of the stove warming up soup, she felt cold descend upon the kitchen. She knew Naomi was present but decided to ignore her. She whispered under her breath. "I think I'm more afraid of the prowler than I am the ghost." Eventually, the coldness in the kitchen began to disappear. "She probably wanted me to be aware she was still here. Don't you worry, Naomi, I'm getting close to finding out who murdered you that night. I can't be sure, but I am pretty sure I already know. But why did he do it?"

CHAPTER THIRTY-FIVE

She poured her soup into a bowl and walked into the living room. Jessie sat down in her favorite chair near the fireplace. It was almost nine o'clock before she ate her soup. "Tonight, I'm going to start from the beginning and write everything down. I'll start from the beginning of my journey all the way up until today." Jessie opened the drawer of the end table next to her chair and pulled a tablet and pencil out. She began to write about her journey from her life in Chicago to where she was now. She wrote about Mr. Wilson and why she stole the money. "He was an evil man and I want everyone to know the truth about him. Maybe people will understand why I did what I did."

She continued to write until midnight. The alarms never went off that night. Jessie was relieved and decided she would go up to bed. Several days went by without any incidents. She began to think the prowler had given up. Then one night around eleven o'clock the alarm on the back door began to go off. Jessie grabbed her gun as Rusti began to bark at the back door. She waited to see if they tried to come in. All she could see was a shadow of a man standing outside the back door. It was as if he wasn't afraid of the alarm or the dog. He stood there for almost five minutes. Suddenly he disappeared. Jessie walked over to the window and looked out in hopes she would get a glimpse of the man.

She couldn't see anyone, so she decided to sit down in her chair and wait. She held her gun in her lap as she waited to see if the man tried anything else. Rusti settled down on the floor near the fireplace. After a while, Jessie decided that the man had left. She turned the light on and began to write in her tablet. She had written fifty pages already when she decided to stop for the night. The clock on the mantel said it was 2 am. "I think I'll sleep down here tonight, Rusti." She opened the coat closet and retrieved a pillow and a blanket. After a while, she slipped off to sleep.

In the morning, Jessie was awakened by a loud noise. It was as if something had fallen off a shelf. She jumped up from her chair startled by the sound. Rusti was barking and running toward the kitchen. Jessie glanced at her watch. It was only five o'clock in the morning. Someone had busted in the window of the kitchen door. Glass was all over the floor.

"Apparently the alarm went off and your barking scared them away, Rusti. Just look at this mess. What's going to happen next?" Jessie had a slight chill as she realized her life was in danger.

After cleaning up the glass from the floor, she went to the pantry and pulled out a large roll of plastic. She looked in the utility drawer and found a roll of masking tape. She covered the open window with the plastic and taped it up so it would stay. "I guess I'll have to try to get someone to repair this. If I'm not careful, I'm going to run out of money." The coffee pot was due to come on at 6 am. She needed a cup because she began to feel physically ill. It was 5:55 am as she glanced at her watch again. "I sure hope whoever is trying to break in this house is gone. I hate to think they are still outside watching us."

The coffee pot came on as 6 am rolled around. She poured herself a cup and went into the living room and sat down. The fire in the fireplace was still burning with the last glow of its embers... "I guess I better put some more wood on the fire, Rusti. It's getting a little chilly in here." She noticed her legs felt weak and her hands were shaking. After making a good fire, she sat down in her chair and began to think about everything. She started thinking out loud. "What am I going to do about this situation. It's getting out of hand now and my life is in danger. I'm afraid someone is going to try to kill me."

Jessie sat there feeling disappointed and discouraged. She had tried to solve this mystery on her own for the past three years. Now she was feeling defenseless against the intruder. What more could she do? She had no one to turn to. Tears began to well up in her eyes as she cried uncontrollable. Daybreak appeared through the window as she sat crying. She wiped her nose with a Kleenex and sipped a little of her coffee. "If things continue to escalate, I just may have to breakdown and go to the police." Her voice was cracking as she spoke. Rusti lay silent in front of the fireplace as if he was listening to her.

Later that morning, Jessie decided to get dressed and drive into town. Joyce and Bill had already left the island. Jessie felt relieved that they had gone home. She wore her disguise as always. She still didn't want to take any chances on being recognized by someone else. After they arrived in town, she parked in front of the hardware store. Jessie was happy to see Sandra behind the counter. "Hi, Sandra, how are you today?"

"Fine, Miss Jessie, how may I help you today?"

Jessie was a little hesitate to tell Sandra what she needed. "Do you have someone that is willing to come out to my home and replace the glass in my kitchen window?"

"Oh no, Miss

Jessie, what happened?"

"I locked myself out of the house and had to break the window to get in. Isn't that just like a woman to forget her keys?" The two women laughed and joked about the incident. "I think I know someone who would be willing to go out and replace the window for you. Let me give him a call while you're here." Jessie waited patiently as Sandra made the call.

The thought of going through the night with the window broken was scary to Jessie.

"Miss Jessie, I found someone to fix the window. His name is Walter Higgins, and he works for us when we need him. He's a very pleasant man and can be trusted. He said he would come out this afternoon."

"That's great, thank you, Sandra. Can you tell me how much it will cost?"

"Walter charges by the hour, so the drive out there plus the glass and installation should come to one hundred dollars."

"That's an expensive window, to say the least." She paid Sandra and thanked her for her help.

CHAPTER THIRTY-SIX

She headed to the café. She figured she would pick up lunch while she was in town.

Janice saw her coming and began to get the lunch ready. Jessie entered the café and sat down at the counter. "Hey, Jessie how are you today? You weren't feeling very good the last time I saw you."

"I'm okay Janice, thank you for asking."

"I'm a good listener if you need someone to talk to. Is something wrong?"

"Do you have a family Janice."

"I'm basically, on my own. I was married once, but I'm divorced now. I couldn't have any children, so, he just up and left me."

Jessie thought that was a horrible thing for a man to do. She wondered if Janice could be trusted. She needed a friend to confide in, someone to talk to. "Jessie, you look like you could use a friend."

"I do need a friend, but I need someone I can trust. Can I really trust you, Janice?"

"Of course, you can. You can ask anybody that knows me."

"Janice, do you believe in ghost?" Well, I have an open mind and I know there are things in this world we can't explain."

"Do you know how to get to the Cannon Hill house?"

"Isn't it way out in the country?"

"Yes, it's about an hour's drive from here."

"I've heard of it and have thought I would love to see the old place."

While she stood there trying to decide if she could trust Janice, she decided she just needed to get home. Walter would be coming out in the afternoon to replace the window. She wanted to invite Janice to come to see her but wasn't sure what she should do. Suddenly, it just popped out of her mouth. "Janice, when are you off from work?"

"I have Saturday off."

"If you don't have any plans, would you like to come out to tea, on Saturday?"

"Oh, that sounds delightful, Jessie."

"How about noon?"

"Okay, I'll be there at noon on Saturday."

On the drive home, Jessie wondered if she had done the right thing. "Rusti, I hope I was right inviting Janice to our place. When she hears about our ghost, she may want to leave.

Should I tell her about everything that has been happening?" She had her doubts and worried that she had spoken too quickly. "Maybe I shouldn't have asked Janice to come here. I won't tell her about myself. We'll just see where our conversation leads us. I can tell if I can trust someone or not right away. She seems like a very nice and trustworthy lady and I like her, Rusti. I hope my instincts are correct."

Jessie didn't have any prowlers for a while after the incident with the back-door window. She had it replaced and installed more locks on the doors. "Rusti, this house is beginning to look like a prison. We have alarms systems and locks all over the place. Why a man would be a fool to try to get in here. Especially with my wonderful watchdog, Rusti." She knelt on the floor and hugged Rusti around the neck and rubbed his ears. "You are the best dog anyone could have. Rusti, I love you so much."

"Rusti let's take a ride into the village today. I need to pick up some things from the local grocery store. Janice is coming out Saturday for tea, so I might as well pick up a few things for lunch too. Rusti ran to the door with his leash in his mouth. "Just look at you boy; all ready to go. You want a friend too, don't you?" The drive into the village was a pleasant one that day. "Let's turn on the radio and listen to some music." For the first time in a long time, Jessie sat back in the car seat and relaxed while she drove.

Jessie pulled up in front of the café and looked around. She wanted to make sure there wasn't anyone she recognized. "Rusti, you stay in the car and wait for me. I'll be right back."

Rusti sat in the front seat anxiously waiting for Jessie. Janice saw her coming in the door of the café and called her order in to the other waitress.

"One chicken salad sandwich on whole wheat with curly fries to go, Edith." Jessie entered the café with a smile on her face for the first time. "Look at you, Jessie. All smiles today. What's going on?"

"Oh, not much, Janice. I just drove into town to pick up a few things from the store. You're still coming out on Saturday, aren't you?"

The beginning of a true friendship began to emerge between Jessie and Janice. "Of course, I'll be there right at noon. Is there anything I can bring for lunch?"

"No, just yourself."

"I'm looking forward to it. I go out highway 281 for forty-eight miles till I come to Cannon Hill Road. The house will be on the left; is that right, Jessie?"

"Sounds like you have been there before."

"No, not really, I looked it up on a map." The two women laughed as they said their goodbyes.

As Jessie was walking out the door of the café, she turned and said, "Janice, you might want to bring an overnight bag with you. It's a long way out there and you may not want to drive home"

"Can I bring Coco, my little Yorkie?"

"Yes, of course. You shouldn't worry about Rusti hurting Coco either. He's a really good dog."

"Okay, see you Saturday." Jessie stopped by the local grocery store to pick up a few items before leaving the village.

On the ride home she began thinking about her adventures since she left Chicago. "Rusti, this island is so beautiful, and the people here are so kind and pleasant. Even with all that has happened at Cannon Hill house, I am so thankful I came here. I wish I could let go of the past and live like other people on this island. Maybe one day things will be different. When we get home, I need to clean the house and make sure we have plenty of wood for the fireplace. I want everything to look nice when Janice comes out on Saturday. I just hope the ghosts will stay away while she's here." Rusti let out a loud bark as if he understood.

CHAPTER THIRTY-SEVEN

After arriving home, Jessie set out to clean the house. She first cleaned both bathrooms upstairs. She decided if Janice stayed the night, she would let her stay in her bedroom. "Rusti, you and I'll sleep in the back bedroom. I've never detected any interference in that room." She went about changing sheets and making the room feel comfortable. "This bedroom feels warm and cozy now, Rusti." The dog followed Jessie all over the house. He never let her out of his site. "Our bedroom is lovely and I'm sure Janice will feel relaxed and at ease in there."

After cleaning the upstairs Jessie and Rusti went down to the kitchen. She brought an arm load of wood from the back porch. She placed it in the log holder which sat at the end of the brick fireplace. She stood back away from the fireplace and looked at the living room with pleasure. She then went into the kitchen and began to gather the things she would need to make the casserole for Saturday. She decided to make an Amish chicken casserole. "I read about the Amish people and their cooking in a magazine the other day. This Amish casserole sounded so delicious; I decided I would make it for our company."

Amish Chicken Casserole

Mix a little flour with melted butter

Add a little milk, salt and pepper, chicken broth, chopped onion and parsley

A small can of mushrooms, chopped cook chicken, cook wide dumpling noodles and mix with the mixture. Sprinkle Parmesan cheese over the casserole before placing in the oven at 350 degrees for about 30 minutes

After cleaning the kitchen, she decided to set the dining room table. She sat two plates and two salad bowls out. She looked down at the loose board on the floor and thought to herself, "I sure hope Janice doesn't ask me anything about that board. It makes a squeak when you walk over it. I'm not sure I'll tell her about the mystery of this old place, just yet. Maybe in time I will, but not Saturday. I want to have a nice lunch and conversation with someone without involving them in my mystery, or should I say, misery."

●　　●　　●

The month of April on Prince Edward Island was simply beautiful. The weather had warmed up a bit and the flowers were beginning to show their lovely heads above ground.

"Rusti, what a nice day for a ride out to Cannon Hill house. I hope Janice will be impressed when she comes out today." She had the casserole ready to pop into the oven as she took the lettuce, tomatoes and cheese out of the refrigerator. "I want everything ready when Janice arrives. Now what should we drink? I have some nice red wine or maybe she would rather have a cup of tea. What to drink, that is the question. Oh well, I guess I'll have to wait and ask."

Jessie was excited to have company. "Rusti, the only people that have been in this house are maintenance people. We haven't had any guests here. And we can't count the prowler, who I hope got scared away the other night. I truly hope he doesn't ever come back." It was 11:30 and Jessie had everything ready for her guest. She went about the house making sure things were in place. She wanted everything to be perfect so Janice would feel at home and comfortable. "If things go well today, maybe Janice will come back and visit us some other time."

Rusti let out a loud bark and ran to the front door. "That must be Janice, Rusti. She's bringing her little dog Coco, so you better be nice to him." Jessie looked through the peep hole in her front door to make sure it was Janice. She was coming up the steps of the porch holding her little dog in her arms. She rang the doorbell twice as she stood there waiting. Jessie opened the door with a smile and said, "Hi, come on in, Janice. Oh, this must be Coco? The dog saw Rusti and started getting anxious. "Lay your things down and make yourself at home."

The two women sat down in the living room and chatted for almost thirty minutes.

"What a beautiful day for a ride in the country. I really enjoyed it too."

"Yes, it's a nice drive out here but a long way from the village. I'm sorry you had to drive so far."

"It was no problem at all, Jessie, I didn't mind one bit."

"Janice, look, Rusti and Coco are getting along just fine. They are playing with each other. Rusti hasn't had another dog to play with since he left the shelter. I've been thinking about getting another shepherd, so he would have somebody to play with."

"Well, living way out here, you probably need another dog."

"Come on, Janice, let's have lunch. What would you prefer to drink? I have red wine, hot tea, cold tea or coffee."

"Red wine sounds good to me, Jessie."

"Okay, red wine it is." She poured red wine in the two glasses and sat them on the dining room table. She took the casserole out of the oven along with the French bread and sat them on the counter. "Wow, that smells so good, Jessie. I can't wait to taste it. "Do you mind if I go ahead and fill your plate?"

"No, of course not." The two women sat down at the table and had a nice time talking and laughing. They talked about their high school days as they ate a delicious lunch.

CHAPTER THIRTY-EIGHT

After lunch, Janice helped Jessie clear the table. Jessie poured them another glass of wine. The weather outside was beautiful, but still a little cool. Jessie had the fireplace going with a nice fire in it. They sat in front of the fireplace and talked. "Were you born here, Janice?"

"No, I wasn't, I lived in Atlanta and wanted to get away after my divorce, so I chose Prince Edward Island. I have lived here almost ten years. I'm originally from Austin, Texas."

Jessie continued to ask Janice questions about her life. She wanted to know as much as she could if they were going to be friends. "I don't think I'll ever leave this island. I love living here."

"I love it here too."

"How long have you been here, Jessie. I know you aren't from Canada."

"No, I moved here from California about five years ago. I bought Cannon Hill house because I am a writer and needed a private place to live." Janice asked Jessie if she had ever been married before. "No, I haven't been married, came close a time or two though. I like to be private and alone most of the time."

• • •

Jessie knew she had to lie to Janice about her past, so she continued to tell her stories that weren't true. She knew she couldn't reveal who she really was. "I love this place, Jessie.

Was it a mess when you found it? You know how people talk in town. I heard the house had been unoccupied for several years."

"Yes, it was, but I painted and cleaned it up by myself. It took a long time, but I managed to finish most of it."

"I also heard it was haunted. I'm not one to believe everything I hear, so I just shrugged it off."

The women continued to drink wine and talk about the house. "Well, sometimes I hear things here, but I'm like you; I just shrugged it off as being an old house. I haven't seen anything." It was getting late in the day when Janice said she should be going. When she stood up she could hardly walk. "I feel so dizzy. It's probably from all the wine!"

"You better sit down. I feel a little dizzy too. I guess we both had too much wine. Why don't you stay the night, Janice?"

"I may have too, Jessie; I really don't feel like driving home."

Jessie and Janice started talking about silly things they have done in their lives. They laughed until tears ran down their faces, and still they continued to drink wine. "Pour me another glass of that delicious wine, Jessie."

"I think we are both drunk, Janice." They both laughed and laughed until Janice passed out in her chair. It was seven o'clock by now and Jessie was too drunk to go upstairs to the bedroom. She decided she would stay downstairs too. "I need to get up so I can get us a blanket. I guess I should let these two dogs go out and potty first." Jessie staggered a little when she got out of her chair. "Whoops, I feel dizzy. I hope I can make it to the back door."

Suddenly, the dogs started to bark and run along the fence in the back yard. Jessie ran over to the front window and looked out. She noticed a strange car parked behind Janice's car in the driveway. She saw a man running to his car. He looked young and had dark hair. She couldn't see his face very well. She couldn't imagine her intruder coming back after the scare he got the other night. She felt sure she would recognize the car if she saw it again. It looked like a light gray Camry, maybe an older model. She let the dogs in the back door and locked it up tight.

She went over to the coat closet, located near the front door. She pulled out two blankets for her and Janice. She made it to her chair and fell into it. "I bet we sleep like babies tonight. I haven't drank that much wine in years." She covered herself up with the blanket and began thinking about the man she saw. She wondered if he was the same one that had been prowling around. Jessie's eyes began to get heavy as she slipped off to sleep. Rusti and Coco snuggled up together in front of the fireplace and went to sleep.

•   •   •

Jessie didn't wake up until 7:30 in the morning. Janice was still asleep in the chair.

Jessie let the dogs out into the back yard and put the coffee on to brew. As Janice began to move around, she could smell the coffee brewing. "Oh, my goodness, that smells so good."

"Good morning Janice: how did you sleep last night. We both had a little too much wine and slept in chairs."

"I know, my back is killing me, and I have a horrible headache."

"Come on in the kitchen and have a cup of coffee. That will make you feel better."

Jessie cooked bacon, scrambled eggs and toast for breakfast. "Jessie, thank you so much for the delicious breakfast. The coffee made my headache go away. Do you mind if I have another cup?"

"Of course not, drink as much as you want." They sat at the kitchen table chatting and drinking coffee until almost eleven o'clock. Janice glanced at her watch and said she needed to head home. "I haven't laughed this much in years. I really have enjoyed the visit. Next time I want you to come to my place for lunch."

"Okay, just let me know when. I am so glad you came, Janice. I really enjoyed your company and all the laughs."

Jessie didn't go into town for almost three weeks. She was glad to have a new friend, but she didn't want to get too close to anyone. The prowler never came back after that night. "I guess that intruder finally gave up, Rusti. I sure hope so. I think I have almost got this mystery figured out. I just need a little more time." Suddenly the room became very cold. "Rusti, we have a guest again. I think Mrs. Carmichael is here." Jessie started shivering and shaking from the cold. "I wish she would leave this house. Jessie grabbed one of the blankets off the chair and wrapped up in it. Almost as quickly as the cold descended upon the room, it disappeared.

CHAPTER THIRTY-NINE

Jessie wasn't afraid of the ghost of Mrs. Carmichael any longer. She believed the ghost of her husband was also in the house. Mr. Carmichael only appeared once or twice since she had moved in. "If only I knew someone that could help me solve this murder, maybe an investigator. Obviously it would have to be someone I could trust. If I could get the fingerprints off that gun, I believe I could finally solve this mystery. I know that prowler is after the gun. He's either the killer or someone hired by the killer to come and get it. I think he's hired by the killer."

Jessie thought about telling Janice about the whole situation but thought better of it. She needed someone to talk to besides her sister. Joyce was too far away, and she didn't want to involve her. "Rusti, it's been three weeks since Janice was here, so I think we'll take a ride into the village today. I need to pick up a few things from the local store. Maybe we'll go by the cafe and pick up lunch." It was May and the weather had started to warm up a little. Jessie loved this time of year and didn't mine the long drive into town.

• • •

Arriving in the village, she pulled up in front of the grocery area. The first thing

Jessie always did was buy ice for the cooler. She would put all her frozen groceries in the cooler just in case she decided to stop off someplace else. "Let's go see Janice and pick up lunch, Rusti." Jessie parked in front of the café. "Rusti, you stay here, I'll be back shortly." She patted the dog on his head as she got out of the car. Janice saw Jessie and called in her order.

"Well, it's about time you showed up, Miss Jessie. I was beginning to worry about you."

"Jessie, I wanted to tell you how much fun I had and to thank you for inviting me over.

I'm so glad you came by today because I wanted to invite you to come to my house." Jessie began to think about the offer before she answered Janice. "If I except her invitation, that means leaving Cannon Hill house empty for the night. I'm afraid to do that. I better not except her invitation at this time."

"Well, will you come for lunch?"

"Janice, I would love to come for lunch, but no wine because I can't spend the night. I don't like to leave Cannon Hill house at night."

"Okay then, how about this coming Saturday?" Jessie acknowledged she would be there the following Saturday.

"Now that it's all settled, how about giving me a cup of that wonderful smelling hot chocolate you make. Oh, would you put some whip cream on top of it too?"

"Give me a minute, Jessie, we are so busy. We desperately need help around here." After Janice poured Jessie a cup of hot chocolate things began to slow down. She came over to where Jessie sat and leaned up against the bar. "It's good to be able to take a deep breath for a few minutes. It's been so busy here and we are one person short. What about you, Jessie? Would you like a part-time job a couple of days a week?"

•   •   •

On the ride home, Jessie thought about Janice's job offer. "I could sure use the extra cash, but this rental car is not that great on gas. Maybe I should exchange it for a smaller more economical car. Seems I've been leasing this SUV for quite a long time now." She decided to drop by the car rental lot before she headed back to Cannon Hill. Jessie drove into the car lot and met with one of the leasing agents. She decided to lease a Toyota Corolla for a year. "I sure am going to miss my SUV. It's a hundred miles to and from town; and this car gets better gas mileage than that SUV did. I think we made the right decision leasing this car, Rusti."

The following Saturday was a beautiful day. The sun was shining brightly, and the flowers had started popping out all over the island. Jessie woke up early, took a shower, and headed downstairs. She looked in the mirror and noticed how thin her face had become. "I've lost so much weight and it makes me look so old these days. I need to go to a doctor and have a check-up. I haven't been to a doctor in years. Maybe I could get something for my nerves." She dressed and went downstairs. She put the coffee on, scrambled eggs and made two pieces of toast. After breakfast she was ready to drive into the village to have lunch with Janice.

•　•　•

Jessie and Janice had a wonderful lunch of fried chicken, potato salad and green beans.

"Janice, you shouldn't have gone to all this trouble for me. I could have eaten a sandwich."

Janice said, "I also made a lemon pie for our desert. I hope you'll like it."

"Everything so far, is delicious. You are a fine cook."

"Hurry up and eat, I want to talk to you about a job opportunity." After lunch the two women went into the family room and sat down. "Jessie, would you like another cup of coffee?"

"That would be nice, Janice."

"Jessie, we need someone at the café two or three days a week and I have suggested you for the job."

"But I don't know anything about cooking in a restaurant, Janice."

"You won't be cooking. We just need someone to take orders and clean off tables. I know you can do that. What do you say, Jessie?"

"I admit I could use the extra money. When do you want me to start?" Janice reached out and hugged Jessie. "I am so happy you accepted the job. It will be fun working with you." The women sat and talked for the next hour when Jessie realized how late it was getting. "It's four o'clock already; I better be going if I'm going to get home before dark."

•　•　•

On the drive home, Jessie began to think about the job. "Rusti, I'll have to leave you at home on the days I work. I don't want to leave you, buddy, but

I really need the money." She reached over and patted the dog on his head. She was anxious and excited about the job at the café. "I just hope I don't see anyone who will recognize me. With my disguise and all this weight, I have lost; I don't think anyone would know who I really am." That evening she decided to go ahead and dye her hair again. "Come Monday morning I want to be ready to start my new job."

CHAPTER FORTY

Monday morning, Jessie woke up early and dressed. She pulled her hair back into a ponytail and wore black slacks and a white blouse. She applied a small amount of foundation on her face and wore her black rimmed glasses. "There is no way anyone would recognize me looking like this. I don't look anything like I did when I first came to the island." She fed Rusti and gave him fresh water. "You be a good boy today, Rusti. I'll be home in a little while." After she left the house, Rusti laid down in the living room and never moved until she got back home.

• • •

Jessie was exhausted when she arrived home from the café. When she opened the door,

Rusti jumped up on her and started licking her face. "Oh, my goodness, Rusti! I missed you too. The dog was excited to see Jessie as he followed her through the house. "Well, everything looks okay. I don't see anything out of place. Rusti, you are a good watch dog." She went into the kitchen and poured dry dog food in Rusti's bowl. "There you go, boy. Eat your dinner." She filled the kettle with water and sat it on the stove to heat. "I need a hot cup of tea to revive me tonight." She went upstairs to her bedroom to change clothes while the water heated.

As Jessie started back down the stairs she heard a noise in the back bedroom. She turned around suddenly with a start. "Rusti, Rusti come upstairs with me." The dog ran up the stairs barking as he too heard something unusual. Jessie thought it was either an intruder or Mrs. Carmichael making herself known. "It couldn't be an intruder. Rusti was here all day. She's probably getting impatient for me to solve her murder. I bet she's getting agitated." Jessie and Rusti stood outside of the door to the bedroom. She was hesitant about opening the door.

Jessie looked down at Rusti and whispered to him. "Should we open the door, Rusti? I'm scared to death someone is going to be in there. Oh well, this is my house and I need to find out what that noise was, so here we go." Jessie put her hand on the doorknob and slowly opened the door. Rusti ran inside the room barking, but there was no one there. "Well, Rusti, I guess the ghost are acting up again. Oh, how I wish they would go away. My nerves can't take much more of Mrs. Carmichael."

• • • •

The next week, Jessie worked hard at the Café. She bussed tables, swept and mopped the floors, and cleaned all the tables. She was so tired after working, she could hardly drive home. Janice asked her to stay at her house the days she worked, but Jessie refused. "I would love to Janice, but I need to go home and see about Rusti."

"Okay, Jessie, but you are always welcome to stay at my home anytime you don't feel like driving home."

"Thanks, Janice, I may have to take you up on that one of these days."

• • •

Jessie and Janice began to get closer as the days went by. Janice was the first friend she had on the Island. Jessie wanted to confide in Janice about Mrs. Carmichael and the murder, but just couldn't bring herself to talk about it. One afternoon after work, Janice asked Jessie if she would like to have dinner with her. It was Saturday and the Café closed at 4 pm. "Sure Janice, as long as I can get home before dark. I don't like to drive that far after dark." "I understand, Jessie, and of course, there's Rusti to think about."

• • •

The two women closed the Café around four O'clock on Saturday. They walked down the street to Oreille's bar and restaurant. "Wow, this is a nice place, Janice."

"I thought you would like this place, Jessie. I come here from time to time. The atmosphere is nice, and it makes me forget all my troubles."

"Now what kind of troubles could you have?"

"It's nothing really. My ex-husband won't leave me alone. He's been harassing me lately." Jessie thought to herself, "If only that was all I had to worry about. Janice would probably have a stroke if I told her all my troubles."

"Hey, I have an idea: why don't we sic Rusti on him. I bet that would get rid of him."

The two women laughed so hard; they could hardly control themselves. The waiter came around to the table and asked what they would like to have. "I'd like a glass of red wine, please. I also would like a chicken salad sandwich with fries."

"Is that all Ma'am"

"Yes, thank you. What would you like, Jessie? Dinner is on me tonight." Jessie was hesitating about ordering wine. "Well, thank you, Janice. Next time dinner is on me." The waiter stood there waiting for Jessie. "I think I'll have a Coke to drink. And please let me have one of those chicken salads sandwiches with fries too."

"You know, Jessie, a glass of red wine would relax you. Surely one glass of wine won't hurt you."

"Oh, believe me I would love to have a glass of wine, but I can't take any chances driving home." The two women talked and laughed while eating their dinner. "Now, I'm going to tell you my whole life story, so don't laugh at me. I was born Janice Ronda Carlton. When I was five years old, my mother passed away from cancer. We lived in Austin, Texas at the time. My dad couldn't find work there, so he packed my two brothers and me up and moved here to the Island. He found a job as the caretaker at the local Prince Edward Island elementary school. He passed away in 1969 from a heart attack. I stayed here for several years after that but moved away around 1984."

Jessie sat there with her arms propped under her chin, listening. She wondered if

Janice expected her to tell her life story. She wanted to tell Janice all about her life, but now wasn't the time to do that. Jessie continued to listen to Janice. "I moved right out of high school to Atlanta, Georgia. That's where I met my ex-husband, John. After we divorced I wanted to get away from everything and everybody, so I moved here to Prince Edward Island.

I have lived here ever since."

"How long were you married to John, Janice?"

"We got married in 1987 and divorced in 1995. No children of course, but I always wanted to have some."

CHAPTER FORTY-ONE

Jessie looked at her watch and noticed it was already 6 pm. "Oh my gosh, Janice, it's getting late. I really need to get on the road. I wish I could stay and hear the rest of your story, but I really must be on my way. I don't remember when I have had a more enjoyable time than today."

"I know you have to leave, Jessie, but I sure wish you could stay a little while longer."

"Maybe next time." Jessie rose from her seat at the table and asked Janice to walk out to her car with her. "This tab is on me."

"Are you sure, Janice; I don't mind paying the tab."

Janice paid the waiter and picked up her purse. She followed Jessie out to her car. "Well look at that. I didn't know you traded your SUV. I love the Corolla though."

"Thanks, Janice, I just wanted something different. Thank you for lunch and the nice conversation. I really enjoyed today."

"Next time I want to hear your life story. You have a great day off tomorrow." Jessie said, "I'll see you Monday morning." The two women waved goodbye as Jessie backed out of the parking lot. "I bet Rusti is wondering where I am. I didn't mean to stay so long."

Rusti was happy to see Jessie as she came in the front door. He jumped up on her and ran circles around her. "I'm happy to see you too, Rusti. I am so sorry I'm late coming home."

She bent down and hugged the dog and patted him on his head. "Come on boy, let's get your supper." Jessie went upstairs to her room where she undressed and turned the shower on. After she showered she put her pajamas on. She went downstairs and filled the kettle with water. "I'm going to make a cup of tea and go sit in the living room for a while. I didn't realize how tired I was." She had put Rusti outside to potty while she made her cup of tea. He started barking and running up and down the fence. Jessie knew someone was out there. She got her pistol out of the kitchen drawer and went out on the back porch. "Rusti, what is it, get'em boy. Okay whoever is out here better be on your way. I have called the police and I have a gun in my hand. Believe me, I'll use it if I have too."

Rusti calmed down and ran up onto the back porch. "Good boy Rusti, you stay outside for a little while. Whoever it was may still be there." Jessie checked the front door to make sure it was locked, then walked over to the windows and closed all the curtains. She didn't hear Rusti barking anymore, so she went to the back door and called Rusti to come in. He was exhausted from running and barking. "Come on, Rusti and drink your water. I think our intruder has probably left. Rusti, I'm sure you scared him off. You are such a good dog. What would I do without you?"

Rusti sat in the kitchen until he caught his breath, then ran into the living room and stretched out on the floor. "I'm so sorry, Rusti. Whoever that was is very persistent and keeps coming back here. I think tomorrow after work I'm going to go over to the hardware store. I want to pick up one of those outdoor cameras. Perhaps we will be able to find out who keeps trying to break in." As Rusti laid on the floor his ears stood up straight every now and then. It was as if he heard something but wasn't quite sure.

Jessie poured water into her cup. She added one tablespoon of sugar and a little cream.

She went into the living room and sat down in her favorite chair. She reached over to the side table and pulled out a tablet and pen from the drawer. She started to jot down all the names of the men that were involved with Mrs. Carmichael. "I wish I knew for sure I could confide in Janice. I need help with this situation and Janice is the only friend I have here on the Island." Jessie thought about all the times she encountered Mrs. Carmichael. The ghost never had any intentions of hurting her; she just wanted help.

The next day was Monday and Jessie needed to get up early. She fell asleep in the chair and didn't wake up until 1 in the morning. "Oh my gosh, Rusti look at the time! We'd better head to bed. I really must get up early to get to work tomorrow. Jessie and Rusti headed upstairs to their bedroom. Jessie took a quick shower and glanced at herself in the mirror. "Wow, I look like I've aged ten years. No wonder, that's what happens when you're living in a house with ghosts. Trying to solve a murder takes a lot out of a person. I feel like if I don't get help with this situation, I'm won't be able to keep it together."

• • •

Jessie set the clock for 6 am as she always did on workdays. When it rang, she reached over to turn the alarm off and dragged herself out of the bed. "I feel like I've been hit by a Mac truck this morning. I wonder if I'm coming down with a cold." She got dressed and went downstairs to the kitchen. The coffee had already started to perk. "Come on, Rusti, you need to go outside to potty. Jessie reached into the kitchen cabinet and got the Tylenol bottle. She took two tablets and made a cup of coffee. She hoped to feel better by the time she got to town.

• • •

She pulled in her usual parking space, got out, and locked the car. As she walked in the door, Janice said, "Well, good morning to you, Miss Jessie. What's wrong Hon, you look like you've seen a ghost." Jessie said, "Funny you should say that" as she laughed under her breath. Jessie said, "Janice, I need to run over to the hardware store to pick up something. I'll be back shortly."

"Okay, Jessie, I'm going ahead and eat my sandwich. I'll see you in a little while." Jessie crossed the street to get to the hardware store.

CHAPTER FORTY-TWO

As soon as she walked in, a friendly clerk asked if he could help her find something. "Hi, yes, I'm looking to install an outside camera. I have a computer in the house. Will I need anything else to see outside my house?" "You should be able to connect it to your computer. Do you have Wi fi?" "Yes, I do, and I was hoping that's all I needed." The young man showed Jessie where the cameras were. "Follow me and I'll show you what you need to do. I'll show you how to hook it up, if I can without seeing your house. It may be a little difficult, but I'll try my best." Jessie said, "Thank you so much for helping me. I really don't have any idea where to start."

Jessie and the young man went over the instructions several times. "I think I have the hang of it now. Thank you again for helping with this. I don't think I could have done this my own." You are so welcome, Miss. If you have any problems at all, just come by and I'll try to help you." Jessie felt relieved after purchasing the camera. She crossed the street and got back to the café as quickly as he could. She realized she had used up all her lunch break. Janice said, "Jessie, go ahead and eat your sandwich. We're not busy right now. What in the world did you get at the hardware store? Seemed like you were gone a long time."

"Well, to tell you the truth, I bought a camera to put outside my house. I've had a prowler and I want to find out who it is. The young man at the hardware store was teaching me how to install it. I didn't realize how long I was gone." Janice said, "Oh no, Jessie, that would scare me to death."

Jessie responded to Janice by saying, "Well to tell the truth, it has been a little scary, not knowing who is out there. I wish I knew what they wanted."

"Why don't I come out this weekend and help you watch for them. If we catch the creep, we can have him arrested by the island police."

"I would love for you to come out this weekend, but there's no guarantee the man will return. He's been coming around two times a week for the past couple of months. One night he busted out my kitchen door window. That cost me a hundred dollars to repair."

Janice said, "Jessie, why haven't you said anything about this. I could have helped you in some way."

"I really don't like people knowing my business, Janice. I'm a very private person and I like to take care of things on my own. To tell you the truth, I haven't had anyone to confide in until I met you. I have trust issues with people; so, I keep things to myself."

"Jessie, I thought you knew you could trust me. What do I have to do to convince you I'm your friend and trustworthy?" On the drive home that evening, Jessie really pondered what Janice had said about trust. She began thinking about friendships. "Janice has really proven to be a good friend to me over these last three years. I really believe I can trust her now. I just won't tell her about my escaping Chicago and why. One day the detectives may find me, but until then, if I want to have a peaceful life, I've got a murder to solve. The next time Janice is off on a Saturday, I'll invite her for a visit. Maybe just maybe, Janice can help me solve this mystery at my Cannon Hill house. I never thought I would admit it to myself, but I guess I do need help."

·   ·   ·

Rusti was happy to see Jessie when she arrived home that afternoon. As soon as he heard her car come into the driveway; he started barking. "Hello my sweet dog. I'm so happy to see you. She knelt to hug Rusti and pat him on his head. Have you been a good boy today?"

Jessie kicked off her shoes as soon as she walked in the front door. She flopped down in her favorite chair exhausted. Suddenly the room became very cold. "Looks like we have company, Rusti. Please go away Mrs. Carmichael. I'm doing the best I can." Finally, the room began to warm up. As usual, the ghosts left the room.

·   ·   ·

The following week was busy at the café. Jessie and Janice worked as hard as they could to keep up with the visitors. It was summer on the island so there were a lot of people arriving every day. In the back of Jessie's mind, she wondered if anyone was going to recognize her. "Surely no one will recognize the new and different me. My appearance is different from my Chicago life." Jessie stood next to one of the tables just thinking. "Jessie, are you okay? You look like you are lost in another world."

"Yes, my friend, I'm okay. I was just thinking about an old flame."

"Oh, is that all? He must have been someone really special."

Jessie thought to herself, "Get a hold of yourself, woman. No one is going to recognize you. If I keep feeling guilty, I'm going to look guilty!" Still, she was concerned that Janice was suspicious of her past. The decision was made. She would only tell her about the mystery she was trying to solve. "Jessie, I'm off tomorrow. Why don't I come out to Cannon House and visit with you? Then you can tell me all about this prowler of yours."

"Sure, Janice, I would love for you to come out. I need a little help programing that camera anyway."

"Well I'm no computer buff but I can probably help you with that."

It was time for Jessie's shift to end for the week. She decided to stop by the grocery store before she left for home. "I need dog food for Rusti, milk eggs and coffee. I wonder if Janice likes spaghetti. That sounds good to me, so, I think I'll make spaghetti and French bread and maybe a salad. Oh, I don't want to forget to get a bottle of wine, maybe two bottles." As Jessie was coming out of the grocery store, she heard someone call her name. It was James Walton, one of Mrs. Carmichael lovers. The very one she was suspicious of murdering the woman.

CHAPTER FORTY-THREE

Jessie began to get nervous. James Walton walked up to her, took the groceries out of her arms and walked her to her car. "How have you been since you came to my office? Have you solved Naomi's murder yet?" Jessie knew he was fishing to find out what she knew She wondered why he was on the island. "No, I haven't, Mr. Walton." Jessie knew she'd better not let him know what she knew so far. She played it calm and as cool as she could. "What brings you to the island, Mr. Walton?"
"Oh, I had a little business to take care of. I'm on my way home now; I just dread that long drive."

"Well, good luck to you, Jessie. If anyone can solve a mystery, I am sure it's you." Mr. Walton left, just like that. Jessie was relieved to keep the encounter short. She hurried to get in her car and head home to Cannon Hill. "That man makes me so nervous. I just know he is the murderer. I think he was fishing to get some information out of me. He probably knows I suspect him. I'll bet anything someone tries to break in tonight." She suddenly turned her car around and went back to the café. She found Janice just in time. "Janice, I am so glad I caught you. Why don't you come on out tonight, to Cannon Hill. I have a sneaky suspicion someone is going to try to get in tonight."

Janice wasn't expecting the invitation. "Well, I guess I could make it tonight, Jessie. I was planning on getting some things done around the house tonight; but I can come if you want me too."
"I would feel so much better if you did, Janice."
"Okay then, I will see you around eight O'clock."
"That's perfect, Janice. I hope you like spaghetti?"

"Yes, I love spaghetti, especially with a little red wine."

"I've got you covered, Janice. I just bought two bottles of red wine."

"That sounds so good, Jessie, I'll see you later, then." The two women left the café and went their separate ways.

Jessie was happy the weekend was here. She was tired from the busy week she'd had. Rusti was excited to see her and jumped up on her as she entered the front door. She knelt and hugged the dog as she always did. "Come on, Rusti, let's take you outside to potty. Miss Janice is coming out to dinner and I need to hurry. While Rusti was outside, she went upstairs and changed her clothes. She put on a pair of jeans and a pullover cotton shirt. She washed the workday from her face and pulled her hair back into a ponytail. Before going downstairs, she decided to check the guest bedroom. Jessie wanted to make sure, everything was okay for Janice.

As she opened the door a figure of a man was standing by the window. She drew in a deep breath and stopped in her tracks. The man never turned around, he just disappeared. She just stood there, feeling like she couldn't move. In an instant, Jessie decided, "I need to tell Janice about this house. I bet that was Mr. Carmichael." She finally spoke out loud into the silence of the room. "Please go away and leave me alone." Jessie was still trembling as she went downstairs. "Now I really need to tell Janice about this house. What if Mr. Carmichael should appear in her room again? It would scare her to death. Yes, I'll tell her tonight after dinner."

Rusti was sitting at the back door wanting to come in the house. She opened the door and said, "Come on in, Rusti and eat your dinner." She poured his bowl full of dry dog food. As she prepared dinner, she began thinking to herself, "I wonder how many times, the ghosts appear to Rusti during the day. Poor dog probably sees them a lot when I'm not home."

Jessie arranged the table for two. She checked to see if the spaghetti was ready, then prepared a loaf of French bread to go with the pasta. For dessert she was ready with two bowls of strawberries topped with whipped cream.

She glanced at the clock on the kitchen wall. It was 7:45 and Janice should be there any time now. Her hands were still shaking a little as she poured herself a glass of wine. She went into the living room and sat down in her favorite chair. She hoped the glass of wine would help settle her nerves. She sat there drinking the wine and in just a few minutes, she nodded off to sleep. Ten minutes later, Janice knocked on the front door.

• • •

The knock at the front door woke her up. She looked out the peep hole before she opened the door. She wanted to make sure it was Janice. Rusti started barking as Jessie tried to get him to calm down. She opened the door slowly. "Hi, Janice, come on in. I drank some wine while I waited on you and dozed off."

"I guess you were tired from working all week. It was so busy with all the visitors on the island."

"Yes, it was, and I know you must be tired too. Especially having to drive all the way out here." Janice assured Jessie the drive wasn't bad at all. "I always enjoy the drive out here. The countryside is so beautiful. But I am glad it was still daylight. I would probably get lost if it was dark."

"Well you made in just in time. You did beat the darkness. Lay your things down and let's go eat dinner. The wine is waiting." Jessie and Janice had a delightful dinner. They chatted about the long hard week they both had at work. Jessie said, "Janice, we shouldn't drink too much of this wine, I want to talk to you about something important and I want our heads to be clear."

CHAPTER FORTY-FOUR

The two women cleared the table and went into the living room to sit down.

"Before we do anything else, Janice, I need you to help me get that camera set up. I've had a problem getting the outside of the house to show up on my computer screen."

"Sure,

Jessie, where is the computer?"

"It's upstairs in my bedroom."

"Okay, let's go look at it. I think I know what the problem is. Do you think the prowler is going to come around tonight?"

"I'm not sure, Janice, but I've had a feeling all day he might. I wanted to be prepared."

Jessie and Janice went upstairs to Jessie's bedroom with Rusti right behind them. As they entered the room, Janice said, "What a lovely room you have, Jessie. It's so warm and comfortable."

"Thank you Janice, I wanted the room to feel like home."

"This is your home, Jessie."

"I know, but sometimes it doesn't feel like it. Remember you telling me you had an open mind about things?"

"Yes, I remember."

"Well I have something to tell you about this house, but let's get this camera going first. I want to see who keeps trying to get in my house."

"Okay, Jessie let's get it started."

Janice programed the camera in the computer. Suddenly the outside of the house appeared on the screen. "Wow, look at that Jessie, you can see your whole yard."

"Thank you Janice, I am so grateful to you for helping me with this. I feel so much safer now." Jessie said, "Why don't we go downstairs and get a glass of wine. We can come back up here and watch the computer while I tell you a story."

"That sounds wonderful to me. Let's go." Jessie and Janice went downstairs and retrieved the bottle of wine and two glasses. As they were walking up the stairs Jessie said, "Why don't we put our pajamas on and get comfortable first."

So, Janice went into the guess bedroom to change clothes, while Jessie went into her bathroom and put on her pajamas. When they were finished getting changed, Jessie sat at the computer and Janice sat on the bed. "Are you comfortable Janice?"

"Yes, I'm fine. Now tell me that story you were going to tell me."

"They were like two schoolgirls having an overnight party. Jessie said, "Janice, I have known you for three years now and consider you my best friend here on the island. I know I can trust you to keep whatever I tell you a secret."

"Of course, you can, Jessie. If it's something I can help you with, I'm here for you."

"I have thought long and hard about this and have come to the conclusion, I need help."

Jessie was hesitating at first but continued to tell Janice how the mystery all came about. I ran away from a very difficult situation. I traveled a long way to get here. When I arrived on the island, I stayed in a bed and breakfast for a few days. It was nice and the people who ran it were wonderful. But one day I decided to take a ride out into the countryside. I just wanted to get a feel for the island. I always wanted to visit Prince Edward Island, but I never expected to be living here. I ended up way out here in the country. I wasn't sure where I was when I came to a stop sign. I either had to go left or right. As I was sitting there at the stop sign, I started to look around.

"Go on, Jessie, this is getting interesting. I can't wait to hear what happened next." Jessie continued her story. "That's when I saw this house. I backed the rental car into the driveway of this old place. It looked abandoned and in bad shape. I got out to get a better look and found an old faded for sale sign laying in the yard." Janice said, "You know, years ago I heard about this place. A woman was murdered here on Christmas Eve. I don't think the police ever found the murderer."

"Yes, I know all about the murder here. Anyway, I picked up the faded sign and called the number written on it."

Jessie told Janice all about the house and how she bought it at such a low price. Janice was in awe of the story and wanted to hear more. Jessie's story was suddenly interrupted by a noise she heard. Rusti began to bark and ran down the stairs. "Did you hear that, Janice?"

"No, I didn't, what kind of noise was it?"

"Look, Janice, someone is outside the house." Janice got up off the bed and ran over to the computer. "I recognize that man. He has come into the café on several occasions. But I don't know his name." Jessie said, "Let's see what he does. Look Janice, he's heading for the back yard. I'll go let Rusti out back. That should run him off."

Rusti was barking and anxious to get outside. Jessie ran down the stairs and followed the dog to the back door. As soon as she opened the door, Rusti raced out into the back yard. Janice continued to watch the man on the computer screen. Jessie locked the back door and ran back upstairs. "What's happening, Janice? What's that guy doing now?"

"Jessie, look, he's at the front door now. Do you have a gun in the house?"

"Yes, in the kitchen cabinet drawer."

"Come on, let's go get it." Jessie and Janice ran down the stairs. Janice stood by the front door as Jessie ran into the kitchen to get the gun.

CHAPTER FORTY-FIVE

Jessie was ready for the prowler now. She had a nine-millimeter fully loaded. "Janice, open the door, I'm ready for him now." Janice slowly opened the front door, but no one was there. "Where did he go?" Jessie opened the screen door and looked all around the yard. "I don't know, Janice, but something must have spooked him. Something besides Rusti." The two women went back inside the house and locked the door behind them. Rusti was still barking and running up and down the fence. Jessie said, "Rusti does this every time someone comes in our yard. I think I'll leave him outside for a while longer."

"Jessie, I don't know how you stand this. I would be scared to death all the time."

"Janice, you don't know the half of it. I just know he's gone for the night, so let's go back upstairs. I want to finish telling you my story."

"What about Rusti?"

"He's stopped barking, so I'll bring him in." Jessie let Rusti in the house and patted the dog on his head. "What a good boy you are. I am so proud of you, Rusti." Jessie laid her head down on Rusti's head and hugged him at the same time. She glanced at the clock on the kitchen wall. "Oh, my goodness, I didn't realize it was after midnight. Janice, since it's so late, why don't I finish telling the story tomorrow. Why don't we go to bed."

Janice was disappointed. She wanted to hear more of Jessie's story. She followed Jessie and Rusti up the stairs and told Jessie good night. Janice was a little scared but as soon as she got under the warm comforter, she fell asleep. Jessie sat up for a while watching the computer.

Since there didn't seem to be any further activity outside, she decided to try to get some sleep.

While Janice slept, the ghost of Mr. Carmichael stood by the window. He was in the same place, and in the same position. Janice slept and never knew he was ever there.

•   •   •

The following morning, Jessie woke up early. She took a shower and dressed for the day. She pulled her long black hair back with a rubber band. She put on a small amount of foundation and rouge. "Where are my glasses, I know I laid them on the table beside my bed." She finally found them lying on the bed. "I must have laid them there before I went to sleep. Come on, Rusti, let's get breakfast started." Jessie and Rusti went downstairs to find the back door partly open. "Oh my gosh." She ran to the dining room to see if the board under the chair had been disturbed. "I sure am glad I moved that gun. At least if he gets in here, he won't find the gun."

Jessie went all over the house. She looked in closets, under beds and anyplace someone could hide. "They could be in the cellar. I think I'll let Rusti go down there and check it out.

There is no other place in the house they could hide. Come on, Rusti, go down in the cellar and check it out for me." Rusti ran down the cellar steps and sniffed the air. The dog never barked and finally ran back up the steps. "Good boy, Rusti, at least we know no one is down there. I just can't figure out how that door got open, unless it was the ghosts. I am positive I locked it."

Jessie decided to go ahead and start cooking breakfast. She put six slices of bacon in the frying pan, she turned the coffee pot on and got a dozen eggs out of the refrigerator. She went to the pantry and got Rusti's dry dog food out. She filled his bowl and patted him on his head.

"Rusti, you are such a good boy. I don't know if I could live in this house without you." In the meantime, Janice woke up. She gathered her things from her overnight bag and went into the hall bathroom. She showered and dressed and went downstairs to the kitchen. "Good morning, Janice how are you feeling this morning?"

Janice said, "I slept like a baby all night. I was so comfortable in that bed of yours. I had some bad dreams though."

"Well, come have a cup of coffee and tell me all about your dreams."

"I dreamed someone was in my room standing by the window. It was a tall man, but I couldn't see his face. He just stood there as if he was staring out the window. All I can remember is he had on a gray suit." Jessie knew in her mind that it wasn't a dream. Mr. Carmichaels ghosts really was standing by the window. Oh, how I wish these ghosts would go away. Jessie's thoughts were all over the place. I must tell Janice about the Carmichaels.

CHAPTER FORTY-SIX

After breakfast, Jessie and Janice sat at the dining room table drinking coffee. "Janice, I want to tell the rest of my story; but I need to know for sure what I tell you today, will not go out of this room."

"Jessie, I give you my word of honor, I'll not tell a living soul." Jessie felt like Janice was telling her the truth, so, she began where she left off the night before. "As I said last night, I bought this house really cheap. It had not been occupied for seven years and very run down. So, the real estate lady was glad to sell it to me. After signing the papers, she left me with a folder that contained the names and history of all the people who had lived in this house before I did."

Janice just sat there listening as if she was watching a movie on television. Jessie continued as she sipped on her coffee. "Janice, would you like more coffee?"

"Yes, I do, but I'll get it for us." After Janice sat back down at the table, Jessie began again. "Delores, the real estate woman, failed to tell me the house was haunted."

"Haunted, oh no, Jessie, what did you do when you found out?"

"Well, I decided I wanted to keep this house and the ghosts were not going to run me away. So, the first thing I did was to clean the whole house. I wanted to make it suitable to live in. Then, I read as much as I could about the people who lived here. I wanted to find out why the house was haunted."

Janice was intrigued and wanted to hear more of the story. Jessie said, "Why don't we go sit in the living room and get more comfortable. Why don't we get a coke?" Janice couldn't wait to hear more of this adventure. "Go ahead, Jessie, I'll bring us two Cokes."

The two women went into the living room and got comfortable. Janice flopped down on the sofa. Jessie sat down in her favorite chair and propped her legs up on the ottoman. "Come on, Jessie, don't keep me in suspense. Get on with this story."

"Don't be so impatient, Janice. Okay, where was I, oh, I know; I was telling you about the ghosts. I kept reading about the people who had lived here before me. I came across the Carmichael family. I found out that Mrs. Carmichael was shot and killed on Christmas Eve while having a Christmas Eve party. Mr. Carmichael lived here alone for almost five years after her death. After I read about Mrs. Carmichael, I began to get little hints around the house. I found a picture of a man lying on the top step as I was going downstairs one day. The room I was in would get cold or one of the bedrooms would have this awful smell in it. There was always little signs that they were here."

"Jessie, how long have you been living with this nightmare?"

"Five years now, Janice.

After all the activity in the house, I decided to get a dog, one that would protect me. So, one day I went to the animal shelter and found Rusti. And he has been a Godsend for me. He has been my protector and friend."

"Janice said, "Rusti is a fine dog. I wish I had one like him. You really need a dog like Rusti living way out here in the boonies."

"I knew from the beginning I would need him. I was lucky when I went to the shelter that day. He was just six weeks old and he was ready for a forever home."

The clock on the mental struck 12. Jessie said to Janice. "I can't believe it's noon already. Are you hungry, Janice?"

"I want to hear more of the story, but I could eat a sandwich."

"Well, why don't we go in the kitchen and make some lunch and then I'll tell you some more of the story."

"Sounds good to me, Jessie." Janice and Jessie made chicken salad sandwiches, chips and another Coke. Janice was anxious to get started on the story. "Come on, Jessie, I'm dying to hear more." The two women sat down in the living room as Jessie began to talk.

As Jessie began to tell more of her story, the room suddenly got very cold. Janice found a shawl lying on the sofa and pulled it up around her shoulders. Jessie said, "Mrs. Carmichael is visiting us. Don't be afraid Janice;

she won't hurt us. She just wants her presence known. She comes and goes all the time. The cold descended above the room like a deep freeze. The two women were shivering. Then, the cold suddenly disappeared. "Jessie, how can you stand that."

"If I could solve her murder, I believe she will leave this house. I have been trying to find out who murdered her for three years now."

Jessie told Janice how she had investigated all of Mrs. Carmichaels lovers. She told her how she had found the trinket box in the back of the closet. "The past two years have been particularly hard. Every night I would read one of Richard's letters. The letters are what lead me to the other two men. Then after I had the chance to talk with Richard, he had a heart attack and dies. Richard was my main source and hope to find the answers for this mystery. I feel quite sure, he wasn't the murderer." Janice said, "I've got chills running up my spine just listening to all this. The visit from the ghosts hasn't helped either. Jessie, I don't know how you have stayed here in this house with all this going on."

"I've come to the end of my rope, Janice. That's why I decided to confide in you. I need someone to help me solve this mystery. I am tired of living this way. The ghosts must go. The prowler has some connection to the murder. I believe there is something in this house he wants before I find it. Maybe it will lead me to the killer."

"Of course, I'll help you, Jessie. I'll need to see all the evidence, you have. I also want to hear more about this lady ghost of yours."

"I hope you aren't in a hurry to get home today."

"Oh, no, Jessie, I'm not leaving until I know the whole story."

CHAPTER FORTY-SEVEN

Jessie and Janice decided to clean up the kitchen and take a break. The clock on the mantel rang out. Janice said, "I can't believe it's 3:00 already. My how time flies when you're having fun." Jessie and Janice laughed until they cried. "Oh, my goodness, I never expected to hear all this. I heard this house was haunted several years ago, but I never expected all this was going on here."

"Now you know why I have always been so private and secluded, Janice. Then I found a friend and confided in you."

Janice couldn't understand why Jessie never went to the police with her findings. "Jessie, you know you could have turned all the evidence over to the police and let them handle this."

"No, I couldn't do that. First, the police wouldn't believe the ghosts story.

Secondly, they would descend upon this house like vultures. Thirdly, they would investigate me because I know so much. They would never believe my story about the trinket box and all the things that have been happening since I moved in here."

Janice knew Jessie was right. "What are you going to do if you do find out who murdered the woman. What then, Jessie?"

"To tell the truth, I haven't figured that out yet. I do know if I don't solve this mystery, the Carmichaels spirits are never going to leave this house."

"What about the prowler? He has something to do with all this or he wouldn't keep coming around here."

"I know what he's looking for and he's not going to get it. I found evidence hidden under the dining room table floor."

"What did you find, Jessie?" Janice was so excited about all this; she could hardly control herself.

"This is the most exciting story I have ever heard in my life, Jessie. I don't think I'll ever be able to sleep at night again. Finish telling me what you found in the dining room floor." Well," said Jessie, "one morning I decided to sit at the dining room table and eat breakfast. As I pulled out the chair from the table I heard a loud creak. I started looking at the floor and there it was."

"What, Jessie, what did you find?"

"It's already 4 pm, Janice, why don't you stay another night, then I can bring you up to date on everything."

"Jessie, you couldn't make me leave now. I want to read those letters Mrs. Carmichael got from Richard."

"Of course, I want you to read them and maybe understand why I'm so certain Richard wasn't the one who murdered her."

"Jessie, I would love to have a cup of coffee."

"I would love to have one too. Let's go put on the coffee pot." Jessie and Janice went out to the kitchen and made themselves fresh coffee. It was a beautiful day outside and Rusti had been out almost day. It was August and very hot. "I think I'll let Rusti in for a while. I'm going to go ahead and feed him. The poor boy is probably burning up out there."

"Janice, did I tell you I was thinking about screening in the back porch?"

"That would be nice, Jessie. You would be able to sit out there and read or just relax and drink your morning coffee. I love that idea."

"That's what I was thinking, Janice. Do you know anyone that does that kind of construction?"

"What about the guy that repaired the door window for you?"

"Sandra at the hardware store recommended him to me. I think I'll stop over there next week and talk to her." Janice was ready to get back to the story. "Jessie, show me the board in the dining room where you found something."

"Okay, Janice, if you insist."

Janice couldn't understand why Jessie had gone all this time without contacting the Island police. "Jessie, I know you don't want people coming out here and searching your home, but what are you going to do if you solve this murder?"

"I'm not sure yet, Janice. I was hoping you could help me. You are the first person I have ever told about this place."

"I do have a nephew that is a private investigator. He lives in Halifax and has his office there. Maybe he could be of some help."

"Let's don't go there just yet, Janice. This is between you and me and we'll consider that later."

"I understand, Jessie. I won't say a word to anybody. I promised you I wouldn't, and I won't."

"Good, Janice. I told you about all this because I felt I could trust you."

"And you can, Jessie. Come on, I'm anxious to see what you found in the dining room floor."

"Well, I was walking through the dining room one night when I heard the floor creak. I stopped and backed up and heard it creak again. I got down on my knees and started touching the boards. Suddenly one of the boards popped up a little. I pulled it up very carefully. Guess what I found? A box with a loaded gun."

"A gun, what kind, Jessie?"

"I think it's a nine-millimeter. Come on, Janice, and I'll show it to you."

"Is it loaded, Jessie? I'm afraid of guns."

"It was loaded, but it's not now." Jessie went upstairs to her bedroom and got the gun from under her bed. She took it back downstairs to show Janice. "Look at this, Janice. I believe whoever has been stalking this house is trying to get this gun."

"I bet it has the killer's fingerprints all over it, Jessie."

"I thought of that too, Janice, that's why I picked it up with a washcloth. This is only the second time I have handled it."

CHAPTER FORTY-EIGHT

Jessie and Janice just stood there staring down at the gun. Janice said, "What are you going to do with it, Jessie?"

"I'm not sure yet, but one thing's for sure, whoever is coming around here at night is after this weapon. I bet he hid it here and intended to come back and get it. He wasn't worried about it when the house was empty. But since I'm living here now, he's afraid I might find it."

"Jessie, how do you think he hid it here?"

"Whoever he is, he was probably a friend of Mr. Carmichael's too. I'm guessing that he came by one day to see Mr.

Carmichael. My guess is that while Mr. Carmichael was out of the room, he hid the gun in the floor. He must have known there was a loose board there."

The two women decided to prepare dinner. Janice said, "Jessie, I am so creeped out right now. I have chills running up and down my spine again. This mystery of yours is getting intense. I don't know how in the world you have gone this long without telling someone."

"I talk to my dog a lot. Old Rusti here knows everything about it. Don't you, boy." Jessie knelt to pet Rusti on his head. "Jessie, you are so lucky to have such a good dog. German Shepherds are so smart." Jessie said, "Rusti is the best. I don't know what I would have done without him. He has been a lot of company for me too. I love him as if he was my child."

Jessie had a small grill on the back porch which she used from time to time. "Janice, why don't we grill some steaks out. I have two beautiful rib eyes in the refrigerator."

"That sounds delicious."

"How about a bake potato and salad with your steak?"

"Do you have any more of that red wine, Jessie?"

"I have a whole bottle left. That will taste wonderful with our steak."
After the two women grilled the steaks and enjoyed their dinner, Janice
asked to read the letters from Mrs. Carmichael's lover, Richard. Jessie said,
"Why don't we take our glass of wine and go in the living room where we can
be comfortable."

Jessie sat down in her favorite chair and reached over to the side table
and opened the drawer. She pulled out the trinket box which held the letters.
Janice had gotten comfortable on the sofa holding a glass of wine in one
hand. "Janice, before you start reading these letters, I want to tell you a little
more about Mrs. Carmichael. She had three lovers while married to Mr.
Carmichael. Richard Mitchell seemed to be the one who was truly in love
with her. After speaking to him on the phone and arranging to go and meet
with him, he suddenly died of a heart attack. I believe the shock of me
finding the letters and wanting to see him, might have brought on the heart
attack."

Janice was in shock. "You mean he died right after you spoke with him
on the phone?"

"Apparently, and I never got the chance to talk with him again. I felt
terrible about the whole thing. When I came across these letters, I just had
to find him and talk to him."

"It's okay, Jessie, I would have done the same thing." Jessie continued
to tell the tale. "Richard was in his sixties and apparently had a bad heart. I
spoke with his sister after he died, and she said he had been in poor health
for a while."

Jessie was ready to get off that suspect and move on to telling Janice
about the other possibilities. Jessie said that Jeff Parks, was suspect number
two. Mrs. Carmichael had only seen him a few times. They went to dinner
every now and then. Jessie didn't think he was the killer. "Well, it all seems
strange to me, Jessie. You said Mr. Walton was arrogant and
contemptuous."

"I traveled over to Halifax one day just to see him. I called first and made
an appointment. When we met each other, he was distant and a little
arrogant. It seemed to me he was hiding something. I just haven't felt right
about him since."

"Do you think he might be the one who keeps prowling around here at night? Maybe he's the one whose looking for that gun."

"Yes, Janice, I have thought of that. And I have to say I am a little suspicious of him."

"You know, Jessie, there's a lot to consider in this situation. First, this all happened about seven or eight years ago. So, if you do find out who the killer is, how are you going to prove it. And who are you going to prove it to?"

"I'm not sure yet, Janice. I'm keeping a log of all the things I have found out about this house and the Carmichaels. If I find out who the killer is, at least I can prove it to Mrs. Carmichael. She is the main one that needs to know who took her life. I really think she will go away once she knows."

"I hate for this weekend to end, Jessie. Don't you worry, I would never tell anyone about what you have told me. I just want to help you solve this mystery. Jessie, what happens to the person who killed her. I mean if you find out who really did kill Mrs. Carmichael, what happens to the killer?"

"I'm not sure yet, Janice. I'm still trying to work that out in my mind. All I know is, when I find out, I'll know what to do."

"Okay, I trust you, Jessie and I know you'll do the right thing. It's four o'clock, I guess I had better head home. Tomorrow is a workday and I have a few things to do at home. I have really enjoyed this crazy weekend."

CHAPTER FORTY-NINE

After Janice left for home, Jessie sat down in the living room and propped her legs up on the ottoman. She felt a sense of relief come over her. "Rusti, I am so glad I told Janice about our mystery. At least someone else knows now and it felt good to confide in her. I just know the killer is Mr. Walton, but I still must prove it. I'm not sure who that is that keeps coming around here at night. I think Mr. Walton has probably hired someone to get the gun. I'm going to go ahead and have Walter come out and enclose the back porch. It might be a little harder for the prowler to get in with the porch screened in."

• • •

On the drive back to the center of Prince Edward Island, Janice thought about all the things Jessie told her. "There's got to be a way to solve this mystery. I think Jessie is right. Mr.

Walton seems to be the guilty person. We just need to prove it. Listen to me, now I'm talking to myself." Janice couldn't stop thinking about the man who was prowling around outside Jessie's house. He looked so familiar to her. If only she knew his name. I bet Mr. Walton hired this guy to get his gun back. Jessie is smart to enclose the back porch. At least this guy, whoever he is, can't just walk up and try to get in the back door."

• • •

On Monday it was time to go back to work at the café. Jessie woke up extra early. She took a bath and decided to go ahead and dress for work. She looked at herself in the bathroom mirror and thought about how thin she was. "I just keep losing weight. It's got to be all this worry I've been going through. I think I'll stop by the local pharmacy this morning and pick up some vitamins. I need supplements. If that doesn't help, I may have to go to a doctor. That's the last thing I want to do."

• • •

On the drive into Prince Edward Island township, Jessie thought about all the things she told Janice. She hoped that she didn't have to worry about Janice telling anyone what she now knew. As she pulled into her parking place in front of the café, she noticed a man standing outside waiting to go into the café. "He sure does look familiar to me. Oh, my goodness, I think that is the man, that was outside my house Friday night." She got out of the car and walked up to the man. "Good morning Mister, uh, what was your name again?"

"It's Ross, but I don't remember giving you my last name."

"Oh, I'm sorry, I'm Jessie. I work here. We are just about to open. It should be just a few more minutes." Mr. Ross said, "Thanks, I'll wait."

Jessie opened the door to the café and went inside. She locked the door behind her since they didn't open until 8 am. She glanced at her watch to see exactly what time it was. It was seven fifty-five. She saw Janice and motioned for her to come over. "What's up?"

"Look, Janice, I believe that is the same man that was outside my home Friday night. What do you think?" Janice looked out the window and saw the man standing next to the building. "Jessie, I think you're right. That man does look just like that guy in your yard." Jessie said, "I found out his last name is Ross. Why don't you see if you can get him to say his first name."

Janice wasn't sure how she was going to get this man to tell her his first name, but she was willing to try. It was time for the café to open, so Janice went over and opened the door. Mr. Ross was the first person to come into the restaurant. Several other customers followed behind him. Ross sat down at the bar and ordered a coffee and scrambled eggs. Janice said, "Good morning sir, how are you today?" In a grumpy voice he said, "I'm okay, just hungry. Where's those eggs I ordered?"

"Now calm down, Jack, they are on their way."

"My name is Nick, not Jack, and I have waited long enough."

After serving Nick Ross with his eggs and toast, Janice went over and whispered in Jessie's ear. "His name is Nick, probably short for Nicholas."

"I knew you could do it, Janice.

Thank you for getting his name," Janice said, "He's about a grumpy old coot." Jessie felt so relieved. Finally, she knew who had been prowling around her house. Mr. Walton probably hired this man and she was going to prove it. After the man left the café, Janice and Jessie huddled together and talked about him. Jessie said, "Yeah, that was him alright. Now I have a name. I think I'll go over to the library at lunch and do some research on this Mr. Nick Ross."

CHAPTER FIFTY

Jessie's lunch break was at one o'clock. It was 12:55, so she went to the back of the café and took her apron off and clocked out right at 1:00. She grabbed her purse and headed out the door. On the way out, she shouted at Janice that she would be back at 1:30. "Okay, Jessie, see you then." Jessie was in hurry to get over to the library and look up whatever she could find on Nick Ross. In the library, she told the lady at the front desk she was looking for information on a certain person. The lady behind the desk directed her to the newspaper section. "Thank you, I'll just be a few minutes."

Jessie pulled up the microfilm for the years 1998 through 2009. "I'm not sure what years to look for, so I guess I'll start with these." It didn't take long for Nick Ross's name to appear in the newspaper. "Oh my gosh, it says here when he was nineteen he was convicted of armed robbery and spent five years in jail. He looks to be about thirty-five years old now." She came across another article that was dated 2006 in which he was convicted again of robbing a liquor store. This time he spent another five years in jail. "This guy has a track record of burglary for sure. No wonder Mr. Walton hired him to do his dirty work."

Jessie was intrigued with the articles. She glanced down at her watch and saw it was

1:35. She finished the article, grabbed her purse, and hurried to her car. By the time she got back, she was fifteen minutes late clocking in. "Janice, I am so sorry for being late. I got so involved with what I found on the microfilm, I completely forgot to watch the time." Janice said, "Don't worry about it, Jessie, we aren't busy anyway. Now tell me what you found out about this guy Nick?"

"Well, for one thing, he is a very dangerous character. So far, I have found out he has spent ten years of his life in prison for burglary." Janice said, "I figured he was a rough character by his demeanor. What did he rob, Jessie?"

"He had two-armed robbery convictions; one was a liquor store."

"He's just the type someone would hire to break into your house, dangerous and unafraid."

"If you don't mind, I would like to go back to the library tomorrow and see what else I can find. I want to know this guy inside and out."

"Of course, Jessie, don't worry about being a few minutes late."

• • •

The following day, Jessie took her lunch break and went back to the library. She looked through the microfilm again and found more information about the devious Mr. Ross. Jessie found a rap sheet a mile long on this guy. "I can't wait to tell Janice what I found out about Ross." She glanced at her watch and saw it was 1:20. She decided to return to work. She got back at the café right at 1:30 and clocked in. Janice was surprised to see Jessie back so soon. "What happened to you? Couldn't find any more information on our Mr. Ross?"

The café was slow in the afternoon, so Jessie said, "Janice, why don't we sit down for a minute. I want to talk to you about what I found out today at the library."

"Yeah, why not, it's not busy now anyway. Besides, I can't wait to hear what you found out about Mr. Ross." Jessie said, "Janice, I told you about his rap sheet. Well, it seems he was married for five years when suddenly, his wife disappeared. She was never found."

"Did the police investigate him as a suspect in the case?" Jessie said, "Yes, he was a suspect, but they never could convict him of anything. I guess it was because they never found her."

Janice was in shock. "Jessie, that means he probably killed her and did away with her body. Now I'm afraid for you. If this Nick Ross killed his wife and got away with it, he could do it again."

"Well, if he comes in my house, he might get shot or Rusti will get a hold of him. I have a gun and I know how to use it. I have just got to prove the murderer of Mrs. Carmichael hired this man to find the weapon. And I have the weapon, so he will never find it anyway." Janice said, "If you find out who the murderer is, what then?"

"I'm not sure, Janice. I'll cross that bridge when I come to it."

Janice said, "Look, Jessie, you may not want company this weekend, but as soon as the café closes Saturday afternoon; I'm heading out to your place. I don't want you to be alone this weekend. That crazy coot is probably planning on coming back out there." Jessie said, "Walter is coming out Saturday to screen in the back porch, so if that guy does come, he won't be able to get to the back door anymore. Of course, he could cut the screen, but I plan to have Rusti waiting for him. Janice, you know you are always welcome to come out to Cannon Hill."

Jessie was hoping to have a quiet peaceful weekend alone, but she liked Janice and enjoyed her company. "Okay, then come on out, Janice. Maybe we can relax on my new back porch. I am so excited about getting it screened in. Oh, and guess what, I have ordered some new patio furniture for the porch: two wicker lounge chairs with cushions and a wicker table. I can't wait to see them."

"Wow, Jessie," said Janice," that is going to look nice. Did you get white wicker?"

"Sure did, and I can't wait to lay on those lounge chairs. Hey, Janice, maybe you could help me decorate the porch."

CHAPTER FIFTY-ONE

Saturday morning, Jessie got up at 7 am. She got her shower, dressed and ran down to the kitchen to put the coffee on. She knew Walter would be arriving at 9 and wanted to be ready for him. "Here you go, Rusti, now eat your breakfast because we are having company soon." Rusti ran over to his bowl and started eating his dog food. "Good boy, Rusti. I think I'll have a cup of coffee while we wait for Walter. I'm so excited about my new porch this morning, I think I'll just have a piece of toast; I'm not very hungry."

. . .

Janice got off from work at the café at 3 pm on Saturday. She decided she would go ahead and drive out to Cannon Hill as soon as she got off. It was Margaret's turn to close-up that weekend. "Margaret, Jessie is having her back porch screened in today and this afternoon she is getting porch furniture delivered. I want to be there when they bring it." Margaret said, "Oh, that's exciting. I bet Jessie can't wait. You go ahead and go, Janice. It takes an hour to drive out there, doesn't it?"
"Yes, it's quite a long drive to Cannon Hill. Thank you, Margaret, I'll see you Monday morning. Have a good weekend."

. . .

On the drive out to the country, Janice sat back in her seat and thought about the mystery of Mrs. Carmichaels death. She decided to talk Jessie into letting her get in touch with her nephew, Jack. He was a good investigator and had connections with the police department. Maybe he could help them find out about the gun Jessie found in the floorboards. Identifying the fingerprints on the gun would lead them to the killer. She knew Jessie didn't want to involve anyone else. She decided to try and talk her into using Jack.

As Janice arrived, she pulled up in the driveway to find a big furniture truck already parked there. "Wonderful, the furniture has arrived. I made it just in time. I guess I'd better park over to the side of the yard so the truck can back out of here." As she was getting out of her car, she looked down at the ground. She found several half-smoked cigarettes lying in the mud. "Well, look at this, I bet they belong to that prowler. Here is another clue to the murderer. I am surprised Jessie hasn't found these. I'll show her these after everyone has gone." Janice pulled a Kleenex out of her pocket and put the cigarettes in it.

The front door was unlocked, so Janice went on in the house. She called out for Jessie as she came in. "Hey, Jessie, where are you?" Jessie was on the back porch and heard Janice call her name. "I'm on the back porch, Janice. Come on back." The two delivery men were leaving as she passed them on the way to the kitchen. Jessie was right behind them. "I'll be right back, Janice. I just want to see these guys out and lock the front door. Go on out on the porch and see the new furniture. "Okay, I can't wait to see it."

Janice walked out and was surprised to see the new porch. Jessie locked the front door and went back to the kitchen and poured two glasses of wine. She took them out to the porch and handed one to Janice. "Have a seat, Janice, and drink your wine."

"Jessie, the furniture is just beautiful, and I love the new porch." They sat down on the new lounge chairs and drank their wine. Jessie said, "I have always wanted a screened in back porch. I think this was one of the smartest things I have ever done, and I owe it all to you, Janice." Janice said, "To me, why is that Jessie?"

As the two women sat talking on the porch, Jessie explained. "I would have never been able to have this done, if it had not been for the job at the café'. I saved every paycheck I earned since starting to work there."

"Wow, Jessie, now that's determination. I admire you for doing that. Cannon Hill house is really a lovely place since you moved here. I just love it out here in the country." Jessie said, "I do too, Janice. It's so peaceful out here, at least most of the time anyway."

Janice said, "Hey, where's that bottle of wine?"

"I'll get it; you just sit there and enjoy the fresh air." Janice felt like she needed another glass of wine to get up her courage to talk to

Jessie. She wanted to show her what she'd found in the driveway. Jessie came back out to the back porch carrying a bottle of red wine and two chicken salad sandwiches. Janice said,

"Thanks, Jessie, those look delicious."

"I made the chicken salad this morning, so it's fresh."

"This red wine really compliments the sandwich, Jessie. It's all so good."

The two women sat there in the new lounge chairs eating the sandwiches and finally Janice spoke up. "Jessie, I wanted to talk to you about something I found in your driveway."

Jessie said, "Well, what in the world did you find, Janice?" Janice pulled the tissue out of her pocket and unwrapped the cigarettes butts. Your prowler must have left these out there while he was watching your house." Jessie was surprised she had not found them herself. She said, "Well, here's more evidence Nick Ross has left for me."

"Yes, and that's what I wanted to talk to you about."

"Listen, Jessie, I told you before about my nephew, Jack. He's a private detective and lives in Halifax. He has all kinds of connections with the police department. He can find out things in private for us. Like the gun for instance. He could find out who's fingerprints are on it and what caliber it is. He does this kind of thing all the time for his clients. He's discreet and honest. You can trust him with your life. Besides he's my nephew and he loves his Aunt Janice." Jessie said, "I don't know, Janice. I'll have to thank about this. I don't want to involve anyone else if I can help it."

CHAPTER FIFTY-TWO

The two friends sat a while in silence, drinking their wine, and eating. Finally, Janice spoke up, "You know, Jessie, you can't continue to go on like this. Sooner or later that Nick Ross is going to get inpatient and Lord knows what he might do to you. I'm afraid for you, Jessie. You need help in solving this mystery." Jessie said, "I know you are right, but at this point I just don't know what else to do. Janice, have you said anything to your nephew about this?"

"Of course not, you asked me not too."

"Okay, I just wanted to be sure, that's all. Let me think this over for a while."

As they sat there enjoying the fresh air and wine, Jessie asked Janice to finish telling her about herself. "How about telling me more about your family, Janice. You said you would finish your story next time we were together."

"Okay, but you need to tell me more about your family too, Jessie." Janice tried to remember where she left off last time they talked. "Where did I leave off, Jessie. I can't remember." Jessie said, "Why don't you start by telling me about your nephew, Jack?"

"Oh, okay, Jack is my sister's son. He is the youngest of three children. Jerrie has a girl named Peggy, who is in college at Biltmore right now."

Jessie was enjoying hearing Janice talk about her family. She wanted to know more about her nephew, Jack. "Hold on Janice, while I get us something from the kitchen. We may have to go inside soon; it's beginning to get dark." Janice said, "Maybe we should go inside, I don't want to be out here if that Nick character comes around tonight."

"Neither do I, so let us go ahead and go in. You can finish your story while we eat our dessert."

"What did you make, Jess?"

"I made us a lemon pie!"

"Sounds good! I can't wait to taste it."

Jessie and Janice locked the screen and cleaned up the porch before going inside. Jessie said, "After I feed Rusti and Coco I think I'll let them stay out here on the porch for a while. Rusti will start barking if anyone comes around."

"Good idea, Jessie, Coco will bark if Rusti does. So, we'll know if anyone is out there. I just have a feeling that Nick character is going to try to get in tonight. I don't think he is ever going to give up until he gets that gun." Jessie went through the house turning on lights. After she got all the outside lights on she went to the kitchen and turned the coffee pot on. "Janice, would you like a cup of coffee with your pie?"

"Yes, I would love one."

They took their coffee and pie and went into the living room to get comfortable. "Janice, go ahead and finish telling me about your sister's children." Janice went back to talking about her family. "My sister has another daughter named Christine. She is married and has a new baby."

"Have you been over to see the baby yet, Janice?"

"No, I haven't had the time to go, but I was thinking I would go sometime this summer." The clock on the mental chimed and startled both women. Jessie said, "Oh, my goodness, I never dreamed it was this late. How can it be 10 O'clock already? Why don't we go up and put on our pajamas? When we come down, I want to hear about your nephew, Jack."

As they we're heading up the staircase, the dogs started to bark. Jessie and Janice stopped in their tracks and looked at each other. Janice said, "He's here, Jessie, what should we do?" Jessie said, "Let's go make a lot of noise and scare him off." Janice agreed, "Yes, let's do it. I bet he won't ever come back after we scare him to death." Jessie and Janice slowly walked back downstairs. Jessie said, "Let's go to the kitchen and get some pans and something to bang on them with."

"Good idea, Jessie. Boy, when he hears all the racket were going to make, he'll probably run for his life! Hopefully he won't ever come back."

Jessie got two big pots out from under the kitchen cabinet and gave one to Janice. The women went out onto the back porch and started banging on the pots. Rusti and Coco starting howling and barking as they banged. It worked! The racket drove the intruder back to his car and out of sight! The women were as excited as two little kids. They started yelling and clapping. Janice said, "He's gone, Jessie. We did it!"

"I'm so relieved! Do you think he'll come back, Janice?"

"After all this ruckus, I really doubt it. Whoever is paying this guy to come here is going to be upset for sure. Old Nick is probably going to tell him he doesn't want any part of this job."

Jessie took a deep breath and said, "I sure hope you're right.. I am so tired of all this. Let's go sit in the living room and have our coffee while we settle down." The women carried their coffee and pie into the living room and tried to get comfortable. "Janice, tell me some more about your nephew, Jack."

"Okay, I would be glad to, Jessie. I don't mean to interfere in your business, but three years of trying to unravel this mystery is enough. You need help and I'm not sure I'm the one to do it. Jack is a private investigator and a darn good one. He has been written up in newsletters and the newspapers. Oh, and he has written two books on his investigations. He is a smart and honest boy and I just know you'll like him."

CHAPTER FIFTY-THREE

Jessie sat silent as Janice continued to talk up her nephew. "So, don't you think he's a better choice than the help I can give you, Jessie?"

"Your nephew sounds like a good investigator, but I am concerned about my privacy." Janice said, "Like I said before, at the very least, let him take the gun and get the prints for us. Once you have that, you should know for sure, who killed Mrs. Carmichael. And Jack will be discreet about the whole thing. He won't tell a soul about anything we tell him. Believe me, I know my nephew. You can trust him, Jessie."

"Okay, Janice, I'll think about it. I can't give you an answer right now, though." Janice replied, "I know you can't, but you will think about it?"

"Yes, I'll think about it."

The two women sat in the living room talking until they were so sleepy they could hardly hold their eyes open. Jessie said, "Janice, before we pass out down here in the living room, why don't we go up to bed. I am really tired." Janice yawned and stretched as she pulled herself up off the sofa. "Oh, my goodness, I think you are right. Let's just go to bed. We can talk more tomorrow." The clock on the mental chimed and startled both women. "I didn't realize it was so late. It is 12 am already. Go ahead and go on upstairs to bed, Janice. I just want to make sure everything is locked up before I go up."

• • •

The next morning Jessie woke up first. She glanced over at the clock on the bedside table. It was only 6 am and still quite dark outside. She laid in her bed thinking about Janice's nephew, Jack. All kinds of scenarios were going through her head. She thought, "There is no way I can go back to sleep now. I just can't stop thinking about everything Janice told me." She decided to get up and head downstairs. "Come on, Rusti, let's go potty and make some coffee." Jessie and Rusti went down to the kitchen. Rusti watched Jessie as she filled the coffee pot and turned it on. "Look at you, sitting there so patient and waiting on me. I'm sorry, boy, come on I'll let you go outside."

After Jessie let Rusti out the back door, she poured herself a cup of hot coffee. Even though it was barely light, she decided to take her coffee to the new screened porch. She sat down in her new wicker lounge chair. Jessie got back to thinking about Jack. Her thoughts rambled on about the situation she was in. "Maybe I should talk to Jack and see if he can help me. After three years I have not solved the mystery. I feel quite sure that Mr. Walton is the killer, but I still need to prove it. He thinks he has gotten away with murder, but I'm going to show him how wrong he is."

She sat on the porch for almost an hour when she decided to go in and start breakfast.

Jessie knew Janice was tired from last night, so she decided to let her sleep in. She put four slices of bacon in the frying pan. While the bacon was frying she got the eggs out of the refrigerator. She cracked four eggs and beat them with a fork. She glanced over at the clock on the wall to see what time it was. "Good heavens, I must have sat on the porch longer than I thought. It's already 8:30. I'd better take the bacon off the stove before I burn it." Jessie poured herself another cup of coffee, just as Janice walked into the kitchen.

"That coffee sure does smell good."

"Well, my friend, come on and have a cup. Why don't you take it and go sit on the porch while I finish making breakfast."

"Let me help you, Jessie."

"No, no, you take your coffee and go sit outside. It's a beautiful morning and you'll enjoy it."

"Why don't we eat our breakfast out there, Jessie?"

"Well, you are just full of good ideas, Janice." When she finished cooking the eggs and toast, Jessie took a plate to Janice and sat it on the table between the two lounge chairs. She went back inside, got her plate, and joined Janice on the porch.

Jessie decided to talk to Janice about her nephew. "Janice, I want to talk to you about

Jack. If you think he can find out who the prints on the gun belong too, I'm going to let him. But he has to be very discreet about it." Janice said, "Of course, he will be, Jessie. I'll give him a call right after we finish eating."

"Okay, that sounds good. I just want to get this mystery solved. I'm tired of trying to solve this by myself." The two women sat back in the lounge chairs and relaxed while drinking their after-breakfast coffee. Janice said, "Jessie, do you really think Mrs. Carmichael will leave this house after you find out who killed her?"

"Well, I researched this kind of thing at the library. I read that if a ghost has not crossed over yet, it was because of something they needed to take care of first.

She has led me to believe she wanted me to solve her murder. She has left me clues around the house on several occasions. So yes, I do believe she will leave."

"What about her husband?" Jessie said, "I think he is waiting on her. So, when she leaves, he will probably go with her." Janice was confused and asked. "I don't understand why some people don't cross over to the other side?"

"Those people are called earthbound ghost. They don't realize they are dead. It's sad because they don't immediately cross over to the light. I think sometimes they have unfinished business to take care of, so their spirits linger earthbound.

CHAPTER FIFTY-FOUR

Janice did you know there are some people that try to help these spirits cross over. It is like a tunnel with a light at the end of it. These spirits are reluctant to go into the tunnel. They are aware they have died."

"Wow, Jessie, you really have read up on all this paranormal stuff."

"Well, when you live with a spirit, or ghost, you want to know more about them and why they are still in your house. I lived here alone with Rusti for five years before I got to know you, Janice. I had plenty of time to research the spirit world."

"You must have been scared to death, Jessie, when you realized you had ghost living here."

"I was, Janice, and at times I still am. After much research, I know why they are still here. That's why I have been trying so hard to solve this mystery."

"You must be more than ready for these spirits to go away."

"I've been ready for a long time, Janice." After breakfast, Jessie and Janice went into the living and sat down. Jessie said, "Listen, Janice, why don't we meet Jack some place and talk to him. I really don't want anyone coming out here to Cannon Hill. I've allowed you here and a handful of workers but as far as this situation goes, I would rather meet Jack someplace else."

"Okay, Jessie, why don't we meet him in Halifax. We could take a day trip one day and meet him at a restaurant." Jessie gave it only a brief consideration, and said, "Okay, Janice, that sounds like a good idea. Call him now and see if he can meet us next Sunday. With both of us off on Sunday's, that's the perfect time to go." Janice pulled her cell phone out of her back pocket and dialed Jack's number. His phone rang three times when he finally answered. "Hello, this is Jack Grant, how may I help you."

"Hello, Jack, this Aunt Janice."

"Aunt Janice, how the heck are you?"

"Oh, I'm doing pretty good. How have you been?" Jack said, "Well, I can't complain, Aunt Janice. What's going on?"

Janice spoke up and said, "Jack, I was wondering if you could meet me and friend next Sunday. We will come over to Halifax. We need to discuss something important with you."

"Sure, Aunt Janice, why don't we meet at a restaurant downtown Halifax for lunch. Let's say 1 for lunch?" Janice looked over at Jessie and asked Jack to hang on a minute. "What about lunch next Sunday at 1 pm, Jessie?" Jessie replied, "Okay, find out where and don't forget the address."

"Hey Jack, where do you want to have lunch?" Jack said, "Let's go for seafood, Aunt Janice. The Press Gang Restaurant and Oyster Bar is a really nice place. Oh, and by the way, lunch is on me."

"You silly boy, I just might let you do that. Do you have the address, Jack?"

"Yes, Aunt Janice, got a pencil?"

"Yes, go ahead, Jack."

"It's 5218 Prince Street, downtown Halifax."

"Okay, Jack we'll see you next Sunday at 1 pm. It was wonderful talking to you. You take care now." The two women just sat there quietly in the living room as if they were relieved. Jessie spoke up first, "Janice, should I take the gun with me Sunday?"

"Yes, Jessie, we'll probably have to give it to him. Nobody is going to know you have that gun on you. Just wrap it up in a small towel or something and put it in your purse."

Janice, I am so scared to talk about all this with someone I don't know. What if he decides to tell the police and they come out here and go through my house. Oh, Janice, I don't want that to happen. That's why it took me so long to confide in you."

"Listen, Jessie, you have given this problem over three years of your life. I haven't been much help to you. So now, it's time to let someone who knows about these things step in and help you. I would have never contacted my nephew if I thought for one minute he couldn't be trusted. Jack has never been in trouble a day in his life. He is an honest and good man. You will sense it as soon as you meet him. Oh, and he is a good-looking guy too. You just might like him, Jessie. He's single too, so don't judge him just yet." Jessie said, "You are kidding me, aren't you Janice?"

• • •

It was late Sunday afternoon by the time Janice left Cannon Hill house. She had been visiting Jessie since Friday afternoon. Jessie was tired and ready for a nap after Janice left. She decided to go out on her new screened in porch and relax for a while. She laid back in her new lounge chair and slipped off to sleep. Rusti laid beside her lounge as if to protect her. While she slept she dreamed about the gun and the man that had been trying to break in to get it. In her dream, he broke into the house and came after her with a knife. The dream was so real, she suddenly woke up frightened and sweating profusely.

After Jessie woke up from her horrible dream, she decided to check all the doors and windows. As she walked from room to room, she thought about her situation. "I'm such a scaredy-cat these days. I just hope I have done the right thing meeting with Jack Grant. What if he finds out about my past. I guess I was foolish stealing that money from Wilson, but I just had to get away from that place and start a new life. I love it here on the island. I hope I'll never have to leave here. Come on, Rusti, let's go make dinner. I'm getting hungry."

CHAPTER FIFTY-FIVE

It was Monday morning when the alarm clock on her side table chimed 6 am. Jessie reached over and turned the clock off. She climbed out of bed reluctantly and grabbed her robe. She suddenly felt a wave of elation come over her. All the events of the past three years were whirling through her mind. "At last I feel like I'm on the final leg of a too long journey. I've done a lot of hard work and sacrificing, and I've done it alone. I finally feel a change heading my way." Her worries that she might never solve the mystery, were disappearing.

Jessie took a quick shower and put her robe back on. All the while thinking about Jack

Grant. "This feeling of freedom I have this morning, must be because of him. I have finally decided to get help with this situation. I just know in my heart he is the answer to my prayers. I truly hope I am doing the right thing by telling Mr. Grant my problems. I trust Janice and surely she wouldn't betray me." Jessie put on her jeans a white blouse and tennis shoes, pulled her hair back into a ponytail and dabbed just a small amount of rouge on her cheeks.

After looking into the mirror and seeing how frail and old she looked, she began to feel sadness and fear again. The world seemed to be spinning and slowing down. She felt a tightness in her lungs she couldn't explain. Jessie's thoughts once again began to ramble on and on. "I am so afraid I am doing the wrong thing now. I should never have agreed to meet with Jack Grant. Oh, how I wish this feeling of regret would go away. Mrs. Carmichael is probably wondering why I told other people about her. I wish I could take it all back now. But I need help; I'm tired of trying to solve this mystery on my own."

After telling Rusti goodbye and locking up the house, she drove into Prince Edward Island township. She entered the café and went straight back to the time clock. After clocking in she ran into Janice. "Good morning, Jessie, how are you this fine Monday morning? You seem a little down today."

"I'm just worried about meeting with Jack on Sunday. I can't decide if I'm doing the right thing or not."

"Of course, you are Jessie. You can't continue to carry this burden around by yourself."

"I know, Janice, but I'm afraid of the outside world. I don't want people knowing about Cannon Hill House."

It was time to open the café, so Janice unlocked the door. There were four people waiting outside to come in. Janice took their orders and poured herself a cup of coffee. Bryan, the cook was busy in the kitchen preparing breakfast orders. Jessie also poured herself a cup of coffee and asked Bryan if she could help him. "Oh, no Ma'am, I'm fine for now. You can go ahead and take the first order in if you want."

"Sure, I would be glad too." As she was walking toward the dining room, she saw Janice coming her way. "Jessie, Nick Ross just came in the café."

Jessie began to shake and tremble as she carried the tray of food to her customer. She sat the tray down on the customer's table. As she did, she knocked the coffee over. "Oh, I am so sorry. I'll have this cleaned up in a minute." Janice saw what happened and came over to the table to help Jessie clean up the mess she had made. She brought a fresh pot of coffee and two cups. The couple were very understanding and nice about the situation. Jessie said, "Thank you both for being so understanding. I am so sorry for this accident." The man and woman told Jessie not to worry about it.

Jessie went back into the kitchen and stood by the counter trying to catch her breath. Janice said, "Jessie, get a hold of yourself. Nick Ross can't hurt you in here."

"I know, Janice, but I had a bad dream about him last night. He was trying to kill me with a knife."

"Well, no wonder he makes you nervous. Listen, Hon, why don't you stay in the kitchen while he is here. I can handle everything up front."

"I don't want you to have to do everything, Janice."

"It's okay, Jessie, besides he isn't going to be here all day. He's almost through eating anyway."

Jessie decided she would clean the dishes while she waited. Eventually, Nick Ross left the café. After the breakfast shift was over, the two women sat down in a booth and drank another cup of coffee. "Jessie, are you alright now?"

"Yes, Janice, I'm not trembling like I was before. That man makes me so nervous. Now I'm having bad dreams about him. And I am sure he is the one who continues to try to break into my home. No wonder I'm a nervous wreck every time I see him."

"Are you having second thoughts about meeting Jack on Sunday?" Jessie replied, "This morning when I got up I felt a wave of relief about the whole thing. I was ready to turn this situation over to him. Then my mood changed, and I started having doubts."

"Listen Jessie, everything is going to be okay. You don't have to worry about Jack. He has never been in trouble in his life. He has always been a good kid and he loves his Aunt Janice. So, there is no reason to fear him. He will be discreet and honest in every way, believe me. You can trust him with your life. He's going to find out who the prints on that gun belong too for us, and then you can decide if you want him to continue with the case. It's all going to be up to you, Jessie."

CHAPTER FIFTY-SIX

The women decided to ride over to the bus depot. They wanted to find out what time the bus left to go to Halifax Sunday morning. Janice asked one of the men who oversaw the buses about the times. "Sir, can you tell me what time the bus will be leaving here on Sunday morning?"

"Sure, lady, the bus leaves at 9 am sharp."

"What time does it come back to the island?"

"There's only one time on Sunday to get back here, and that would be 7 pm. If you miss the bus, you can't get back here until Monday." Janice thanked the man and walked to her car. "Well, Jessie, I guess we better get here early Sunday morning, or we'll miss the bus."

• • •

Janice dropped Jessie off in front of the café. Jessie said, "Thanks, Janice, I'll see you Sunday morning around 8 am."

"Okay, Jessie, have a good weekend." As Jessie was driving home to her Cannon Hill house, she had time to think about everything that had happened recently. It was already 7 pm and she thought about Rusti. "Poor Rusti, having to wait on me all day and then I'm late getting home. The good thing about this drive is there is no traffic." She didn't miss the traffic she had in Chicago. You always had to leave early to go anywhere.

• • •

Jessie finally arrived home around 8 pm. It was still light outside and very warm. It felt like a storm was brewing in the air. "I just want to get out of these clothes and take a cool shower. I am so tired from the whole week and thankful tomorrow is Saturday." As she unlocked the front door, Rusti was waiting for her on the other side. She could hear him barking at her. "Hi, buddy, how was your day," she said, as she knelt to pet the dog. Come on, Rusti, let's go outside for a little while." Rusti was excited to see her and ran in circles around her. "Now you be a good boy while I take a shower."

She ran upstairs to her bedroom and undressed. She took a quick shower and put on her pajamas. She looked in the mirror and noticed again how thin and pale she looked in her pajamas. She looked in the mirror and noticed again how thin and pale she looked in the face. "All this worry has caused me to look like a scarecrow. I desperately need to gain some weight. My face is all sunken in and on top of that I have no tan at all." She brushed her teeth and hair and put on her bedroom slippers. "I think I'll make myself a bowl of soup and a sandwich."

She called Rusti to come in and eat his dinner. Rusti ran up the back steps and went into the house wagging his tail. Jessie bent down and hugged Rusti around the neck. "I love you so much, Rusti boy, I don't know what I would do without you." As she hugged him, she said,

"Rusti, you are still my best friend and confident. Now eat your dinner and we'll go get comfortable in the living room." Rusti loved to lay by the fireplace while Jessie sat in her favorite chair reading or sleeping. Jessie carried her soup and sandwich into the living room.

After she ate, she began to get sleepy. She decided to close her eyes, just for a few minutes.

•   •   •

She didn't wake up until the following morning. "I guess I was really tired last night,

Rusti, I slept in this chair all night. I think I'll go make the coffee. She took a cup of hot coffee back into the living room and sat down. Jessie began to think about going to meet Jack Grant and all the things she needed to tell him. She decided it was best if she told Jack that she found the gun and wanted to know who it belonged to. He doesn't have to know everything. He may not believe in ghosts or anything I tell him. He could be one of those skeptical people who must have facts and figures about everything."

After Jessie finished her coffee, she went upstairs to get dressed. She put on a pair of jeans, a tee shirt, and her favorite tennis shoes. "This house needs a good cleaning and it's going to get it today. That's the only way I can keep my mind off my problems." She got the mop and broom out of the kitchen closet. She first swept the floor and then mopped it. When the mopping was done, she went outside and sat on the porch. "It's so nice out here. I made a good decision when I had this porch screened in." She sat down in her new lounge chair and watched Rusti as he dug something up in the back of the yard. "Rusti bring that here boy. What did you find out there?"

Rusti came running up to the back-porch door with something in his mouth. "Let me see what you found, boy." Rusti laid it down on the ground and wagged his tail as Jessie looked in horror. "Oh my God, it's a human skull. Rusti, what in the world have you done? Let's go see if there is anything else back there." Jessie walked slowly to the back of the yard with Rusti by her side. "That head is very small, like an infant's head." As she got closer to where Rusti had been digging, she could see a pink blanket partially sticking out of the ground. "I can't look any further. I think I'll go call Janice and see if she will come out here."

CHAPTER FIFTY-SEVEN

Jessie ran to the back-porch and went inside the house to find a phone. She called Janice and let it ring until she finally answered. "Hey, Janice, are you busy right now? I need you to come out to Cannon Hill right away."

"Okay, Jessie, but can you tell me what's wrong?"

"No, you'll see when you get here. And Janice, please hurry." Janice didn't know what to think about the call from Jessie. All she could think about was Nick Ross. "Maybe that guy has come out there and approached Jessie. What else could it be, I wonder." Janice quickly changed her clothes, grabbed her purse and keys, and headed out the door.

Janice drove as fast as she could out highway 211. There was only one four way stop between turning on 211 and Jessie's house. She slowed up but didn't stop. She looked in the rear view mirror and saw a police car right behind her. Their lights were on, so, she pulled over to the embankment and stopped. The police officer got out of his patrol car and walked up to her car window. Janice said, "Hi, officer, what did I do wrong?" The patrolman said, "You ran a four way stop back there, miss. May I see your license and registration?" As Janice pulled her license and registration card out of her purse she said, "I am so sorry, officer, but I was in a big hurry to help a friend who is in trouble."

The officer spoke up and said, "Okay, Miss Janice, I'm going to let you go this time with a warning. You got lucky today. Do you think there is something I can do to help your friend?"

"No sir, sometimes she exaggerates, so I'm hoping it's nothing to worry about."

"Well, if you need us, please give us a call. I hope she will be okay when you get there." Janice thanked him for not giving her a ticket as she watched him walk back to his car. She took a deep breath and slowly drove down the road. She hoped he wouldn't follow her.

As Janice drove out 211, she kept an eye on her rear-view mirror. When she approached

Jessie's house, she decided to go pass it for a little way just to see if he was following her. When she got to the four way stop sign, she turned left and continued down this road for a mile. When she didn't see the patrol car make a turn at the four way stop, she felt relieved. Janice turned her car around and headed back to Jessie's house. Jessie answered the door and said, "What took you so long?"

"I got stopped by the police for not stopping at a four way stop. I was afraid he was going to follow me, so I went pass your house for a little way."

"Come on out here in the back yard. I need to show you something Rusti dug up today.

Janice, I don't know what to do, this situation seems to get worse by the day."

"Don't panic, Jessie, let's see what he found first." The two women approached the small grave of a newborn baby; it's little bones were clearly visible. "Rusti brought the skull up there to the porch this morning. I'm so afraid, Janice. What am I going to do?"

"I'm not sure, Jessie, but the first thing I think we should do is dig a deeper hole and rebury all this. We need time to think this thing through."

· · ·

Jessie went in the house and came out with a shovel. She started digging until she was out of breath. Janice took the shovel out of her hands and started digging the hole too. "Jessie do you have a pair of gloves I can use?" Jessie ran back into the house and found a pair of gloves in the utility drawer and gave them to her. Janice placed the gloves on her hands and picked up the pink blanket. She placed all the little bones in the blanket and lowered it into the hole. Both women covered the hole with as much dirt as they could find. Jessie said, "Wait, Janice, I want to place a big rock on the top of the grave." After placing the rock on the grave, they went into the house.

Jessie put the tea kettle on the stove to heat. She got two cups out of the cabinet and placed them on the table. Janice sat down at one end of the kitchen table and covered her face with her hands. Jessie poured them both a cup of tea and sat down at the table with Janice.

Jessie, it's obvious Mrs. Carmichael had the baby and buried it. I just hope the baby was not alive when she did it. She probably had the baby with one of those men she was seeing. What else could have happened?"

"Yes, and I would bet anything it was Richard. They were in love with each other even though she did go out with the other two men."

Jessie spoke up and said to Janice, "I think whoever killed Mrs. Carmichael thought the baby was his. He didn't want anyone to know about it, so he shot her to shut her up. Did I tell you that I had a dream the other night and in the dream I saw the killer. So, I know who did the dirty deed."

"If his prints are on that gun, you'll also have proof. That is why it's a good idea that we are going to see Jack tomorrow."

"If you say so, Janice. At this point I'm not sure what to do. Finding these bones of a baby just adds more to the mystery."

CHAPTER FIFTY-EIGHT

Janice was curious about Richard. "Do you think Richard knew about the baby?"

"He didn't indicate it in any of his letters. If he knew, he never said a word about it to her." Janice said, "The baby could have been still born and she didn't know what to do, so she buried it. She probably never told anyone." Jessie said, "What am I going to do, Janice? I have a creepy feeling now just knowing the baby is buried in my backyard."

"You are not going to do anything right now. Let sleeping dogs lay right where they are. Maybe Jack will have the answer for us. Speaking of tomorrow, I need to get back home before it gets too dark. I don't like to drive after dark."

After finishing their tea, Janice said she needed to leave. "Jessie, are you going to be alright tonight?"

"I hope so, Janice. I probably won't sleep very well, but I'll be okay." Janice said, "Alright then, I'll be leaving now. Call me if you need me; otherwise I'll see you at the bus depot."

"Okay, bye Janice, have a safe trip home and thank you for coming way out here. I'll be at the bus depot at 8 am sharp." Janice pulled out of Jessie's driveway with a horrible headache. She said to herself... "I almost wish I didn't know anything about this mystery of Jessie's. It just keeps getting more and more involved."

• • •

After Janice left to go home, Jessie decided to go ahead and get her shower. She went upstairs and undressed. As she was stepping into the shower a sad feeling came over her. It was as if someone had passed away that she knew. She tried to dismiss it and finished her shower. "I can't stop thinking about the baby. It makes me feel so sad for the little thing, and to think it's buried in my back yard." She put on her pajamas and went downstairs to make a cup of tea. "I hate it, but my nerves are getting the best of me. I'm so nervous about tomorrow and now finding this baby. Oh, how I wish all this was behind me. I want so badly to have a normal life."

The clock on the mental chimed and scared Jessie. It was 11 pm and Jessie wasn't sleepy at all. She decided to get out her tablet. "I'm going to write about today and what Rusti found in the back yard. I want to do it while it's fresh on my mind. I don't want to miss any details." Rusti laid on the floor near the fireplace as she sat in her chair writing. Jessie wrote until 1:00 in the morning. She yawned and stretched and decided it was time she went to bed. "Come on, Rusti, let's head up to bed. I've got to get up at 5:30 and leave the house no later than 7 am." Rusti followed her as she climbed the staircase. It didn't take long for Jessie to fall asleep. She never realized how tired she was until she laid her head on the pillow.

•   •   •

The following morning Jessie woke up around 4:30 am. She had set the clock to go off at 5 am. She decided to just get an earlier start. She could drink coffee and listen to the news before having to get dressed. She tumbled out of bed and put on her slippers. Still sleepy eyed she walked down the staircase. She called out to Rusti to come and go with her. Rusti came running out of the bedroom. "Let's go make coffee and wake ourselves up a little. I still feel tired right now." As she got to the kitchen, she heard someone rattle the screen door on the back porch. Rusti began to bark and put his paws up on the door.

Jessie knew in her heart it was Nick Ross trying to get in the house again. This time she opened the door and let Rusti out onto the porch. Rusti was growling and trying to get to the man. Jessie decided she had enough of this man and screamed out at him to go away. "What do you want? I am tired of you coming around here trying to get in. Go away or I'm going to shoot you. I have a gun in my hand right now." The man ran to his car and drove away as fast as he could. Jessie couldn't believe she had finally said something to that creep. "I guess I told him. Maybe he won't come back."

• • •

That afternoon, Nick Ross decided to call Mr. Walton. After Walton answered the phone, Nick said, "Listen man, I can't do this anymore. That woman knows who I am, and she is on to me. She had a gun and threaten to shoot me. This is getting too dangerous man; I can't go there anymore. You need to find someone else." Walton was surprised to hear what Nick had to say. "So, you are getting chicken on me. Come on, Nick, she's just a woman. She can't do anything to you. She hasn't got the nerve to shoot you." Nick replied. "Walton, she has a German shepherd dog and he would tear me apart if he got a hold of me."

CHAPTER FIFTY-NINE

Walton didn't know Jessie Harris had a dog. "I guess she felt she needed protection living way out in the boonies like that. Okay, Nick, I'll pay you double the price if you'll continue to try to find the gun. Listen, I must have that gun. I don't know anybody else that can do this for me. Don't give up now, Nick, I need you. "what about the dog?"

"Why don't you shoot it. He won't give you any more trouble then." Nick shook his head and said, "Walton, I'm guilty of a lot of things, but I don't harm animals. I love dogs and he's a fine-looking dog."

"Well, Nick, I don't know what to tell you about the dog. I guess you'll have to make friends with him somehow. Take him a snack or something. Listen, Nick, I hid the gun in the dining room floor. One of the boards is loose and all you have to do is pull that loose board up and get the gun out."

"Listen, Walton, that woman knows who I am. She said my name and had a gun in her hands. She said she was going to report me to the police if I didn't stay away from there."

"Okay, Nick, I guess I'll have to find someone else. I'll pay you what I owe you and you can be completely out of it."

"Thanks, Walton."

Walton was furious with Nick Ross. He didn't know anyone else he could get to retrieve his gun from the Cannon Hill house. His thoughts rambled on about Jessie Harris and how he was going to get that gun. He wondered if Jessie had already found the gun. Maybe she has hidden it someplace else in that house. "I guess I'm going to have to go out there and get it myself. If she tries to stop me I'll kill her and the dog. Her body won't be found for months because she doesn't have any friends that I know of. Yeah, that's what I'm going to do." Walton walked back and forth across his office floor, as he chewed on a cigar.

The prowler, Nick Ross had finally vanished from the property. Jessie was amazed at how brave she had become. "I actually held a gun on that man. It scared him away, too." Jessie glanced at the clock on the kitchen wall. It was 6 am already and she should have been just getting up. After today, he may never come back. At least I hope he doesn't." After she drank her coffee and ate a piece of toast, she went upstairs to get dressed. Rusti followed her up the staircase and sat by the bedroom door as if he knew she was leaving.

· · ·

She was ready to leave the house at 6:45. Jessie knelt to hug Rusti. "Now you be a good boy while I'm gone. Don't let any intruders get in this house. I may be a little late getting home tonight, Rusti, but I'll be here all day tomorrow." Rusti was anxious and breathing fast. "Calm down boy, I'll be home in a little while." As she patted him on his head, she told him she loved him. Jessie always felt bad when she had to leave Rusti alone. "I wish I could take him with me today. She suddenly had an idea. She picked up her phone and called Janice. "Hello, this is Janice."
"Hi Janice, this is Jessie. I was wondering if Rusti could stay with Coco today?"

Janice was delighted for Rusti to come and stay with Coco. The little dog was lonesome and needed another dog to play with. "Sure, bring Rusti with you, but you better hurry, don't forget the bus leaves at 9 am sharp."

"We are on our way." Jessie ran into the kitchen to get Rusti's leash. Rusti knew he was going with Jessie and began to turn around in circles. As they we're driving into town, Jessie thought about Nick Ross again. "Jack Grant will know what I should do." Jessie pulled up in front of Janice house at 8:40. After Janice got the dogs settled, she ran out and got in the car with Jessie. "We should make it just in time."

The two women made it to the bus depot in time. Everyone was on the bus except the two women. Jessie parked the car and ran over to the bus. "Jessie, I just knew we were going to miss the bus. "I hurried as fast as I could. I just couldn't leave Rusti today, he seemed so sad. I just had to bring him with me."

"He should be fine at my house. The two pups will keep each other company. Well, Jessie, here we go to Halifax. This should be an interesting day."

CHAPTER SIXTY

Jessie decided to tell Janice about Nick Ross. "Janice I wanted to tell you what kind of morning I've had."

"I hope you got plenty of sleep last night."

"No, not really, I woke up around 5 am this morning and couldn't go back to sleep. I was getting up at 6 am anyway, so I decided to go downstairs and make coffee. As I was going into the kitchen I heard something outside near the porch. Rusti started barking and jumping up on the back door. I got my gun and opened the door. Nick Ross was trying to get the screen door open."

"Jessie, you mean you opened the door not knowing who might be out there?"

"I sure did and with a gun in my hand."

Janice was in shock. Jessie continued to tell Janice about her morning. "I pointed the gun at him and told him he'd better leave and never come back. I told him I was going to report him to the police. He ran and got in his car and left. By this time, it was almost 6 am and I had to get ready to come here."

"Jessie, I am surprised and shocked at how much nerve you had. I am also proud of you for standing up to that creep." Janice reached over and gave Jessie a hug. "Be sure to tell Jack about this. Did you bring the gun you wanted him to see?" Jessie whispered in Janice's ear. "Yes, I brought it wrapped in a towel. It's in my purse."

The bus was slow getting everyone aboard, but the view was unbelievable along the way. "Look Janice, have you ever seen a more beautiful sight than this?"

"I believe it's the most beautiful place on earth. I love living in Nova Scotia and I hope I never have to leave this place." Jessie agreed with Janice and prayed silently she too would never have to leave. She began to have second thoughts about telling Jack Grant her mystery story. "Janice, what if this whole thing explodes and gets in the paper. I could be the laughingstock of the whole island. Oh, Janice, I don't know if I'm doing the right thing by telling Jack."

Janice couldn't believe what she was hearing from Jessie. "Listen, Jessie, I thought we talked about this. We had it all settled and that is why we are on our way to Halifax. Jack will be waiting for us at the restaurant. I have already told him that everything we tell him today must be confidential. No one else should know anything about this except the three of us. Now if you want to turn back now and continue the same path you have been on for the past three years, so be it. But if you do, I refuse to be a part of it any longer." Jessie felt anxious and scared and decided to keep silent the rest of the trip.

•   •   •

It took an hour to get to Halifax. When they finally arrived, Janice took her cell phone out of her purse and called a taxi to come pick them up. As they waited for the taxi

Jessie was conflicted and forcing enthusiasm because she knew it was the right thing to do. She had lost all self-confidence. Jessie's head hurt and her stomach was upset but she didn't want to say anything to Janice. She knew Janice was upset with her. She decided to continue to be silent on the ride to downtown Halifax.

Jessie and Janice were silent as they road in the taxi together. After they arrived in downtown Halifax, Janice finally spoke. "Jessie, since we have an hour before meeting Jack, would you like to do a little shopping?"

"Yes, let's go over to that dress shop across the street. I want to see if I can find a couple of shirts to wear with jeans."

"Jessie, look, there's an outside café over there. Why don't we go there first and have a latte."

"That sounds wonderful, let's go." The two women sat down at a small table under the umbrella that was attached to the café. They ordered a vanilla latte and once again began to talk about anything and everything, except why they were there.

Jessie began to feel better and not as anxious as she had been before. "Janice, we better go, it's getting late and I want to do a little shopping before we leave today." Janice looked at her watch and couldn't believe they had sat there for over an hour talking. "Come on, Jessie, I think we have enough time to go in that shop across the street before meeting Jack." They crossed the street and went into the little dress shop. Jessie found four tee shirts she liked and a beautiful blouse. Janice bought a pair of jeans and a white button-down blouse. Jessie said, "We better go before I spend all my money."

The restaurant was two blocks from the dress shop, so they decided to walk instead of getting a taxi. It was a beautiful summer day for walking. Jessie loved the old buildings and wanted to see more of the city. "I would love to come here one day just to sight see. I love these old buildings and the sidewalk cafés."

"So, do I, Jessie, maybe we can take a trip over here before it gets too cold. I would love to go shopping again." As they approached the restaurant Jack was getting out of a taxi. He looked up and saw his Aunt Janice. Jessie couldn't believe how good-looking Jack was. "Aunt Janice, how the heck are you."

As they hugged each other Jack noticed Jessie standing behind his aunt. "Aunt Janice, you didn't tell me you were bringing a beautiful woman with you. Hi, I'm Jack Grant and you are?"

"Hi, Jack, I'm Jessie. I'm the one with the strange story to tell."

"Hey, I like you already. Come on ladies, let's have lunch, I'm starving." Jack held the door for the women and told the waiter to seat them in a private booth. The waiter led them to the very back of the restaurant where there was a private booth. "Thanks, Kevin, this is perfect." Janice told Jack the seating arrangements were fine for the kind of conversation we were about to have.

CHAPTER SIXTY-ONE

Their waiter brought them three menus. After they had ordered their meals, Jack wanted to know what his Aunt Janice had been up too. "It seems like years since I last saw you."

"Oh, Jack, I saw you at your mother's about six months ago."

"I know I just wanted to tease you. Now tell me what all the secrecy is about."

"Well, my friend Jessie has a long story to tell and we want you to find out something for us. I know we can trust you to be discreet and private about all this."

"Of course, you can, Aunt Janice. Whatever you ladies tell me today stays right here with me."

Jessie was hesitant at first. "To be honest, Jack, I'm not sure where to begin. You see I came to Prince Edward Island almost five years ago looking for a place I could be alone and write. I'm a writer and I wanted seclusion. I just happened to stumble across this house which had been empty for several years. I found the realtor who owned it and was lucky enough to buy it. There was a catch that wasn't revealed to me until later. I hope you have an open mind about things, Jack."

"Are you about to tell me the house is haunted?" Jessie looked at Janice and then back at Jack. "Janice, did you tell him about the house?"

Janice was just as surprised as Jessie when Jack asked that question. Jessie continued to tell him about the house. "Yes, the house is haunted by a couple that lived there eleven years ago. The Carmichaels had a Christmas party on the eve of Christmas, and someone shot her through an open window. Her ghost has haunted the house ever since. Believe it or not, I believe she wants me to solve the mystery of her death." Jack just sat there listening to Jessie as if he already knew the story. "Jack, have you heard about the Carmichaels before?"

"As a matter of fact, I have. I was just a young man at the time, but word got around about her getting shot."

Janice asked Jack exactly what he knew about the Carmichael family. "Not much, only that the woman got shot on Christmas Eve. Of course, I didn't know she haunted the house now. I had heard that it was one of her boyfriends who shot her."

"She has left me clues. When she wants me to know she is there; the room will get extremely cold. Then it returns to normal."

"Aren't you afraid to live there by yourself?"

"No, I'm not afraid of her or her husband. They have never harmed me or caused me to harm myself." Janice said, "Besides Jack, she has a big German Shepherd that protects her."

Jack was impressed and wanted to hear more of the story. "Tell me what kind of clues she has left you, Jessie?" Jessie was reluctant to tell Jack about the trinket box. "She has left different things like pictures left on the staircase. What I really wanted your help with is this. She opened her purse and brought out the gun wrapped in a towel. I don't want anyone to see this, so I must be careful." Jack said, "Where in the world did you find that?"

"It was hidden under a loose board in the floor in my dining room." Janice spoke up and said, "We need you to find out who the prints on the gun belong too."

Jack was excited and thrilled listening to the story. "This is really quite an interesting story you are telling me. I want to hear more, Jessie." Jessie began to tell him about the three men Mrs. Carmichael was involved with and how she had tracked each one. She told him about what she knew of each man and how Richard had a heart attack. The story became more and more interesting to Jack. Before they knew it, they had been in the restaurant for three hours. Janice said it was 4 pm already. "I think these people want us to leave."

After they left the restaurant, Jack wanted to know what time they had to catch the bus.

Janice said, "We need to be at the bus depot at 6:30 and no later."

"Good, we still have at least two hours. Come on ladies, I know of a park just around the corner. I need to hear more of this story of yours, Jessie."

The three of them walked down the street and crossed two lights before coming to the park. They found a park bench that was quiet and isolated and sat down. "Jessie, do you think the murderer hid the gun in that floor?"

"Yes, I do, and he has sent a man named Nick Ross to get it. Nick Ross has made many attempts to try and break into my house."

Jack knew this Nick Ross. He had run in's with him before. "I know that guy. He's a crook all right. I've had problems with him before. So, Jessie, what has he been doing to you?"

"He's been sneaking around at 3 or 4 am on the weekends. He has been trying to get into my back door for several weeks now. My dog Rusti scares him away."

"Do you have a gun, Jessie?"

"Why are you asking me that, Jack?"

"Because Nick is a dangerous man and you need more protection than a dog." Jessie looked at Janice as if to say, 'Help me out here Janice, I don't want anyone to know I have a gun'.

Janice spoke up and said, "I hate to say it but it's almost 6:00 and we really must go. There's only one bus leaving for the island tonight."

"You guys haven't told me the whole story. Aunt Janice, why don't I come over to your house Monday night after you and Jessie get off work. We can continue our talk."

"What do you think, Jessie?"

"It's up to you, Janice, but I'll need to bring Rusti with me tomorrow. I can't leave him at home that long."

"Jessie that's no problem at all, just bring him on the way into work. He can visit with Coco."

CHAPTER SIXTY-TWO

Janice told Jack that would be fine. "Jack, we won't be home until about 6:00. Is that okay?"

"Yes, that's fine and don't worry about dinner, I'll bring Chinese."

"You are a God send, Nephew. Thank you, that sounds delicious."

"Jessie, how about keeping that gun in your purse until tomorrow night. I'll take it with me then. Someone might see you taking it out of your purse and report us."

"Sure, Jack, whatever you say."

"Aunt Janice, let me get us a taxicab." Jack stood on the curb and hailed a taxi down. Here you go, ladies, have a nice bus ride home." As they all said their goodbyes, Jack hailed another taxi down the street and disappeared into the evening.

On the way to Pei, Janice asked Jessie if she liked Jack. "Yes, he's very charming and good looking."

"Jessie, I mean do you think you can trust him?"

"I sure hope so, Janice, because I have told him things I wouldn't tell other people."

"Don't worry about it,

Jessie, you can trust Jack to keep his mouth closed. To tell you the truth, I believe he wants to come here tomorrow night to see you. I think he liked you a lot."

"Don't be ridiculous, Janice.

He just wants me to finish the story. I didn't get to tell him everything he needs to know."

"Whatever, I think he liked you more than you know."

• • •

The taxicab pulled up to the bus depot right on time. Janice paid the fee as they got out of the taxi. Jessie and Janice boarded the bus and sat down by a window looking out over the city. Jessie was in awe of the views. "I can't get over the beauty of this place and even now, it's hard for me to believe I am really living here. You know, Janice, I have wanted to come to Prince Edward Island my whole life. I hope I never have to leave this place."

"Why should you ever leave, Jessie? This is your home now and Jack is going to help us straighten this mess out. You wait and see."

The day was long and frustrating for Jessie. Everyone seemed to be irritable or cranky that morning. It was all Jessie could do to hold her tongue. "Janice, have you noticed how rude most of the customers are this morning?"

"Well, it's Monday, Jessie and some are probably hung over from the weekend. Don't let it get you down; just ignore them."

"I'm trying to, but it isn't easy." As the day continued, Jessie and Janice were so busy, they didn't even notice Nick Ross when he came in the café. Suddenly, Janice noticed him sitting at the counter. "Look, Jessie, guess who just came in."

Janice started walking towards him and talking to Jessie as she did. "I'm going to get to the bottom of this today, Jessie. I'm tired of this man always bothering you."

"Janice, please don't say anything to him, it may put your life in danger."

"Don't you worry about me,

I'm not afraid of him." Janice whispered in Nick Ross's ear to follow her over to a booth. She told him she needed to have a word with him. Nick did as he was told and sat down in a corner booth. The café had cleared out by then.

Janice slid in the booth seat across from Nick Ross. "I'm Janice by the way. Nick, I don't know who you are working for, but I do know that you have been harassing my friend out on Cannon Hill Road for several months now. We have both seen you on camera so you can't deny it. I think I know what you are after in that house, but you might as well forget it because we have already found the object and turned it in. Now when the fingerprints come back, guess what Nick? Your boss is going to be in a lot of trouble, and so are you." Nick had a look of shock on his face and stuttered when he tried to talk.

Nick sat silent for just a moment. "Look, lady, I don't know what you are talking about.

You must have me mixed up with someone else. I haven't been anywhere near that woman's house."

"Of course, you have, Nick. I've seen you myself and I think you know it. So, you might as well stop lying about it. Now I want you to tell your boss what I just told you about the gun. And I want you to stay away from my friend's house on Cannon Hill. The next time I see you out there, will be the last. I will turn you and your boss into the police."

"Ok, ok, listen, lady, I need that gun, I have got to have that gun."

Janice was very curious at this point and wanted to question Nick, but she was afraid she might overstep her bounds. "Look, Nick, the gun has gone to the lab to be tested for fingerprints. You may tell your boss that if his prints and the caliber of the gun should match the murder weapon, well I believe the police may be paying him a little visit." Nick's face turned a deep red. He was stunned at what she knew, and he didn't know what to say. "I've got to go see a man about a job."

"Ok, Nick, I'm not stopping you from leaving." Nick left the café and Janice knew he would never be back.

CHAPTER SIXTY-THREE

Jack arrived at Janice's house at 7:00 pm that evening. When Janice opened the door, she was surprised to see him so early. "Come on in, Jack, I didn't expect you to be so prompt."

"Well, I was caught up on a job, so I decided to head on over here. You know it takes a while to drive here."

"Yes, I know it's a long way for you to have to come. Come on and sit down in the living room. Jessie will be right out; she's feeding her dog Rusti."

"I heard about Rusti and I'd love to see him."

"After he eats, he will be coming in here along with Coco, of course. Those two are big buddies now."

"Aunt Janice, I picked up dinner. I stopped at the best Chinese restaurant in Halifax.

Their food is delicious." He handed her three white bags of Chinese food and two bottles of red wine. "Bless you, Jack, you are an amazing young man. This was so sweet of you." Jack said, "Come on let's eat while we talk." Jessie finally came into the living room and said, "hello Jack."

"Hi, Jessie, I hope you like Chinese food?"

"I love Chinese food Jack, it's one of my favorite foods."

Jack had another job he was working on, so he wanted to get to his office early. He went through his messages and found one from his other client. He was spying on a woman's husband who was suspected of having an affair. So far, there was no evidence of his infidelity, but it was his job to find out for sure. His client was quite certain her husband had a girlfriend. She had plans to change her Will but wanted the evidence before she saw her lawyer. She was an heiress to the Orkin family and was quite wealthy. Jack was making a lot of money on this job, so he didn't want to make any mistakes.

Jack tried to keep his mind focused on the client's needs, but he seemed to have Jessie on his mind. He started thinking about her situation. "I'd better run by the station and drop off this gun Jessie gave to me, and I know how anxious she is to hear the results. The sooner she finds out who the prints belong to, the closer she will be to figuring out the murderer. I'm still having doubts about the ghosts in that house even though I did feel something when I entered the door. I wonder if Aunt Janice has ever seen or felt something? I think I'll give her a call today when I get a free moment." He knew Janice had stayed in that house before, so she should know. I want to reassure Jessie of my loyalty and commitment to her mystery. He wanted to believe in ghost too, for some reason, he really did want to believe.

Jack wasn't completely convinced that the cold air he felt was the ghost. He wanted to believe it was for Jessie's sake, but he still had doubts clouding his mind. Later that day, he decided to take a few minutes and call his Aunt Janice. Since it was almost six, he thought his aunt would probably be home. He got his cell phone out of his pocket and dialed Janice. "Hello, this is Janice."

"Hi, Aunt Janice, how are you today?"

"Hi, Jack, I'm doing fine, how are you doing? I understand you spent the night on Jessie's sofa last night." Jack felt a little embarrassed and didn't respond at first. "Well, it was so late when we finally got through talking, she said I could sleep on her couch. And that's all there was to it."

Jack hesitated at first to ask Janice about the Cannon Hill ghosts. He decided to just go ahead and ask her. "Aunt Janice, I know you have spent the night at Jessie's home before."

"Yes, I have on several occasions, why?"

"I was wondering if you have ever had an encounter with the so-called ghosts living there."

"Jack, they are not so-called ghosts, believe me they are real. Yes, I have had encounters with them."

"What happened, Aunt Janice? I mean how did it happen to you?"

"Jack, you must have felt something yourself. What did you see or feel?"

He told his aunt Janice how the cold breeze hit him as he entered the house. "I wasn't sure what it was. It was so strong, I thought it was going to knock me down." Janice said, "I've experienced the coldness before and had a dream about a man standing over my bed, except it wasn't a dream; it was real."

"I want to believe Jessie, but I have to admit, I still have doubts. The ghost leaving her clues and things like that."

"Listen Jack, you either believe her or you don't. She is a very private person and it took a lot for me to convince her to tell you the story. She has always been honest and truthful with me, so you need to decide if you're going to believe her."

•   •   •

That afternoon, Jack was sitting behind his desk reading a book on ghosts. His phone rang several times before he answered it. It was his friend, Jim, at the crime lab. "Hey, Jack, the results are back on those fingerprints you wanted. You want to come by and pick the gun up this afternoon?"

"Yes, Jim, I'll pick the gun up later today. Thanks for doing this for me. I really appreciate it."

"No problem, Jack, anytime." As Jack hung up the phone he decided he would go ahead and go to the crime lab. He wanted to pick up the results because he knew Jessie was anxious to get them.

CHAPTER SIXTY-FOUR

Jack decided to call Jessie and see if he could stop by her house that evening and give her the testing results. It was Wednesday and he had not seen her since Sunday night. Something tugged at his heart about her. He wasn't sure what it was, but he knew he wanted to see her. Jessie was happy to hear from Jack so soon. "Yes, come on by, Jack. You know it's almost fifty miles from town. Are you sure you want to drive that far?"

"I don't mind at all, Jessie. I have those results for you, and I would love to hear any other details you might have about those men that were seeing Mrs. Carmichael."

Jessie asked Janice if she could leave work a little early. Janice was only too glad to let her go. She knew that Jack was going out to Cannon Hill today to give Jessie the results of the test. She also wondered if Jack had another reason for going to Jessie's. "I think he likes her more than he is telling me. I think they would be perfect for each other." Jessie interrupted

Janice's thoughts as she asked her for the keys to the freezer. "Oh, sure, Jessie, they're in my apron pocket: here you go."

• • •

Jessie finished her work for the day and told Janice she would see her tomorrow. Janice asked Jessie to give her a call later and let her know what the results of the test were. "Ok,

I'll be very happy to share that news!" Jessie decided she would stop by the local grocery store and pick up a few things. She got a pound of roasted turkey and Swiss cheese for sandwiches along with potato salad. She also bought a bottle of red wine. On her drive home, she began to think about the results of the test.

"What if they are Walton's, what should I do next? Surely the police had checked out most of what she had found out. Well, if Walton was at the party the whole time, how did he manage to shoot Mrs. Carmichael? And why did he hide his gun in the house? Maybe when she got shot, he didn't want the police to find a gun on him. That would have clinched it for him. All this time I was sure Walton was the killer. Now I'm back to not being sure of anything." She worried about Jack coming to Cannon Hill again so soon. She wondered why he couldn't tell her the results on the phone. She liked Jack but she was not going to get involved with him.

Jessie arrived home just in time to change her clothes and feed Rusti. As she was getting ready to make the sandwiches, Jack pulled in the driveway. "It's such a lovely afternoon, maybe we could sit on the back porch." She had just reached up into the cabinet to get two wine glasses down, when the doorbell rang. As she opened the front door, Jack stood there holding a bouquet of flowers in his hand. "Hi, Jessie, these are for your thoughtfulness and hospitality. I hope you like flowers?"

"Thank you, Jack, they are beautiful. Come on in, I was about to make us a turkey and Swiss sandwich. I thought we could sit on the back porch while we ate."

"That sounds great, Jessie, let me help you."

"Sure, come on in the kitchen. You can carry the wine glasses."

"Wine too, that does sound good." Jack reached down and patted Rusti on his head. "He is a fine dog. I wish I had a dog like him."

"Rusti is my best friend and my partner in crime as they say. He has always been by side from the time I got him." They opened the back door and went out to the back porch. They sat down in the lounge chairs and talked as they ate. "This really is a nice place, Jessie. It's so private and secluded. Do you ever get afraid of being by yourself way out here?"

"Just when Nick Ross was trying to get in. But I had Rusti for protection, he is all I need."

After they finished their sandwiches, Jack sat up in his chair and pulled a paper out of his shirt pocket. "I have those results for you, Jessie. It looks like this gun was not the one that killed Mrs. Carmichael. The caliber is different than the one used." As she read the letter she said, "Well at least I know who the gun belongs too. Mr. Walton as I suspected." Jack said, "Well, maybe he carries a gun everywhere like I do. When she got shot, he figured he'd better hide it. He sure didn't want to be accused of shooting her."

"That makes sense Jack, but then, who shot her?"

All along Jessie had been certain James Walton was the one that shot Mrs. Carmichael. Now she was left with more doubts. "I have been trying to investigate this situation for three years. I was sure Walton was the one that killed Mrs. Carmichael, but now I am not sure."

"Look, Jessie, I am going to help you solve this mystery. I want you to start from the beginning and tell me everything you know about those three men she was involved with." Jessie began to tell Jack about the letters she found in the trinket box. She told him how she read each one every night. "I went to visit Richard Mitchell once. He was very surprised that I had found his letters to her."

CHAPTER SIXTY-FIVE

Jack sat in the lounge chair listening to Jessie. It was getting dark, so they moved inside to the living room. Jessie continued to tell Jack how Mitchell was accused of shooting Mrs. Carmichael but was later released. "He was afraid of me bringing all this up again. We were supposed to meet and discuss the letters, but he died two days later of a heart attack." Jack pulled his glasses down and looked over the rims. He had a small intake of breath. All this was so unbelievable and yet obviously true. "Sounds to me like there was a little guilt hanging over him."

Jessie had never thought of Richard Mitchell as the shooter before. "What about the other guy you told me about. Jeff Parks was his name, wasn't it?"

"My understanding was they didn't really have much of a relationship. They were more friends than anything else. At least that's what it looked like to the outside world."

"I think there may have been more to the relationship than you thought, Jessie. You can't rule out everybody just because you thought they were only friends. Listen, Jessie, everyone she knew is a suspect until proven innocent."

"I guess you're right, I just thought since there was no romance involved, well, at least that's what I thought. With or without romance, Jeff Parks didn't seem to have a motive to kill her."

Jack wasn't as sure as Jessie was about the lack of motive. "Was Jeff Parks at the party that night?" Jessie replied, "As far as I know, he was not at the party and come to think of it, neither was Richard Mitchell. So, Jack, do you think it was one of them that shot her?"

"I'm not sure, Jessie, but it could have been done out of rage and jealousy. Someone who found out she was seeing other men. Someone who didn't want her to be with anyone else." Jessie was stunned at this idea but knew in her heart it was possible. She didn't want to believe it might be Richard Mitchell who killed her. He seemed to be so nice and Jessie thought he was truly in love with Mrs. Carmichael.

Jack asked Jessie if he could read the letters she found from Richard Mitchell. Jessie was reluctant at first. She finally decided if Jack could solve this case without bringing in the police, he needed to read the letters. "Jack, your Aunt Janice told you we did not want the police involved in this mystery. Please promise me you won't discuss any of this with anyone else."

"Jessie, why do you think I'm a private investigator? Any case I work on is between me and my client and no one else. Besides, I'm doing this for Aunt Janice and you, Jessie." Jessie felt relieved and reassured that Jack was telling her the truth.

Jack glanced up at the clock on the mantel and realized it was getting late. "Jessie, it's

10:00 already, I guess I had better be on my way. Do you mind if I take these letters with me? I really need to read them and try to figure this thing out."

"I would rather you didn't take the letters, Jack. You can come out Saturday evening and read them then. After you read them, maybe we could discuss them together." Jack left without the letters. Jessie decided to invite Janice to come out on Saturday night. That way she wouldn't be alone again with Jack.

Besides, she wanted to show him the baby's grave in the backyard. If Janice was there, she would feel better about it.

It was 11:00 by the time she got to bed that night. She dreamed about Mrs. Carmichael and the Christmas party again. In her dream, Mrs. Carmichael was dancing with Richard Mitchell. Jeff Parks and James Walton were standing by the piano watching them. Mr. Carmichael was sitting across the room with a drink in his hand watching her dance. He had a very serious look on his face. Suddenly she awoke from her dream. She thought she heard a noise downstairs. Rusti started barking and wanting out of the room. Jessie got out of bed and put her robe on. She opened the bedroom door and let Rusti out. The dog ran down the staircase barking all the way.

Jessie went to the computer and looked at the driveway and the surrounding area outside of the house. Rusti was running from the back door to the front door barking as he ran. Finally, the figure disappeared into the night. Rusti calmed down at last and came back upstairs to the bedroom. "If only you could talk, Rusti."

When Jessie was positive no one was around, she ventured downstairs. She checked all the doors and windows just to make sure they were locked. "I can't believe it was Nick Ross again. Whoever it was came to harm me. They probably know I have an investigator looking into Mrs. Carmichael's murder now. I think I will call Jack tomorrow and let him know what happened after he left." Jessie and Rusti went back upstairs to her bedroom. It was almost impossible for her to go back to sleep. The dream kept swimming around in her head. She finally sat up in bed and read a book for a while. She eventually fell asleep and slept until the alarm went off the next morning.

CHAPTER SIXTY-SIX

Jessie got up and shut the alarm off. After she finished her shower, she put on her black dress and white apron for work. She glanced in the mirror to see how she looked. "I believe I have gained a few pounds since I started working at the café." She pulled her hair back and tied it with a rubber band. Jessie's hair had gotten long over the past year. "I am so used to seeing myself look this way; I can barely remember how I looked in Chicago." She looked in the bathroom mirror again and decided her face still looked pale and thin. She decided that she would just put on a small amount of liquid makeup and add a little mascara to her eyes. "Now I don't look quite so pale and thin. This does make me feel much better about myself."

As soon as she walked into the café, Janice noticed the change in Jessie's appearance.

"Well, look at you this morning. Jessie, you look gorgeous with a little makeup on. Why haven't you worn it before now?"

"I don't like to bring attention to myself. Janice you know how private I am about my life. I just thought I would try something different this morning."

"I hope you will keep it up. You look beautiful."

•   •   •

It had been five years since Jessie escaped to PEI. She found the Cannon Hill house and the best friend anyone could ever have, her dog, Rusti. Unfortunately, her life had been in turmoil most of those five years. In the back of her mind she always worried someone would recognize her. She tried not to bring attention to herself by not wearing makeup and pulling her hair back into a plain ponytail. She also wore black rimmed glasses and kept a low profile. For some reason when she woke up this morning, she decided to be different. Her mind kept questioning her reason for the change. She did not want it to be because of Jack.

Early morning was always busy in the café. Jessie cleaned off the tables and washed dishes as fast as she could. By 10 am things began to slow down. Janice and Jessie finally got a break. Janice brought Jessie a cup of coffee and they sat down in a booth together. "Janice, could you come out Saturday and spend the night with me? Jack is coming Saturday evening to read those letters I have from Richard Mitchell and I want to show him the baby's grave. I'd rather you come too."

"I would love to come out, Jessie. I love coming out to your place. What time should I come?"

"Whenever you want too, Janice."

It was a long and tiring week for Jessie. The drive from Cannon Hill everyday had begun to be a chore. It was a two-hour trip for her every day of the week. "I'm beginning to hate the drive, but the money is good, and I need it." Jessie had made enough money since working at the café to pay for her new back porch and lounge chairs. She put every paycheck in her savings account and only spent what she had too. By Friday she was exhausted from working all week. She decided she would splurge a little and buy Jack, Janice and herself a nice steak to cook on the grill. She would make a salad and bake potato to go along with the steak.

Janice arrived at the Cannon Hill house around 4 pm Saturday afternoon. "Hi, Janice, come on in. Look Rusti, Coco came to visit you." Janice said, "I hope you don't mind me bringing Coco with me?"

"Of course not; Rusti loves to play with Coco." Janice handed

Jessie two bottles of red wine. "I thought this would be good with our dinner tonight."

"Thank you, Janice, they will be perfect with our steaks." Jack arrived at 6 pm that evening. Janice answered the door and invited him in. "Hi, Aunt Janice, I'm so glad to see you. I believe fall is in the air. It's beginning to get cooler outside."

Jessie had a nice fire going in the fireplace and soft music playing on the radio. Jack was impressed and a little disappointed that his Aunt Janice was there. He was hoping to be alone with Jessie tonight. "Come out to the back porch, Jack, Jessie is cooking us a steak."

"That sounds great. Lead the way Aunt Janice." Jessie had the dining room table all set for three. As they walked through the dining room; Jack could hear the floor creek. "That must be the place where she found the gun." As they approached the porch, Jessie was coming in the door holding a platter with three large steaks on it.

Come sit down and enjoy your steaks," she said as she poured each one a glass of red wine. "Jack, after dinner, Janice and I have something to show you. It's connected to the case." The three of them enjoyed their dinner while they continued talking about Mrs. Carmichael. They sat at the dining room table for almost two hours talking and drinking wine. Jessie told Jack about all her encounters with the Carmichael's. How they had led her to the trinket box and how she'd left pictures laying on the staircase. Darkness came and they didn't even notice. "Oh no, Jack, it's dark outside and we had something we wanted to show you in the backyard. I guess it will have to wait now."

Jack was not going to be put off by darkness. "Come on, Jessie, let's get some flashlights and look. You have me curious now." Jessie said, "What do you think, Janice, should we take a look in the dark?"

"Well, why not. Jack isn't one to wait till tomorrow." Jessie turned the flood lights on and went to the kitchen and got two flashlights out of a cabinet drawer. The three of them walked to the back of the yard. Rusti and Coco followed them. "Jack, this is a grave of a baby. Janice and I found it the other day after Rusti dug it up. I never knew it was here until then."

"Do you think it was Mrs. Carmichael's baby?" Janice spoke up and said, "Jessie and I assume it was."

CHAPTER SIXTY-SEVEN

Jack Grant was amazed at all the evidence Jessie had collected from the Cannon Hill house. He was still having a hard time with the fact that a ghost lived there. On Sundays, Jack usually relaxed and watched a football game, but this Sunday he decided to go over all his notes. He wanted to try and figure out who the murderer was. He sat down at his kitchen table and spread all the paperwork out. "There's got to be a clue here somewhere that I'm missing. Something has got to lead me to the killer."

He mulled over the paperwork for several hours. Suddenly a light came on in his head.

"It's staring me in the face, but I didn't see it until just this minute. I'm beginning to think it was Richard Mitchell who shot Mrs. Carmichael. He was the one who loved her the most, and he was jealous of the other two men. He told Naomi that in his letters. He was very disturbed by her seeing other men while he was out of town. Now he's dead, so how am I going to prove he was the one who shot her? I need to investigate his past and see what I come up with. Walton was at the party the whole night, so it couldn't have been him. Even if he acts guilty, doesn't mean he is guilty."

Jack made notes and continued to pour over all the paperwork until late afternoon. "I'm too tired to read any more. I think I'll stop for the rest of the evening. Tomorrow is Monday and I'll get back to investigating these men. I'm thinking right now, Richard Mitchell is my culprit." Jessie and Janice decided to spend their Sunday making a nice grave for the baby they found in the yard. They found an old wooden box in the basement and put a nice soft pink blanket in it. They gathered up the baby's bones and placed them in the wooden box. Janice got a shovel and dug the hole deeper and wider. They each took one end of the box and slowly placed it in the grave.

• • •

After Jessie arrived at work Monday morning, she said, "Janice, we gave the poor little thing a decent burial, now I want something to remember her by. I think I'll go to the hardware store on my break." She wanted to look for a cross to put on the baby's grave. Every time she thought about the baby, a sad feeling came over her. She walked to the back of the store and found a nice cross that said: May you Always Rest in Peace. Jessie thought to herself, "This is perfect for our little one." She took it back to the café to show Janice. "Jessie, you're right, this is perfect; I love it."

Jessie took the cross home that evening and placed it on the baby's grave. She sat a vase of spring flowers by the cross. When everything was put in place, Jessie felt a wave of relief come over her. She had wanted to do something for the poor little thing ever since Rusti dug it up. Now the baby could rest in peace. Jessie looked down at Rusti and said, "Now, Rusti, please don't dig this grave up again. You be a good boy and protect this little one from critters. She knelt to the ground to pet Rusti on his head. Remember, Rusti, this is a no touch. From that point on, Rusti never once went near the grave. She felt sure that Mrs. Carmichael felt relieved that her baby had a proper burial. Jessie slept soundly that night for the first time in a long while.

• • •

The following week Jack was busy trying to get all the facts straight in the Cannon Hill case. He was supposed to be working on his other case with the cheating husband. He knew he needed to concentrate most of his time on Mrs. Harper's case. That was a paying case. Even so, Jack couldn't stop thinking about Jessie, or her mystery killer. "I have got to get my priorities straight. Mrs. Harper is waiting to get an update on her husband, and I'm sitting here at my desk thinking about other things. What is wrong with me?" Jack decided to put more effort on Mrs. Harper's problem.

Jack waited across the street from the building where Mr. Harper worked. It was 12:15 when Mr. Harper came out of the building and headed down the street towards Jim's Bar and

Grill. Jack followed him into the restaurant and sat in a booth toward the back of the room. He held his camera close to his side. He made every effort to be inconspicuous. Mr. Harper had also taken a booth, but near the other end of the room. About ten minutes later, a dark-haired woman came into the restaurant and sat down in the booth with Mr. Harper. Jack walked back toward the other end of the room and snapped a picture of the two people in the booth. There was just enough light for him to get a good shot of them together.

CHAPTER SIXTY-EIGHT

He waited patiently at the end of the bar to see what might be happening. Mr. Harper put his hand on top of hers and slowly slid closer to her. They were awfully close to each other. Jack glanced at the clock over the bar; it was 1 pm. The woman suddenly got up and left the restaurant. A few minutes later Mr. Harper paid his bill and left the bar. Jack saw the woman get into a taxi but had no idea where she was heading. Jack followed Mr. Harper all the way to his workplace.

Jack's client, Mrs. Harper, only wanted proof that her husband was seeing another woman. Once she got that, she was ready to file for a divorce. Her attorney was waiting for her go ahead. Jack paid Mrs. Harper a visit the next afternoon. He wanted to give her the pictures he had taken. Once she saw the pictures, she picked up the phone and called her attorney. "Michael, go ahead with the divorce. I'm holding the evidence in my hands." After hanging up the phone, she thanked Jack and gave him an envelope with three thousand dollars in it. "You did a fine job for me, Jack. I have rewarded you well."

Jack was now free to pursue Jessie's case. He decided to give Mr. James Walton a little visit. Mr. Walton's office was also in Halifax, so Jack didn't have to go very far to see him. After locating the address to Walton's office, he hailed a taxi and directed the driver to the address he had found. He entered the office and saw a young woman sitting behind a desk. Jack asked if he could see Mr. Walton. "Do you have an appointment, sir?"

"No, I do not. I'm an old friend of his and happen to be in the neighborhood, so I thought I would stop by to say hello."

"Sir, what is your name?"

"Jack Grant, I'm a private detective."

The woman behind the desk called Mr. Walton and asked if he could see Jack. Walton had no idea who he was, so he told her to let him come into his office. His secretary motioned for Jack to go on in. He was surprised to see such a large man. Walton must have been six feet five inches tall. Jack was six feet and Walton loomed over him. He stood there with a cigar in his mouth leaning on his desk. Jack introduced himself as Jack Grant, private detective. "I was hoping to have a few words with you Mr. Walton. This is in reference to your relationship with Mrs. Naomi Carmichael."

"Good heavens, man, that was years ago. The poor woman is dead now."

"Yes, I know

Mr. Walton. That's why I'm here. Why don't you start by telling me where you were the night she got shot."

"I've already told police my story several times. It's all in my records."

"Listen, Walton, I have a very special reason for asking these questions. I have been hired by an individual to fine Naomi Carmichael's killer. Where were you just before she got shot?"

"I was standing by the piano watching Naomi and her husband dance. There was a lovely lady playing the piano."

Jack was still anxious to hear more from Walton. "Were you carrying a gun that night?" "I always carry a gun, but I didn't have my license to carry with me. When Naomi was shot I was afraid the police would find the gun on me. I accidentally left my billfold at home that night."

"Well, how did the gun get hidden in the dining room floor?"

"Look Mr. Grant, I had to hide the gun someplace. When I walked through the dining room I felt a board move under my foot, so I lifted it up and hid the gun under the floorboard." Jack said, "I suppose that's why Ross has been trying to get in the Cannon Hill house for the past several weeks."

Walton was surprised that Jack Grant knew he was the one who hired Ross to break into the Cannon Hill house. "Look, Mr. Grant, I admit I hired Ross to try and get the gun out of that house. I was afraid I would get charged with Naomi's death. I meant no harm to the lady that lives there now. I just wanted my gun."

"How close were you to Mrs. Carmichael, Walton?"

"We had dinner together a few times. I never stayed at her home overnight, if that's what you were thinking. Why don't you talk to Richard Mitchell. Naomi was involved with him. She even told me she was in love with him."

CHAPTER SIXTY-NINE

Apparently James Walton did not know that Richard Mitchell had died of a heart attack.

Jack decided to give Walton his gun. After Jack had talked to him, he decided it wasn't Walton who killed Mrs. Carmichael. "Thanks for your time today, Walton. You can have your gun back, but I better not ever hear of you or Ross going near the Cannon Hill house again." James Walton was relieved to have his gun back. Before Jack left, Walton showed Jack his permit to carry a gun. Jack said, "You sure went through a lot of trouble trying to get that gun back."

"I know I did. Please tell the lady that lives in the Cannon Hill house how sorry I am for causing her so much trouble."

As Jack was leaving, he turned to Walton and said, "I think you should tell her yourself. She's at the PEI café every day." Mr. Walton just nodded to Jack and turned away. As Jack was driving through town, he thought about Jeff Parks. "I need to find out what kind of relationship Carmichael had with this Parks guy." He decided to pay him a visit at his apartment. Jeff wasn't at home when Jack arrived; but his wife was there. He asked Jeff's wife what time her husband would be home. "I'm not sure, Mr. Grant, probably 7:00 tonight. He may have to work late." Jack gave her his card and asked her to have Jeff give him a call.

• • •

As Jack was driving home, he thought about Jessie. "I think I'll go by the café tomorrow and see her. I need to tell her what I now know about James Walton. I don't think she will have to worry about Ross trying to break in anymore. I should have reminded Walton he could go to jail for sending Ross out to Cannon Hill house. That's a breaking and entering offense. I hope my gut feeling about the man is right. I don't believe he had anything to do with Naomi's death. I just hope Jessie will believe me when I tell her. She really hates the man and she's sure he's the killer."

• • •

Friday was a beautiful day. The sun was shining bright and the weather had turned a little cooler. Jessie loved the fall of the year. She loved the changing of the weather and the leaves on the trees turning brown and gold. She began to think out loud, "I can't wait to buy pumpkins to put on my front porch. No one ever comes to Cannon Hill except Janice, but at least the pumpkins will brighten up the old place." As she made the drive to work, Jack Grant was on her mind. "I wonder when I will see him again. Surely he has found out something by now regarding my murder mystery."

As Jessie pulled into her parking space in front of the café, Jack Grant was getting out of his car. "Good morning, Jessie, how are you this bright and sunny morning?"

"Hi, Jack, what brings you here so early?"

"Here, let me get the door for you." Jack held open the door to the café. They both walked inside. Janice stood behind the counter with a big smile on her face. "Well good morning, you two." Jessie went to the back of the café to put on her apron while Jack took a seat at the counter. "Good morning, Aunt Janice, may I have a cup of coffee, please." Janice sat a cup and saucer in front of Jack and poured his coffee. She sat the creamer and sugar bowl next to him.

The café opened at 8 am and it was only 7:45 am. "I wanted to talk to you and Jessie about James Walton before you got busy." Janice said, "Well, you picked a good time, Jack.

What did you find out about Walton?"

"Jessie, can you spare a minute. I want you to hear this too." Jessie stopped wiping tables and came over and stood behind the counter next to Janice. "I went to see Walton yesterday in Halifax. He was at the party the night Naomi was shot. He said he was standing next to the piano watching her dance with her husband. He had the gun you found in his coat pocket the whole time."

Jessie said, 'Why was he carrying a gun in the first place?"

"He told me he always carried a gun everywhere he went. I guess he felt he needed protection. He had left his carry license in his billfold and left that at home. He thought the police might think he was the one who shot her, so he started looking for a place to hide it. As he was walking through the dining room he heard the floor crack. He said he got down on his knees when no one was around and lifted the board up and hid the gun there and decided he would go back later to get it." Janice spoke up and said, "I guess that's where Ross comes in."

It's 8:00 ladies, so I better not keep you from your work. Aunt Janice, I think I'll go ahead and have some breakfast while I'm here, that bacon smells awfully good."

"Good boy, what would you like to have this morning?"

"How about the breakfast special?" Janice said,

"Two scrambled eggs, bacon, fried potatoes, and toast coming right up."

"That sure does sound good. I don't usually eat breakfast."

"Today you will and it's on the house." Jack ate breakfast and then moved to a booth to read the paper. He wanted to tell Jessie about giving Walton his gun and letting him know that Ross better stay away from Cannon Hill house.

CHAPTER SEVENTY

Jack continued to sit in the booth until noon. Janice said, "Jessie, I think Jack wants to talk to you about Walton. Can you take a few minutes and go over and sit down with him?"

"Sure, Janice, but I only have a few minutes." Jessie joined Jack in the booth. "Jessie, I won't keep you long. I just wanted to tell you that I gave Walton back his gun. I told him that Ross had better not bother you again. He knows I could have had him arrested for sending Ross out to Cannon Hill all those times."

"Thank you, Jack, for helping me. I really was convinced the murderer was Walton. Now you've made me wonder who did kill Naomi Carmichael."

"Listen, Jessie, I'm going to try and find Jeff Parks. I want to see where he was that evening. I know you and Aunt Janice have already buried the baby bones and I hate to do this, but I must open the grave again. I need to try and find out who the father was."

"Oh no, Jack, I hate for you to have to do that. We just put the little thing at peace."

"I know, Jessie, but it may be the only way we can find out who murdered Mrs. Carmichael. I need the DNA from the bones. The father of the baby could possibly be the one who killed her." Jessie was upset about the baby being dug up again. "I guess you have to do what you think is right. But I really wish you didn't have to do that, Jack."

"I know you ladies need to get back to work, so I'd better leave. I'll be saying goodbye for now."

"Good luck, Jack. Please let your Aunt Janice and I know what you find out."

"I will, Jessie. You keep all your doors and windows locked and stay safe. The murderer probably knows I'm investigating now, and they may try to harm you. I wouldn't want anything to happen to you, Jessie." She said, "You stay safe, too, Jack."

• • •

September was a beautiful month on PEI. Travelers from all over the United States had come to visit the Island. The PEI Café was busier than normal. Jessie and Janice worked late trying to keep up with the customers. Jessie washed dishes and swept floors while

Janice took orders and helped the cook in the kitchen. Jessie tried to stay away from the customers as much as possible. She was afraid someone might recognize her and report her to the authorities. By the time Jessie arrived home every day, it was dark. Every morning before she left for work, she turned on her flood lights so she would be able to see to unlock the door when she arrived home.

• • •

On the ride home, she thought about what Jack had said to her. He cautioned her to keep her doors and windows locked. Jessie didn't like arriving home after dark, but it was so busy at the café, she didn't have a choice. She was so grateful to have Rusti to protect her. She knew that when she opened the front door, he would be there to greet her. He kept her from being afraid. As soon as she walked up onto the front porch, she could hear Rusti behind the door barking. Jessie unlocked the door and Rusti jumped up on her to lick her face. "I missed you too, Rusti." She knelt and hugged him. "I am always so glad you're here when I get home."

The weekend couldn't have come any sooner than it did for both Janice and Jessie. They were both so happy to be off for the weekend. Jessie had decided she was going to paint the kitchen on Saturday. When she left the café Friday afternoon, she stopped by the hardware store. She wanted to pick up two gallons of light blue paint. When she was done buying the paint, she decided to go by the PEI grocery store. She needed dog food for Rusti and a few other supplies. As she was going into the grocery store she ran into

Jack. "Hi, Jessie, I'm glad I ran into you today." Jessie was surprised to see Jack and began to have butterflies in her stomach.

Jessie couldn't understand the feeling she had. She brushed it off and thought she was probably hungry. "Hi, Jack, funny meeting you here." They both laughed and continued to talk. "Jessie, would you mind if I came out to Cannon Hill tomorrow to check out that grave? I really hate to disturb what you have done, but I need to find out who the baby belonged to." Jessie was speechless at first but gained control of herself by the time she answered. "I don't mind you coming tomorrow, Jack. I just wish you didn't have to disturb the grave. It's so nice now that Janice and I made it a resting place for that poor little baby."

"Jessie, I promise you I will do my best to return it as I found it."

"Now if you have something planned for tomorrow, I can always come another time."

"No, that's ok, I was planning on painting my kitchen. I just bought two gallons of paint."

"Did you say paint? I'm a terrific painter, and I will be more than happy to help you paint your kitchen. That's the least I can do for you for letting me come out tomorrow."

"You don't have to do that, Jack. Besides, you are the one that's helping me find Naomi's killer." Jack wanted to verify the time. "Would 10 am be ok with you?"

"Yes, that would be fine."

CHAPTER SEVENTY-ONE

The following morning, Jessie woke up early. She stretched and yawned as she rolled out of bed and grabbed her robe. After her shower, she put on an old pair of blue jeans and a tee shirt. She decided to pull her hair back and braid it. She looked in the mirror and thought to herself, "My goodness I still look so pale and thin in the face. Maybe I should put a little makeup on just to bring out the color in my cheeks. I keep telling myself all this is not for Jack, but I wonder if it is? Hmmm, could I have a crush on him? Oh no, that is just too silly."

Jessie tried to forget what just went through her mind, but the thought of caring for someone like Jack, seemed to put a smile on her face. She went downstairs to the kitchen with

Rusti on her heels. She let the dog outside while she put a kettle of water on the stove to heat.

She then filled his bowl with dry dog food. "I think I'll have a bowl of cereal this morning. Then I really need to get started on this kitchen wall. Jack will be here around 10 and I want to have some of this painting done." While she ate her breakfast, she thought about the baby's grave. "I wish Jack didn't have to disturb her resting place. I'm afraid Mrs. Carmichael will be upset."

Jessie ate breakfast and drank two cups of hot tea and was ready to start painting. She had painted a full wall and started on another, when the front doorbell rang. "Oh my gosh, I bet that's Jack. Just look at me; I'm covered in paint. Oh well, he will just have to get over it."

She put the paint brush down on a rag and washed her hands. Then she went to the front door to see who it was. She looked through the peep hole and saw a tall man standing there. "It's Mr. Walton, I don't know whether I should open the door or not." Jessie stood there for a couple of minutes when she decided she would see what he wanted. The doorbell rang again, just as she opened the door."

"Good morning, Miss Jessie."

"Good morning, Mr. Walton, how can I help you?"

"I'm sorry to bother you this morning. It looks like you have been busy painting."

"Yes, I'm painting the kitchen wall."

"I just stopped by to apologize to you for causing you so much anxiety and pain. I want you to know that I did not shoot Mrs. Carmichael. I was at the party the whole time. I was afraid the police would fine the gun on me and accuse me of shooting her. So, I hid it in your dining room floor. I am so sorry for what Nick Ross did to you. He will never bother you again. I know you thought I was the one who shot her but believe me I did not. I wasn't in love with Naomi, but I did care about her very much."

Jessie was shocked at all this confession Mr. Walton was handing her. She wanted to believe him, but for some reason, she was still suspicious. "Thank you for stopping by, Mr.

Walton. I really must get back to my painting now."

"Miss Jessie, I don't think you believe me. I'm telling you the truth. I told the private investigator the same thing I told you. It's all true. Please believe me, Miss Jessie. I didn't drive all the way out here for nothing. I need you to trust me and believe me."

"I'll have to think about it, Mr. Walton. I do appreciate you coming way out here to tell me this. Now I really have to get back to my work." Jessie shut the door and stood there until Walton left her driveway. She took a deep breath and went back to the kitchen.

•   •   •

It wasn't long before Jack knocked on the front door. Jessie said, "Now that has to be

Jack." She opened the front door and there he stood. "Hi, I'm running a little late this morning. So sorry if I inconvenienced you."

"No, not at all, Jack, come on in. You will never believe who you just missed."

"I bet it was Aunt Janice."

"No, it was Walton. He said he came to apologize to me for putting me through so much anxiety." Jack said, "You sound like you didn't believe him."

"I wanted too, but I can't help but be suspicious of him. I don't know how he did it, but I still believe he had something to do with Mrs. Carmichael's death."

Jessie asked Jack to follow her to the back yard. They walked through the house and went out the kitchen door. "I don't think I will go back there with you this time, Jack. I need to continue my painting anyway."

"That's okay, Jessie, I understand."

● ● ●

Jack went around to the front of the house and got a shovel and a pair of men's thick working gloves out of his car. Jessie decided she would finish painting the kitchen. She really hoped she would get finished with it all in one day. She climbed up on her ladder to finish the top of the kitchen door. It wasn't long before she saw Jack carrying his shovel around the house again. Jack knocked on the back door and called Jessie's name. "Come on in, Jack, the door is open." He came in through the back door. "I told you it wouldn't take me long. I hope I repaired the grave the way you had it. Before I leave today you may want to check it." Jessie said, "I will, Jack, but for right now, you can grab a brush and start painting." They both laughed as Jack picked up a brush and dipped it in the paint bucket.

CHAPTER SEVENTY-TWO

Jack and Jessie painted until almost 2 in the afternoon. While they painted, they laughed and talked about their childhoods. Finally, Jessie said, "Why don't we stop for a while and have some lunch. I'm starving." Jack said, "Sounds like a good idea to me."

"I hope you like roast beef sandwiches, Jack. I made them up this morning along with homemade potato salad."

"Wow, Jessie, that sounds delicious. You are really an early bird. I'm going to have to step up my game if I'm going to keep up with you." Jessie prepared their plates while Jack poured them a Coke. She handed him his plate and asked if he would like to sit on the back porch. "That sounds good; let's go outside and get some fresh air. It's a little stuffy in here."

· · · ·

While they ate their lunch, Jessie was curious about Jeff Parks. "Jack, have you found anything out about Jeff Parks yet?"

"Well, I went by his home the other day and spoke with his wife. Jeff wasn't home yet. After I left there I went to his job site and he had already left for the day." Jessie was anxious to get on with the investigation. She was ready to live a normal life and enjoy her home without ghost. They finished their lunch but before they went in, Jessie wanted to look at the baby's grave. Jack had followed her to the grave site. "Thank you, Jack, for keeping everything the way, it was. I know Mrs. Carmichael is glad too."

"I hated disturbing the grave, Jessie, but at least now we can get DNA and find out who the baby's father was."

They went back into the house and started painting where they'd left off. Suddenly the kitchen got very cold. Jack said, "Good heavens, it's freezing in here. What is going on, Jessie?" Jessie said, "Mrs. Carmichael is paying us a visit. She's trying to say thank you for keeping her baby's grave intact."

"You are welcome, Mrs. Carmichael."

"Believe me, she understands you." The cold disappeared and the room began to warm up again. "Jessie, does that happen very often."

"Yes, it does, and Rusti and I almost freeze to death when it does."

"Jessie, I don't understand how you've stayed in this house as long as you have, knowing it's haunted."

Jessie didn't say anything and kept painting. Finally, she spoke up and said, "Well, the ghosts have never hurt me or Rusti. Mrs. Carmichael just wants her presence known."

"Didn't you say she left you clues from time to time?"

"Yes, the trinket box and the picture on the staircase. The trinket box was really a mystery for me. I was surprised when I found it with all those letters in it. I feel sure she wanted me to find the box. When I brought it out of the closet, the hall got cold. I knew then she was there guiding me." Jack said, "Were you scared when that happened?"

"No, I knew it was her. It was her way of letting me know she wanted me to find the letters."

Jack Grant was an experienced private investigator and knew how to read between the lines. He had read the letters from the trinket box. All the letters revealed was Richard's love for Naomi and his jealousy. They did portray a desire for revenge towards the other two men. Jack was suspicious of Richard Mitchell and wish the man had not died. He thought to himself, "I needed to talk to the man. I believe when Mitchell found out Jessie had found his letters to Naomi, he panicked. He thought he was about to get caught. But apparently his bad heart caught up with him first. Love can escalate to jealousy and envy and make a person do unthinkable things."

Jessie and Jack continued to paint the kitchen. By 6 pm they had finished the painting.

"Wow, it looks really nice, Jessie. I love the color you chose." Thanks, Jack, if it had not been for you helping today, I would be painting until midnight."

"Come on, let me help you clean up. I think I had better be getting back to Halifax soon." They began to clean up the kitchen and put everything in its place. Jessie said, "thanks again, Jack, for helping me today."

"To tell the truth, Jessie, I enjoyed it and I especially enjoyed being here with you."

She ignored what Jack just said to her. She asked Jack if he would like to have a cup of coffee before he left. "I would love a cup, Jessie. Just the thing I need right now." Jessie prepared the coffee pot and turned it on. She said, "Let's go sit down in the living room and rest while we wait for the coffee to finish." As they sat waiting in the living room, Jack asked Jessie to show him where she found the trinket box. She asked him to follow her upstairs to the hall closet. As they went up the staircase, a coldness descended upon them. Jessie said,

"Mrs. Carmichael is present and doesn't want us to look in the closet."

CHAPTER SEVENTY-THREE

Jack was curious now about the opening in the closet. "Jessie, it's possible something

could be in the closet that you didn't find." As they approached the closet, the coldness descended upon them with a vengeance. Jessie said, "Wait, Jack, I need to go grab a sweater. I'm freezing."

"Okay, Jessie, I'll wait for you." Jessie ran into her bedroom and grabbed a sweater from her closet. As she started back into the hall, the coldness began to fade. Naomi must have been upset about something."

"Jessie, I think there is something in there you didn't find. Something she doesn't want us to see."

Jessie opened the closet and pushed the clothes hanging there to one side. "Is this where you found the trinket box, Jessie?"

"Yes, that's the spot."

"Did you search every inch?"

"I thought I did, Jack. Why, have you found something else?"

"No, but I think Naomi is back."

Suddenly the cold descended upon them again. Jack said, "There must be something she doesn't want us to find. Why don't we check out the attic. Maybe there is something up there she doesn't want us to find."

Jessie went downstairs to the kitchen and got a flashlight out of her utility drawer. She took it back upstairs to Jack. "Thanks, Jessie, now let's see what's in the attic." Jack pulled the steps down that led to the attic. He slowly climbed the steps and pulled the light cord hanging at the top of the steps. Jessie followed Jack up the attic steps. "Have you looked up here before, Jessie?"

"Yes, I did, but not really well. It seemed too spooky up here, so I didn't look in all the boxes."

"I think I may have found something, Jessie." Jack was hesitant at first to open the box. "Jessie, do you want to open the box?"

"Ok, but let's take it downstairs first."

As Jack knelt to pick up the box, a strong order came from one of the bedrooms. Jack said, "Good heavens, what in the world is that smell?" As he held his nose, Jessie climbed down the attic steps and went into the guest bedroom to see if Mr. Carmichael was in there. She spoke out loud to the ghost as she said, "Mr. Carmichael, I know you are here. Why are you doing this to us. We are only trying to help solve your wife's murder. Please go away, Mr. Carmichael and leave us alone." Jessie walked over to the bedroom window and opened it up as far as she could. The smell disappeared and the room began to fill with a flower smell.

As Jessie came out of the bedroom she called up to Jack. "Well, Jack, do you believe in ghosts now?" Jack replied, "There is no doubt in my mind there are ghosts living in your house. Yes, I am a believer now, Jessie. That flower smell is better, but a little bit overwhelming. I don't understand how you stand it." Jessie explained to Jack as she climbed the attic steps, "The Carmichaels mean no harm to me. Naomi just wants to know who murdered her. I think she will go away once this mystery is solved. Mr. Carmichael is staying around to watch over her. He must have loved her very much." Jack said, "Apparently, true love never dies."

They took the box downstairs to the dining room to open it. "Ok Jessie, open the box."

Jessie opened the box and there lay a beautiful pink baby girl's dress, bonnet and booties. On top of the baby clothes, lay an envelope. "Oh my gosh, Jack the baby was a little girl." Jack said, "Are you going to open the letter, or should I?"

"I'm so nervous, why don't you open it and read it to me." Jack said, "Ok, then I'll read it."

> *To whomever finds this letter and the contents inside the box:*
> *I just want to say I am sorry for my indiscretions. I lost my*
> *sweet little girl and buried her in the back yard. I know now I*
> *was wrong in my actions. I apologize to my husband and the man*

I loved with all my heart, Richard Mitchell. He was the kindest and nicest man I have ever known. He loved me with all his heart, and I betrayed him with other men. He will never know the baby girl was his. He would have been a wonderful father to our baby. But that's never going to happen. My husband, Robert knew about my affairs and the baby. When I lost my child, I wanted to die. I tried to take my life twice, but my husband was always there to pick me up. My husband is a good man and I am ashamed of myself for what I have put him through. I pray when I die, God will forgive me for all I have done.

Naomi

Jessie stood there with tears rolling down her face. Jack reached in his pocket and pulled out a white handkerchief and handed it to her. "Here, Jessie, wipe your face with this." Jessie took the handkerchief out of Jack's hands and wiped her tears. "I can't help it, Jack. That is the saddest letter I think I have ever heard. Can you imagine what Naomi went through? I know she did wrong, but I still feel sorry for her. Who are we to judge her anyway? Nobody is perfect and things happen." Suddenly the room got cold again. "I think she is here, Jessie."

"Yes, she is, and she knows we have found the box with the letter."

Just as quickly as the cold descended on the room, it disappeared. Jessie said, "I think Mrs. Carmichael just wanted us to know she knew someone finally found the letter. Jack, I'm confused over this whole thing. If it wasn't Walton or Mitchell that shot Naomi, then who could have done such a thing?"

"Jessie, I haven't had a chance to talk to Parks yet, so I'm not sure myself. If it wasn't one of the three men she was dating, then who else is there?" Jessie said, "I don't know, but what about Robert, her husband. Where was he when she was shot?" Jack said, "I need to talk to Walton again. I want to know exactly where he was, and her husband at the time of the shooting."

CHAPTER SEVENTY-FOUR

Jack and Jessie quietly sat at the dining room table for almost five minutes before Jack spoke up and said, "Jessie, could I have another cup of coffee. I need something to revive me."

"Of course, Jack, help yourself." Jack said, "This has been a day I won't soon forget." He looked at the watch on his left arm and realized it was 7 pm. "Jessie, I didn't realize it was so late. Maybe I'd better get going." Jessie said, "You need to drink that cup of coffee first. Jack, I really want to thank you for staying and helping me paint my kitchen today. It looks so nice and I do love the color I picked out."

"It's beautiful, Jessie, and I enjoyed every minute of it."

As they sat in the dining room drinking coffee, Jack said, "Jessie, thank you for letting me dig up the baby's grave. I hope I put things back the way you had them."

"Everything looks fine Jack." As Jack got up from the table to leave, he turned to Jessie and said, "I really enjoyed being here with you today." Jessie was taken back by what Jack said, she had feelings for Jack, but she knew in her heart she couldn't get involved with anyone. She said, "I appreciate all you did to help me today, Jack. Helping me paint and finding the box has been an experience I won't soon forget."

As Jack was going out the front door, he turned to Jessie and said, "I'll let you know what I find out, Jessie. I plan to go see Walton again and try to catch up with Parks. Suddenly,

Jack took her in his arms and kissed her." Jessie couldn't believe how receptive she was to his kiss. It was as if she'd wanted him to kiss her. Jack said, "I'm so sorry, Jessie, but I just couldn't help it. I have wanted to kiss you all day." Jessie didn't say a thing to Jack as he turned to leave. As he walked towards his car, he began to worry, "I sure hope I didn't offend Jessie. I could not help it; I think I'm falling in love with her."

•　•　•

As Jack drove the fifty miles to town, he picked up his cell phone and dialed his Aunt Janice's phone number. Janice was outside cleaning her front porch with the hose and didn't hear her phone ring. Jack was disappointed when she didn't answer and decided he would wait for her to call him back. When Janice finished cleaning the porch, she checked her cell phone and saw a missed call from Jack. She sat down in a chair and dialed him back. "Hello, Aunt Janice, how are you?"

"Hi, Jack, I'm doing fine. Did you call me earlier?"

"Yes, Aunt Janice, I wanted to talk to you about Jessie."

Janice was surprised at what Jack had to say. "What's wrong, Jack; are you two not getting along?"

"No, just the opposite, Aunt Janice. I spent the whole day with her today. I helped her paint her kitchen. After all, she let me dig the baby's grave up so I could get the

DNA. So, I stayed with her all day and painted."

"So, Jack, what is the problem?" Jack hesitated and said, "I'm falling in love with her." Janice wasn't surprised at all. She had a feeling Jack and Jessie had feelings for one another the first time they met. Janice said, "Well, that is the most wonderful news I've heard in a long time. Does Jessie know how you feel?"

Jack wasn't sure what to say to his Aunt Janice. "Well, I'm not quite sure if she does or not. Have you heard from her today?"

"No, I haven't heard anything from her. I probably won't hear from her until Monday at work."

"We found another box hidden in the attic."

"What?" Jack repeated himself. "We found another box hidden in the attic."

"What was in it, Jack?"

"It had a baby girl's dress, bonnet and booties in it and....... letter."

"Jack, what did the letter say?"

"Oh, I don't know, Aunt Janice. You need to talk to Jessie about all that tomorrow."

Jack was hoping for more advise and understanding from his Aunt Janice regarding his feelings for Jessie. She seemed happy about it, but he wasn't sure what he should do next. He did not get advice from the one person he thought would be helpful in this situation. After hanging up with his aunt, Jack was still confused and down hearted. He began to wonder. "If I only knew if she was interested in me. I can't stop thinking about her. All I want to do is be around Jessie. Good grief, I sound like a soap box character. Stop thinking, stop thinking."

•　•　•

Monday morning was colder than usual. Fall was in the air and most of the women on the Island wore sweaters. Jessie wore a blue button-down the front sweater over her white blouse that she usually wore to work. As Jessie walked into the café Monday morning, Janice said, "Good morning, Jessie. It's a little cool this morning. I see you came dressed for it. I brought a sweater too, just in case I needed it."

"Good morning, Janice. Yes, it was quite cool this morning. So, I thought I had better wear something warm today."

"Jessie, guess who called me last night?"

"Who, Janice, one of our good products managers?"

CHAPTER SEVENTY-FIVE

Jessie was a little confused and continued to wipe down all the tables and chairs in the café. "No, Jessie, Jack called me." Jessie said, "What does that have to do with me, Janice?"

Janice answered, "He talked about you and how he helped you paint your kitchen Saturday."

"Yes, he came out to dig up the baby's grave. He wanted to get something to test for DNA. Then the next thing I know, he was in the kitchen helping me paint." Janice said, "He also spoke of a box you two found that contained baby clothes and a letter from Naomi."

"Janice, I'll tell you all about it after lunch. Right now, it's about to get busy in here."

Janice could hardly wait to hear what Jessie had to say about the letter. She knew it was too busy in the café to stop until after lunch. She continued to take orders and help in the kitchen with the food preparation. It was 11 am and the café was full of patrons. Janice glanced up and saw her nephew, Jack walk in the café. She thought to herself, "That boy has it bad! I'll bet he's here to see Jessie. I believe love is in the air." Jack sat down on a stool at the counter. He looked around the café to see if Jessie was available. Jessie was cleaning off a table when she looked up and saw Jack. Her face turned red and she began to shake. She thought to herself, "What in the world is wrong with you?"

Janice finished with a customer and walked over to where Jack sat. "Good morning,

Nephew. How are you today?"

"Good morning, Aunt Janice. I'm supposed to meet Jeff Parks in an hour in front of the hardware store, so, I thought I would have breakfast first."

"What can I get you this morning?"

"I think I will have the pancakes and bacon today. How about a cup of coffee first."

"One cup of coffee, coming right up." Jessie finished cleaning the tables and walked over to where Jack was sitting. "Good morning, Jessie."

"Good morning, Jack, what brings you in here so early this morning?"

"I'm meeting Parks this morning. Remember, we talked about it the other day?" Jessie said, "Yes, of course. Let me know what you find out as soon as you can."

Jack ate his breakfast and told his Aunt, he had to go. Jessie walked out of the kitchen just in time to say goodbye to Jack. "Bye, Jessie, I'll let you know what I find out." Jessie missed Jack as soon as he left. She tried to put him out of her mind, but he kept creeping back in. In her heart she knew it was impossible for her to fall in love. She was a fugitive, and nothing was going to change that. She began to discuss it with herself. "If I told Jack what I've done in my past, I'm sure I would lose him forever. He might even turn me into the police. I better stick to business and just find out who shot Naomi Carmichael. That has to be my number one priority."

• • •

After leaving the café, Jack drove over to the hardware store parking lot. A tall young man, with black curly hair was standing next to a car. He had his arms crossed in front of him.

Jack was certain it was Jeff Parks. He got out of his car and walked over to the young man. Jack said, "Good morning, I'm Jack Grant. I assume you are Jeff Parks?" Jeff held his hand out to Jack as they shook hands. Jack said, "I appreciate you meeting me this morning, Jeff. I have a few questions for you regarding Naomi Carmichael."

"Sure, Jack there really isn't much to tell you about Naomi. We were just friends."

"Jeff, were you and Naomi more than friends at any time?" Jeff said, "If you are referring to me having an affair with her, the answer is no."

Jack continued to ask Jeff questions about Mrs. Carmichael. "Jeff, where were you the night Naomi was shot?" Jeff said, "I wasn't invited to the Christmas party."

"Yes, I know, but where were you that night?"

"Actually, I was doing some late Christmas shopping. I was at the mall picking up my mom and dad's gifts. I was nowhere near the Carmichael home." Jack said, "Can you prove you were shopping on Christmas Eve?"

"As a matter of fact, I can. I have a friend who works in the candy shop; I went there to pick out candy for my mom. Her name is Sally Watts. She will tell you I was in the shop around 9 pm.

Jeff was getting frustrated with Jack's questions. "Man, I need to get to work. What else can I tell you?" Jack said, "How about giving me Sally's phone number so I can verify you were there on Christmas Eve." Jeff got his cell phone out of his back pocket and scrolled through his contacts. In the meantime, Jack got his cell phone out of his coat pocket. "Ok, here it is, call her right now, so I can go to work." Jack dialed Sally's phone number. It rang several times before she picked up. "Hello, this is Sally."

"Hi Sally, this is Jack Grant. I'm a friend of Jeff Parks. I just wanted to ask you a couple of questions, if it's okay?"

"Sure, go ahead."

CHAPTER SEVENTY-SIX

Sally verified Jeff was in the candy shop the night Naomi was shot. "Sally, you do realize this was about ten years ago, we're talking about?"

"Yes, I remember because that woman got shot that night and everyone was talking about it."

"Do you remember that woman's name?"

"I'm not sure, it may have been Carmichael or something like that. I don't know for sure, Mr. Grant. It's hard to remember after this long." Jack said, "Thank you for your time, Sally." Jack was satisfied Jeff Parks was not the killer. He began to go back over all the information he'd gathered so far. "So, if Walton and Parks didn't kill Naomi, who did?"

Mitchell apparently loved her, so Jack didn't think it was him. He was dead so he couldn't be asked any questions. Jack decided to go back to Halifax and talk to Walton again. When he arrived at Walton's office the door was locked. "Strange, the door would be already locked at 3 pm in the afternoon. He took out his cell phone and looked for Walton's phone number. The phone rang ten times when Jack finally hung up. "I wonder why his secretary isn't in the office. I'll go home and call him later."

The following morning as Jack was getting dressed for the day, he heard the man on the radio say a body had been found. He listened closely as the man said the body of a man had been found behind Brawta Jamaican Jerk Joint. Jack knew the restaurant was located on Grafton Street. He hurried and dressed so he could go before the traffic rush started. He wanted to see the body, maybe he could help identify him. As Jack pulled up to the parking lot, one of the reporters from The Chronicle Herald came walking towards him. His name was Ed Barnes, and everyone knew he was quite the skeptic.

As Jack got out of his car, Ed Barnes came up to Jack and said, "Hey, Jack, what are you doing here? This is no place for a private eye."

"I heard about this on the radio, Ed. I thought I might be able to identify the body."

"Okay, then that would be helpful. Come on around back of the restaurant with me. The body is still there." Jack asked, "How was he killed, Ed?"

"Shot through the heart with a nine-millimeter." Jack thought to himself, "Well, that's the same kind of gun that shot Mrs. Carmichael." When the two men approached the body, Ed Barnes lifted the sheet away from the dead man's face. Jack said, "Oh my God, that's James Walton. Now I know why he didn't answer his phone."

Ed Barnes asked Jack, "Obviously, you know this man?"

"Yes, I was trying to get in touch with him yesterday. I rang his phone at least ten times and didn't get an answer. Now I know why."

"Who is he again, Jack?" asked Ed. Jack said, "It's James Walton. He runs a car dealership over on Robbie Street, well, he did run the dealership. I think they sell Mazda's." Ed Barnes asked Jack if he knew of anyone that might want Walton dead." Jack hesitated and said, "No, I don't, Ed. I wish I could be of more help."

"Hey, you have helped the police identify him." Jack gave Ed Barnes one of his business cards and said he had an appointment to keep. "Call me if you need to ask me anything else."

Jack couldn't wait to get away from there. His head was killing him. He didn't feel like talking to Ed Barnes any longer. He just wanted to get away from that scene. Jack got in his car and backed out of the parking lot. He began thinking about Jessie and what he was going to tell her. "Walton is dead, Mitchell is dead, and Parks was at the mall the night of the shooting. The husband was dancing with Naomi so he could not have been the one that shot her." He understood Jessie's confusion and the latest deaths only made it a bigger mystery. He just needed to talk to Jessie. It was 11 am and he had not eaten breakfast, so he decided to go over to PEI and eat at the café.

• • •

When Jack entered the café, Janice noticed how pale he looked. "Jack, what's wrong with you? You are white as a ghost."

"Aunt Janice, you are never going to believe this."

"What is it, Jack, tell me honey." Jack had to catch his breath before he could even start to tell Janice. "Walton is dead."

"What happened to him?" Jack said, "Aunt Janice, someone shot him. And the worst part is, the same caliber gun that killed Naomi, killed Walton." Janice said, "So I'd assume the same person shot both of them?" Jack said, "I don't know how to tell Jessie. She's so sure, Walton was the guilty man."

Jessie was in the café kitchen getting water for a customer. She walked out and saw Jack sitting at the counter. She gave him a big smile as she passed. Jack said, "Aunt Janice, this case is nowhere near being solved. And now this new wrinkle. I just don't know what to think." Jessie walked over and said good afternoon to Jack. "What are you two whispering about?" Janice replied. "Nothing to concern yourself with right now, Jessie." Two customers entered the café and sat down in a booth." Janice said to Jack, "Why don't you go out to Cannon Hill house tomorrow and tell Jessie. Don't discuss it while she's working."

CHAPTER SEVENTY-SEVEN

Before he left the restaurant, Jack stopped a minute to speak to Jessie. He asked her if she would mind him driving out to Cannon Hill Road the next day. "I'd like to discuss the case with you. I have some new evidence that has just came to my attention."

"Okay, Jack. Rusti loves seeing you. I'm beginning to think that dog likes you better than me." They both laughed as Jessie started to wipe the counter. Jessie said to Jack, "I think Janice should be there too. After all, she's been trying to help me solve this mystery too." Jack was disappointed because he was hoping to be alone with Jessie. "Okay, Jessie, maybe we can all put our heads together and figure this thing out."

• • •

By Saturday, the weather had really turned cold. The fall air was crisp and cool and made the Cannon Hill house cold inside. Jessie got the few pieces of wood left on the back porch She brought the wood in and started a fire in the fireplace. "There you go, Rusti. A nice warm fire for you to lay by." Rusti stretched out in front of the fireplace and wagged his tail as if to say, 'Thank you.' Jessie had gotten up early to get ready for her visitors. She prepared lunch for the three of them. She prepared chicken and potato salad.

As she was starting the coffee pot, the doorbell rang. Rusti jumped up and started barking. She opened the door to see a strange man. Rusti continued to bark at him. "Calm down, Rusti. May I help you?"

"Yes, Ma'am, I'm John Carmichael. My parents Naomi and Robert Carmichael used to live here. I was wondering if I could come in and just see the old place?"

"It's nice to meet you, John, but I'm expecting company at any time now. It wouldn't be a good time."

"Of course, I understand, Mrs.? I didn't catch your name." Jessie said, "I didn't tell you my name." Jessie thought this man was creepy and she just wanted him to go away."

"Miss, may I come back when it's more convenient for you."

"I don't think that would be a good idea."

John Carmichael thanked Jessie for her time and walked away. Jessie was relieved to see him drive out of the driveway. Ten minutes later, Jack and Janice drove up. Jessie welcomed them into the house. She had lit candles and the house smelled of spice. Janice said, "Jessie the house smells so good and look at that warm fire you have going." Jack thought the house was warm and cozy. Jessie took their jackets and hung them in the front closet. Jack noticed how shaken Jessie seemed to be. He asked. "Jessie why are you so nervous. Has something happened?"

Jessie told Janice and Jack to make themselves comfortable. "I've made chicken salad sandwiches."

"I love chicken salad, Jessie. Do you have coffee brewing in there?"

"Yes, I do, help yourself to a cup." Janice said, "Jack, how about making me a cup of that hot

coffee too. I need something to warm me up."

"Sure thing, Aunt Janice. How about you, Jessie, would you like a cup?"

"No thanks, Jack, I think I'll have a Coke with my lunch." As

the three of them sat down at the dining room table, Jessie spoke up and said, "Did you pass a

car on the way here?"

"Yes, as a matter of fact, we did," replied Jack.

Jessie went on to tell Jack and Janice about her visitor. "Believe me, it was the creepiest encounter I think I've ever had. His clothes were dirty and just hung on him like rags. His hair was a mess and his hands were shaking." Jack said, "I am so sorry you had to go through that,

Jessie. You know we have not considered the son at all in this investigation. Let's look at all the facts while we eat this delicious chicken salad sandwich." Janice said, "How about this wonderful potato salad. Jessie you must have gotten up early to make all this."

"It was no problem at all, Janice. I'm just happy you're enjoying it."

"After we eat lunch, I want to lay everything out on the table and discuss it," declared

Jack. Jessie said, "Yes, I think that is a good idea." They continued to eat and discuss the visitor. After lunch was over, each one carried their plates to the kitchen and washed them in the sink. Jack wiped the counters down and put everything away. No man had ever been this nice to her before. "Thank you, Jack, for all your help. I mean for everything you have done for me." Jack said, "Jessie, I would do anything for you. Don't you know that by now?"

CHAPTER SEVENTY-EIGHT

Jessie was determined she wasn't going to get involved with Jack. She thought it would be way too dangerous with her past. She still worried about being found out and spending the rest of her life in jail. She was lost in thought about her deep feelings for Jack, when Janice snapped her fingers at Jessie. "Hey, stop daydreaming, Jessie. We have serious things to discuss." Jessie came back to reality. "I am so sorry, I guess I'm just tired. I got up really early this morning."

Jack laid all his paperwork out on the dining room table. The two women stood on each side of the table listening to him explain. Jack began by pointing out that they had not discussed Mrs. Carmichaels son, John. "I need to find out where John was the night of the party. As far as I know he wasn't there." Suddenly the room became very cold. Jessie said, "She's here, Naomi is here with us. Jack, she wants to tell us something." Jack said, "How do you know, Jessie?" Jessie replied, "I feel it in the air. I think she is going to appear to us." Janice whispered. "What? You think she is going to appear?"

"Yes, I do. Just wait a few minutes."

The three of them just stood there without moving for almost five minutes when an apparition appeared near the dining room wall. It was a figure of a woman. She looked to be very young and had a long flowing white gown on. She had tears coming out of her eyes. Jessie and Janice gasped and held their hands over their mouths. Jack stood there without moving and said, "Naomi, can we help you?" The woman hung her head as if in shame. Jack asked her another question. "Naomi, do you think your son shot you by mistake?" Naomi moved her head from side to side as if to say no. Jack asked her again, "Naomi, do you think your son shot you on purpose?"

The room began to warm up as the apparition disappeared. Jack, Janice and Jessie took a collective deep breath and sat down in their chairs. Janice said, "Oh my gosh, that was scary." Jessie spoke up and said, "She's gone now. She won't ever come back." Jack asked, "How do you know, Jessie?"

"First of all, she has never appeared to me. If she is gone, then Mr. Carmichael is gone too." Jack said, "I was about to point him out as the killer."

As they looked over Jack's files, Jessie said the house feels different. "How do you mean, Jessie?"

"Well, Janice, there has always been a kind of smell and mist in the air. I was always aware that Rusti and I were not alone here. I tried to ignore my feelings and just act normal but every time I read those letters or thought about the mystery that stood over this house, a cold feeling would come over me." Jack walked over to Jessie and put his arms around her. He held her tightly and said, "You are not alone anymore, Jessie, you have me and Aunt Janice now."

The days that followed were crucial for Jack Grant. He now knew John Carmichael was the one that shot his own mother and Mr. Walton. Jack wrote everything he could in his log about the case at Cannon Hill House. Jessie asked Jack, "Please do not involve me and your Aunt Janice. We don't want the police knowing anything about the baby. They only need to know about John and why he shot Naomi. I don't want the police coming here and asking me questions."

"Ok, Jessie, I won't say anything in my report about you and Aunt Janice. You can trust me."

Jack investigated the background of John Carmichael for the first time. While John was in college, his mother Naomi was seeing Richard Mitchell. He was not happy about her having relationships with other men. He found out about James Walton and Jeff Parks, over time. After two years of college, he was kicked out of school. He called his mother and father for help. They refused to help him because he had been thrown out of school. After a while he got a job with a financial group. His work became sloppy. He struggled but was fired after three years. John began to get more and more frustrated with his life. He went from job to job until he finally became a handy man for an apartment complex.

He was given a small apartment in the basement of the building along with a small salary. When someone's pipes busted, or the air condition was on the blink, John would be responsible for the repairs. At first he did a good job for the building complex. People who lived there liked him and seemed to respect him. After the first year, he became sloppy again with his work. He either didn't show up for the repairs or did a horrible job.

CHAPTER SEVENTY-NINE

As Jack investigated John Carmichael he began to see a pattern evolving. The man was angry with his parents for not helping him through the years. His life became lonely and terribly misguided. His mother cared more for her boyfriends than she did him. His anger built up inside of him like a festering boil. Jack knew the part of town where John lived. He was not looking forward to that trip. It was the nastiest part of Halifax you could imagine. The buildings were run down and children running around in the streets in rags. There were broken water mains causing water to pour down the streets. Men stood on corners just waiting for someone to come along and offer them a day job.

He suddenly felt sorry for John Carmichael having to live in a place like this, but he knew he only came there to do one thing, arrest John. Jack found John's address and parked his car in front of the building. "I sure hope my car will not be trashed while I'm gone." He locked his car and went down the six steps it took to get to John's apartment. Jack knocked on the door. After a couple of minutes, a stout man wearing very shabby clothes opened the door. "Yeah, what do you want?"

"Are you John Carmichael?"

"Who's asking?"

"I'm Jack Grant. I'm a private investigator." Jack took his wallet out and showed Carmichael his credentials.

There was a strong stench coming from inside the apartment. Jack could hardly stand there without holding his nose. He pulled out his handcuffs and asked Carmichael to turn around. Jack said, "John Carmichael, you are under arrest for the murder of Naomi Carmichael and James Walton." Jack read John his rights. "You have the right to remain silent. For example, you do not need to answer any questions about where you are going, where you are traveling from, what you are doing, or where you live. If you wish to exercise your rights to remain silent, say so out loud."

John Carmichael never said a word. After Jack handcuffed him, he locked up the apartment and took him to the police department. As they were walking in the door, the man behind the window said, "Hey Jack, who you got there?"

"John Carmichael, would you get one of the detectives for me Clint?"

"Sure thing, Jack." Clint called Jim Rafferty to meet Jack in the interrogation room. Jack escorted John down the hall to the first room on the left. After almost fifteen minutes of waiting, Jim Rafferty came into the room. "What's going on Jack?" Jack explained the case to Jim. "I will have a full report for you first thing in the morning, Jim."

• • •

John Carmichael was arrested for the murder of his mother, Naomi Carmichael. She was shot on Christmas Eve in 1992. He was also indicted for the murder of James Walton, who was shot on September 5, 2012. Jack was relieved the Carmichael case was over. The mystery of Cannon Hill House was no longer a mystery. The house was free of it's past, at last. Jessie could finally live there in peace and not be afraid. He could hardly wait to see her and tell her John Carmichael had been arrested. He picked up his cell phone and dialed his Aunt Janice. "Hi Aunt Janice, I just wanted to tell you the mystery of Cannon Hill House is no longer a mystery. I'm on my way to tell Jessie."

As Jack pulled up into the driveway of the Cannon Hill house, he wondered how he was going to tell Jessie how much he loved her. He got out of his car and walked up to the door and knocked. Jessie opened the door with a big smile on her face. She had decided whatever happens from this point on was meant to be. She loved Jack Grant and she wasn't going to hide it any longer. As Jack walked into the house he felt a warm loving feeling surround him. He said, "Jessie, it's all over. John has been arrested for the two murders. You are free now and so is your Cannon Hill home."

Jessie said, "Jack, thank you again for helping me solve this mystery. It's been a long way home, but I think I have finally made it. I think you are the most generous, thoughtful and considerate man; I have ever known. And did I mention how much I love you? I just wanted you to know that."

"Jessie, I love you, too. I have from the moment I met you." Jack took Jessie in his arms and kissed her tenderly. Jessie whispered in his ear, "Jack, I hope you'll always make me feel this safe!" They spent a long time locked in each other's arms, laughing and relieved, because the truth was finally out. From now on, the Cannon Hill House would only be filled with love and laughter.

THE END

CREDIT PAGE FOR
MYSTERIOUS HOUSE ON CANNON HILL

1. Editors: Jeannie Madsen Smith and Claudia Schroeder
2. Wikipedia: Diversey Parkway Chicago. West of the North Branch of the ChicagoRiver, the street is known as Diversey Avenue, and separates the neighborhoods of Avondale to the North and Logan Square to the South.
3. Chicago – It is the most populous city in the US state of Illinois' and the third most populous city in the United States.
4. Sault Ste. Marie -City in Ontario, Canada'
5. Magnuson Grand Pioneer Inn – Escanaba, Mi
6. Prince Edward Island – PEI is one of the eastern Canada's Maritime provinces, off New Brunswick and Nova Scotia in the Gulf of St. Lawrence.
7. Brawta - Jamaican Jerk Joint and Oyster Bar – Downtown Halifax, Canada

ACKNOWLEDGEMENT

I want to start by thanking my children, Ronda, Craig, Randy and my husband Jerry, for encouraging me to write. Their sincere advice and for reading my drafts early. I also want to thank my publisher, Reagan Roth for his patience and the Black Rose Writing team for their expertise and cover design.

My editors, Jeannie Madsen Smith and Claudia Schroeder for their excellent advice and great editing.

ABOUT THE AUTHOR

Diane Williams Gordon was born and raised in Atlanta, Georgia where she lives with her husband, Jerry. Diane has written two Amish novels. *Ruby Hope Valley* and *Return to Ruby Hope Valley*. She loves spending time with family and reading Amish Novels in her spare time. Diane is retired from one of the many Professional Golfers Association of America Club Facilities/PGA Tour.

Note from the Author

Word-of-mouth is crucial for any author to succeed. If you enjoyed *Mysterious House on Cannon Hill*, please leave a review online—anywhere you are able. Even if it's just a sentence or two. It would make all the difference and would be very much appreciated.

Thanks!
Diane Williams Gordon

Thank you so much for reading one of
Diane Williams Gordon's novels.
If you enjoy our book, please check out our recommended title for
your next great read!

Ruby Hope Valley by Diane Williams Gordon

Ruby Hope Valley is a delightful and heartwarming book of love,
faith, and friendship.

www.ingramcontent.com/pod-product-compliance
Lightning Source LLC
Chambersburg PA
CBHW010731130726
47899CB00013B/3032

* 9 7 8 1 6 8 4 3 3 7 7 5 0 *